STARSHIP DAWN

E.R. Mason

E.R. Mason

Cover image components compliments of NASA

Editors

Frank MacDonald
Contact:
SciFiProofreadingDoneRight@gmail.com
https://sites.google.com/site/scifiproofreading

Sam Thornton, PE PhD
https://www.facebook.com/SamThorntonPE
SamThorntonPE@outlook.com

ISBN: 978-1-7328697-6-9

Chapter 1

"I have no problem leaving Earth. There are three kinds of Earth people, those who are mature souls, those who are immature, and those in between. The immatures devote themselves to their base desires. They live by the code, *do as thou wilt*. Do anything you like to anyone or anything provided you don't get caught or you don't care. Their conscience either has not yet awakened, or is very elemental. They can be very smart people, seeking political office or lofty business positions. They have no problem with lying and cheating to enrich themselves. On the lower end of the scale they sometimes can be serial killers."

"The matures are those who have gained wisdom over time. They are not governed by their base instincts but rather by reason and compassion. Their code is*, treat others as you would wish to be treated*. It is up to the matures to prevent the immatures from doing too much damage to society. But, as the population grows larger, the percentage of immatures yields so many evil-doers that terrorism and corruption become difficult to forecast and prevent."

"As for me, I have never done well in social gatherings when immatures are present. For some reason I seem unable to accept idiots and egos. The loud ones and the inebriated ones always eventually seek the imposed approval of those around them. Unfortunately I have never been able to give such approval. As a result they often become attracted to me like a moth to a light. They seem to feel an extra push is needed for me to acknowledge their importance. I go so far as to let them into my personal space but am unable to give them a step back. Physical contact is where I draw the line. Afterward, we all help them to get back up off the floor. Napkins are used to wipe up the spilled drink. Usually at that point the maître de suggests it would be better if we both left."

"The irony of these kinds of events is that many, or even most of us are mature, intelligent people. But it only takes one or two immatures to create total chaos. You often see them on passenger aircraft or in restaurants, or theaters. They tend to have tantrums. They seem irritated and offended by others peacefully enjoying each other's company in their presence. Immatures often tend to be temporarily drawn to each other which has led to too many protest groups. Too many ideologies demanding special attention."

"So, I have no problem leaving Earth for a two-year open ended Mars expedition. And, as Captain of the starship New Dawn, I have studied the manifests thoroughly. There will be some immatures within the eighty-two, but since they are all specialists they all will have at least some grounding in logic and common sense. Odds are the powers that be will eventually want me to bring one of the support starships back to Earth so my sojourn won't be permanent, unless I want it to be. The truth is I can't wait for stars to fill the starship windows."

"Computer, end Captain's personal log."

I swiveled in my Airlite seat and considered what pictures should be fastened to the claustrophobic walls of my tiny quarters. The robin's-egg blue, plastic, paper-thin walls do provide good privacy. They were so fresh out of the factory they were giving off a kind of new-car smell to the cool spacecraft air. Captain's quarters had the added luxury of a small desk beneath three display screens and keyboard. The armrests on the Airlite seat fold down to hold its occupant in place during months without gravity. No bed; just a very comfortable sleeping bag to be hung anywhere the user chooses. One accordion exit door on my right to the Command Bridge, another door behind me and luxury access to a joint bathroom and shower shared with my XO, Janet Pars. Although the walls were still bare, I felt very comfortable here.

An attractive woman with long brown hair slid open my main door and smiled at me. "Captain, you're going to be late for the last meeting on Earth you'll probably ever attend."

XO Pars looked me over and laughed. "Is that what you're wearing?"

I compared her gray business suit with my blue flight suit and grinned rebelliously.

"There's going to be press all over the place. You know that of course, plus the VIPs," she added.

"What's the latest?"

"All three cargo ships are still nominal and on course. So far so good."

"I missed the refueling. How was it?"

"Piece of cake. Picture perfect. Happens a lot with this company. We'd better get going. They've already closed the cargo hatches on D and C. Personally I have deck ladder fatigue. It's a long way down to A deck from here. Whose idea was it to put the Bridge on G anyway?"

"You don't want eighty people passing through your command cabin every time they go somewhere, do you? It's also why Engineering is on the lowest deck."

"I *know* that. I was only being facetious." Pars gestured for me to come. I stood and followed her. On the Bridge two technicians in black coveralls were still working on the command consoles. Pars headed for the ladderway. I followed her down. She called up to me as she stepped off the last ladder rung. "Crew cut and a flight suit. That's really what you're wearing, then? You look like you just got off a carrier."

"Hey, you ever landed on a carrier, Jan?"

"I flew Hawkeye II's. What do you think?"

"I did notice you've unfurled your long wavy locks and obviously you hit the salon at full price. Looks nice."

"I want to make a good last impression. With luck we can still get out of here on E."

We passed by busy people on F Deck unloading food packs in the galley area and continued down to E. A number of technicians, again in black coveralls, were running exercise equipment checks and handing gear in and out of open cargo doors. They paused when they noticed us and cleared a path.

We took a place on the crew access arm and waited with others. Pars held up crossed fingers. "The launch tower elevator has been acting up. It was stuck on A deck for a while."

The elevator doors opened. As we rode down she smiled at me. "Have you eaten anything yet?"

"No. I have that revision video of the generator core installations I was supposed to review and acknowledge an hour ago."

"Yeah, me too. Sounds like dinner and a movie to me."

"It should be interesting activating those cores on orbit, don't you think?"

She scoffed. "Can't stay on batteries forever. Miniature nuclear power, guaranteed to be failsafe. What could possibly go wrong?"

"Been using 'em for years on subs."

7

"Not exactly the same but good point."

The elevator doors opened. We waited for those ahead of us to exit. Janet laughed under her breath and looked at me. "Have you started decorating your living compartment with pinups?"

"It will probably be system schematics and drawings."

We followed others along the walkway. Outside at the base of the launch pad the Florida sun suddenly beat down. In the distance trees seemed to be waving goodbye to us. The air smelled like ocean. We both stalled to look up at New Dawn, a glistening white tower against the blue sky mounted high atop a silver super heavy. The staggering size of it made us stand in awe. Pars finally laughed again and asked, "Your Tesla or mine?"

Pars drove. At the Headquarters building, after passing through a few handshakes and waves, we made our way to the seventh-floor meeting room and amid excited greetings from other attendees. We took seats at the worn conference table. Big windows offered a wide view of the Space Center landscape.

CFO Holmes was waiting at the head of the room. We were the last of the stragglers.

She checked off some notes on her pad, brushed back the long, wavy blonde hair and began, "Hi everyone. I see we're all finally here. Let me get right to it. We are looking good for an on-time departure. I'm sure none of you will miss those daily blood screenings; apparently they have worked well. All those included in the isolation mandates have come through without any signs of infection. Also, all eighty-two contracts have now been signed. No one has withdrawn from the program even though some are leaving spouses behind and quite a few are leaving extended family. We must do our best to keep those comm systems at full bandwidth for everyone's sake. At last briefing all three cargo spacecraft remain enroute and are operating nominally and we have no weather constraints forecast for tomorrow's launch. At last update the starships we sent one year and eleven months ago are still talking to us from the planet's surface and are intact and operational just waiting for offloading. We are scheduled to begin offloading the earthmovers in two weeks. If all goes well we should have a nice smooth pad for you land on. So I have nothing but good news for you. Any questions?"

Janet Pars briefly raised one hand. "Status of the last refueling ship?"

"Oh, yes, sorry I missed that. We are stacked and all systems go. You should take a look online. It's a beautiful sight. Any other questions?"

My impression was that there were many but no one was willing to ask. The CFO had made it clear we were going. There was not much else to say.

The CFO closed off her presentation. "Well, I look forward to our next briefing, which will be a teleconference in space. Good luck on your historic journey. I'll next see you online. Captain Easton and XO Pars, would you stay behind please?"

Those at the table rose and began low conversations. CFO Holmes came to us and took a seat across the table. She placed her tablet in front of her, folded her hands and smiled. "Let's go over the late stuff, shall we? Both Cray Compacts are now up and running. I've personally linked to both. They seem to be ready for flight. I've run the program for under floor food packet storage. The RFID system has been tested on all decks. There were a few cases where SAW tags had come off the storage packets, but that problem has been resolved. Inventory shows complete and everything is in its place."

Pars interrupted, "About that. I asked for the number of RFID detectors onboard to be increased to twelve. I know six sounds like enough, but if we ever lost the ability to scan storage for what we needed we'd be in real trouble. We'd never find the supplies we were looking for, especially on Mars."

Holmes nodded. "They begrudgingly rushed six more to us. You got your wish, Jan."

Pars sat back and smiled.

"All the wrist-or-pin communicators have been distributed and tested; no small task I might add. Quite a few people seem to prefer to pin them to clothing rather than wear the band. That's okay as long as they wear them. I will bet Security will have some problems in the beginning with people who forget or disregard them. Some didn't seem to understand the necessity of having them on for emergencies. I've tested the communication voice recognition system myself. When I call a specific person the system does automatically connect me to that person privately. There were some issues with that earlier. They seem to have been worked out."

"The water reclamation system is already up and running. Just so you know, one or two Board members are still arguing against the two-minute showers. Even if some droplets escape the booth the air recirculation system still picks up the water, but of course you know that. You'll have to see how the fingerprint shower allowance works. You may need to make adjustments to the rules. As for the privacy habitats, all privacy cubicle panels are now stored against the walls. The techs will begin inflating the launch seating tonight. I am told that on the Command Deck the navigation and communications consoles, the Captain and pilot consoles, and the life support station are all talking to the Crays, but I'll bet you both are well aware of that too. There are a few other small items. I'm emailing them to you right now." Holmes tapped at her Pad and looked up at us. "How about you two? Any last minute doubts? Any concerns?"

"I believe we are both quite ready to fly, Jen," I replied.

"I know I am," added Pars.

"I believe I envy you two," said Holmes

"Some people are calling it Jen's Ark after you," said Pars and she smirked.

"I'll be mentally willing you there all the way," replied Holmes.

Early the next morning we stood on a balcony outside the Launch Control Center and watched the hulk of a super heavy lift our last refueling starship through the clouds and into space. After the announcement "nominal orbit insertion," we waited until the falling Heavy came back into sight, fell toward the launch pad, then righted itself into the arms of the launch tower. As always I started to choke up a bit but was able to hide it.

The nominal orbit insertion message and rendezvous with the refueling platform was more than a status update. It declared the stark reality that tomorrow morning;

We were going

.

Chapter 2

If someone tells you they got a good night's sleep the evening before a launch do not buy real estate from that person. You lay in bed and launch yourself over and over during those hours. There are a few superhuman exceptions to that particular initiation, like the John Young types who seem unable to get their pulse rate above seventy regardless of any threat of death. Despite a night of shallow sleep, in the morning you are wide awake.

Launch days are always altered reality. All the people around you suddenly become quiet. You feel their silence. They do their jobs with an obvious and intense focus. You have practiced for this day more than a hundred times but the day is suddenly completely new.

In the suit-up room, the B and C Deck passengers were getting lightweight fabric suits with fabric head gear and plastic visors. The six of us who would be on the Command Deck were helped into regular pressure suits and helmets. Both groups lined up for pressure checks.

We came down the ramp of the O&C building in open suits and beheld the strangest prelaunch sight ever seen: a continuous flow of buses picking up suited astronauts. There seemed to be too many.

Pars and I took a Tesla.

Venting was in full swing at the pad but the vapor clouds were being pushed out to sea. That was a good thing because had the wind been coming inland launch criteria would have shut us down. We had to stand in line for the elevator with everyone else. Pars commented, "Don't you Roc-Jocks usually have some kind of amusing quip about now?"

"Look who's talking."

"By the way, I did a last-minute check on our refueler. It's still up there waiting for us."

"I wonder if anyone has gotten sick in their suit yet."

"Just wait 'til we're on orbit."

"Yeah, the med teams are going to have their hands full."

"No pun intended?"

"After you, ma'am"

We squeezed into the crowded elevator with eight other passengers, their fabric hoods still pulled back, stolid expressions on their faces. We rode up in silence. When the doors opened there was a nervous, hesitant push to get out. Pars winked and smiled at me through her raised visor, then she remembered it was the C Deck entrance. She winced at the thought we would be climbing to G Deck in a spacesuit. It made us laugh.

Though we had made the climb many times before, this time it was much more strenuous and at the same time exhilarating. The decks were well lighted. There were colored lights and equipment sounds everywhere. The air was cold and had a fabric smell to it. The ship was alive. People were being strapped in on every deck. The sound of many tense voices filled the air.

We climbed to the Command deck to find the rest of the Bridge crew already there and strapped in. Big smiles from the five of them.

Brent Shaw was at the life support and communications station to the left of my seat. He gave me a thumbs up and gestured toward my position. "The complimentary drink cart will be by shortly," he said.

Pars took the center seat behind us and quipped, "See what I mean about Roc-Jocks?"

On my right at the Engineering station, Steve West looked on and rolled his eyes.

Behind us were Dr. Amanda Bishop, Personnel Director on Pars' right and Paul Descard, Shift One Chief Engineer on her left, all strapped in and ready. Descard called out, "Can you guys believe there are seventy-six passengers seated below us? Do we even believe that?"

"Yeah, seventy-six people is just crazy enough," said West

"Actually, I think the crazy count is eighty-two, Steve," added Pars.

"Now you tell me," replied Shaw.

Pars and I sat sideways on our reclined seats to move straps out of the way.

Shaw added, "The suit techs said to call if we needed help."

"Yeah, it's getting quiet down there. They must be pulling down their hoods," said West.

I swung my legs up in place, found the suit interface cable and snapped it in place on my right leg. The body restraints snapped together easily. A quick click of the display button on my armrest brought the touch screens down into position where I could lay back and still reach them. I shifted into a comfortable position as Pars cursed under her breath, having trouble with a strap.

My touch display flashed alive. Once again, though I had used it hundreds of times, the screen seemed different. Everything in every display was now real.

The speakers in my helmet crackled to life. "New Dawn, GNC on countdown, comm check."

Pars paused to look over at me with another big smile then continued strapping in.

I took a long breath. "GNC, New Dawn, we have you loud and clear."

"Understand GNC is loud and clear. Stand by for comm check by the propulsion engineer."

"New Dawn, Prop on countdown one, comm check."

"Prop, New Dawn, loud and clear."

"Prop, loud and clear, stand by for comm check with avionics engineer."

There was a long pause. The avionics engineer was not ready for some reason. The few free moments made me realized I was grateful for the distraction the comm checks offered. The challenge and response checklists are done so many times in training they become a tedious burden. Not this time.

We worked our way through the remaining checklists, watching the countdown clock hourglass pour down past the T-minus two-hour mark toward zero. For the first time in history eighty-two people were strapped aboard a spacecraft, all monitoring the prelaunch go/no-go checks while waiting in some cases to leave Earth forever.

Completing those checklists was another mental milestone. All external hatches had been installed and sealed. We were now on New Dawn atmosphere and would be for roughly the next six months. Hundreds of simulations had brought us this far but now it was all real. I wondered how many people were having second thoughts. I was not one of them. My soul wanted to get into the sky.

On one of my bright blue touch screens I watched the tracking data from our refueling platform as it uploaded to New Dawn. It was holding course. The sounds of our own fueling had begun from beneath us. There were rumbles, hisses, and vibration. Along with them came the faint hum of the crew access arms being retracted. My display automatically came up with the abort program icon, the program that would allow us to detach and launch away from our super heavy section if there was a catastrophic problem. On my left screen fuels were loading into the routing display diagrams for New Dawn. I had launched on starships five times. I knew what fueling should look like and feel like. In simulations the people below me had heard the sounds of fueling but there was no practical way to allow them to feel the ship actually pumping fuel into the tanks. It felt like New Dawn had awakened and was impatient to go.

My countdown readout said T-minus 7 minutes. I wondered how we had got that far so quickly. Ground control was assuring each other New Dawn was still go for launch. My screen showed a switch to internal power. At one minute it was completely out of my control. My display showed the flight computer racing through final checks faster than any human could even read them. Less than a minute and the Launch Director called out to all that we were go for startup. A rapidly flashing startup notice appeared on my center screen.

Explosions beneath us. A deep loud rumble that sounded as though it might break through the ship's walls. Spacecraft shudder. An invisible hand is pushing everyone back into their seat. It is a sensation welcomed by any experienced flyer because it means you are indeed going up, not out. The noise and vibration gradually steadied to a crackling rumble. The G-force held us. We were flying. All the sensations I had come to expect from a Heavy pressing on us. The numbers on my display looked fine. No out of family engines. As usual we reached max-Q so quickly it would have been easy to miss. Another smooth ride from the super heavy. It must be that so many engines sharing the load makes for a magic carpet effect of lift.

It's a quick two and a half minutes to main engine cutoff but anticipation makes it seem longer. There's an abrupt cutoff of the rumble beneath you and immediately your seat turns you loose from the pull. Your mind knows what's coming next so the new boom of power is expected as you're abruptly forced back into your seat again.

But the ride up on starship is smooth. Watching the engine readouts on the display is a reassurance you don't really need because you can feel the acceleration increasing. As long as those numbers stay constant you know you're inserting properly.

When the voice on the comm declared, "nominal insertion," I dared a look up at those wonderful starship windows. Hazy black sky overhead.

"Standby for RC checks," brought me back to work. I switched my center screen to

Reaction Control Thrusters and watched the firing sequence taking place.

Someone's stuffed praying bear toy floated up alongside me. Its tag read, 'Hope.'

"New Dawn, phase burn in fifteen."

"Boca, New Dawn, phase in fifteen."

The center screen automatically switched to orbital plot. The refueling platform was above us as expected. The burn in fifteen minutes would bring us up to that corridor.

"New Dawn you are cleared to raise seats and screens to deck orientation and raise your visors."

"Boca, New Dawn, raising seats."

The decision had been made long ago to orient the passengers to the deck floor as soon as possible. Medical, HR, and Security would be down there helping them remove their hoods as soon as the seats were up, even though we had not docked with the refueling ship yet. The med people did not want passengers throwing up inside those hoods any more than necessary, so removing them early was considered to be less of a danger than keeping people zipped in. Barf bags would be passed out in ample quantities. It was expected some would have already emptied their stomachs and would need to be dealt with. I wouldn't hear about that until our first staff meeting.

We were chasing the refueling platform and slowly closing in minute by minute. Our refueling platform had already been oriented toward us. We would fly behind it then slowly nose up to it for fuel transfer. The spacecraft probe and drogue system hopefully would interconnect after which the high-pressure exchange would take place. If it did not, our flight would be over.

As we waited to close in, I took a moment to check below. "Easton to Dumars."

Chief Medical Officer Andrea Dumars answered quickly, "Go ahead, Captain."

"How are our passengers?"

"Very much as expected, Captain. Three of my staff have left their seats to attend to early hood removals and clean ups but otherwise we're on track. No problems we can't handle."

"Thank you, Doctor. Easton out."

My center screen had changed to the refueling configuration. On my right screen I had the forward-looking camera showing the bright spot of light that was our refueler in the distance. Center screen showed thrusters were firing to make us just right. I watched as the bright spot of light grew larger and more defined until it came into focus as the feed section of the refueling platform. We drifted up until our rendezvous thruster program kicked it and brought us in line. At the four-hundred-meter imaginary keep-out sphere more thrusters brought us to a stop with reference to the refueler. A few words exchanged with Boca brought an enable command and the next subroutine of thruster firings began to move us in. The camera on my right display monitor let me watch the refueler's feed port moving toward us ever so slowly. I could just make out her drogue baskets open and waiting to capture our short refueling booms.

Starship did it all; no astronaut intervention required. We mated so softly there was barely anything to be felt. When my display began to show fuel flowing I sat back and exhaled as though I'd done the whole thing myself. This was the last milestone. A full load of fuel would mean there was nothing to stop us from breaking away from Earth.

We filled New Dawn to the brim, broke away, and on our monitors we watched the refueler fall back, waiting for more starships to refill it.

My center screen switched back to orbital mechanics. For the first time the orbits now displayed contained one that was marked, TMI. Trans Mars Injection. It was an arc away from Earth and into open space. Following along were the very familiar waypoint designations along with Course Correction burns. I notice XO Pars looking over at me through her open visor with a wide smile.

"We're going, Mark."

"I believe we are, Jan."

"We are a village," she added.

I nodded and as I had so many times tried to imagine eighty-two people locked in roughly the sixty-foot section of a long aluminum tube, surviving that span of time in cold, open space. They'd all been psyche tested, but the reality of the cold just beyond the rocket body walls meant that now there was no option to resign.

When the final Go/No Go poll began my first private shipboard comm message interrupted over my headset.

"Captain Easton, Dumars."

"Kind of busy up here, Andrea."

"I'm required to inform you immediately of any significant problems, Captain."

"Go ahead."

"Two of our citizens are having second thoughts and are insisting they be taken back to Boca."

"How much of a problem?"

"They have been trying to unstrap. We are having to stay with them to keep them down."

"Who are we talking about?"

"Mr. and Mrs Bisley, horticulture specialists."

"Will sedation be required do you think?"

"I believe so. Reminding them of the disclaimer they signed is of no importance to them."

"You have my authorization for the injections. Try to be back in your seats before the TMI burn. Thanks, Andrea."

"Understood. Dumars out."

Pars looked over at me with raised eyebrows. I rolled my eyes and went back to work. Almost immediately there was a call from Mission Director Epstone on a private channel.

"Epstone to Easton, how do you read?"

"Loud and clear, Director."

"Well, this is it, Mark. I can't find a reason stop this. How is it up there? Any deal breakers?"

"We have two horticulturists who have changed their minds, Ben. Dumars is about to put them to sleep. Otherwise we are go."

"Bad timing on their part but we expected this."

"I'll promise them first class seats on the first ship back."

"I doubt they'll see the humor in that. But I guess I have to authorize the burn."

"You've done an outstanding job, Ben. We can't thank you enough."

"Okay, then. God be with us all."

At TMI zero we fired our Raptors and felt the big push, the last sensation of gravity we would have until the midcourse correction. On our rear facing cameras the Earth gradually formed a full globe of blue and white. At engine cutoff New Dawn abruptly became a new way of life.

Chapter 3

On the Command deck we had several hours of checklists and procedures to go through but I knew the real madhouse was below us on C and B decks. I used my left-hand monitor display to create a split screen camera view of those areas. I added a view of the D deck medical area as an insert near the bottom of the screen. C and B looked just as expected. The deck's large center column of toilets and shower stalls were surrounded by people still strapped in their seats while others were up and holding on to anything available including each other. Medical personnel floated from one patient to the next trying to catch midair vomit or help stabilize the person creating it. Security officers were stopping people trying to go into the toilets to be sick. Maintenance personnel were holding to one side of the room, waiting to begin deflating and removing seats so they could be stored under the floor. The hope was they could begin setting up the privacy habitat modules quickly. Because the Maintenance, Security and Medical people had put in a lot of time riding the Vomit Comet they were adapting to zero-G nicely. The general population was clearly not faring as well. Some people were holding on to the ceiling while others hugged the floor for dear life. A few bodies periodically floated by the camera in a frozen comical posture. As we watched, Maintenance did manage to begin deflating and removing a few seats while others began detaching the habitat panel sections from the wall. A few determined but still sick passengers were even trying to help. On the Med Bay camera the entrance to the med area was crowded. There were barf bags in use everywhere and just as many floating free. The situation looked bad enough that at my first break in the checklists, I called down.

"Dr. Dumars, Easton, how are you doing?"

"To quote you Mark, we're a little busy at the moment."

"How many having trouble?"

"Thirty-five at the last count but that's a dynamic number. Hopefully the sick bag estimate was adequate."

"Anything more serious?"

"Maybe. We may have a kidney stone that came loose from the loss of gravity. He's been sedated so we can get through the rest of this mess before setting up the X-ray equipment."

"Anything I can do?"

"I'll let you know. You've got a shipwide announcement coming up, right? They need to know everything's okay. That will help."

"I'm on it, Ann."

"Dumars out."

Steve West called over, "I'm suddenly glad to be doing procedures."

I replied, "Okay, everybody keep the comm channel clear for a minute." I turned to look at Brent Shaw. "Brent can you put me on shipwide and public address?"

"You're on, Captain."

"Attention all personnel, this is Captain Easton. We are still running the post insertion procedures but everything looks perfect so far. It was a good burn, we are on course and all systems are operating within limits. We could not have had a better departure. So we'll focus on converting the ship to travel mode and we should be able to gradually settle into our designated routines without any problems. I'm sure some of you have questions. I will set up a question answer period on ship's text net as soon as we get through our obligations up here. I know many of you are not feeling well. Please hang on. Medical will get you through this. Thank you, everyone. That is all."

"Well, I feel better," joked Steve West.

I declared, "Bridge personnel are now cleared to remove suits." I unstrapped and held to the seat to begin removing my pressure suit. Beneath my seat a blue flight suit was waiting. Behind me Paul Descard and Amanda Bishop were helping each other do the same. I folded and packed my suit in storage under my seat then asked, "Jan, I'm going to break away to do the tour; would you take over? Paul, you want to go with me down to Engineering?"

"By all means lead on, Captain."

"Any space sickness?"

"None at all, surprisingly. John Glenn once suggested older people such as me are less prone to it."

"Well, get ready to be around those less fortunate."

"Lead on, sir."

At the ladderway we pulled cautiously down to find F deck was more populated than expected. A quick look around made it clear these people were also on the edge of sick. They had not removed their lightweight suits. Their hoods were pushed back and floating behind them. Some had locked themselves into seats at the Velcro-covered tables provided to help instill deck floor orientation. The dozen small tables each surrounded by four small chairs with folding restraint armrests had suddenly become popular. Enough seating for half the ship's complement. No one was at the food court area yet, and no one was bothering with the entertainment section. No conversation seemed to be taking place, the object being to keep everything in. The many colorful uplifting-by-design pictures on the walls may have been helping though two had fallen to the floor from the pressures of launch. I took a moment to look everyone over, then nodded my support and waved as reassuringly as the moment allowed. They were content not to respond.

We pushed down to the E deck ladderway and pulled in. Again there were people still in their suits, hoods back, sitting or holding on to exercise equipment at various points around the room. No one was in any condition to exercise. One of them had her face covered by a sick bag. Some of the others gave a sick smile and waved. The food and entertainment area on this deck was again deserted.

I paused at the ladder and collected myself before descending to D deck. I checked to be sure Paul was keeping up. He nodded knowingly.

D deck, the home of sick bay, Security, conference areas, and the emergency airlock was packed. Barf bags everywhere. Expressions of dismay. Medical staff floating around among them. There was no sensible way to make a gesture of support. Paul and I floated past to the ladderway and escaped down.

The C deck habitat area was also crowded but surprisingly a bit more positive. Many people had risen from their seats and removed their suits. Several suits had been abandoned and were floating around the room. Two or three security people in blue flight suit uniforms were hovering around the central column of toilets and shower stalls to prevent people from being sick in them. Maintenance people were in the process of deflating and vacuum packing empty launch seats in preparation for storing them under the floor. Five-foot duffle bags containing all that was left of each person's Earth life were Velcro'd to the walls near the ladderway. We watched as one person talked his way past Security and was allowed to use one of the toilets. The narrow, vertical shower cubicles that separated the toilets were still sealed and tagged shut. The two-minute fingerprint-check showers would not be available until we converted to the three shift New Dawn routine. I made a mental bet the situation down on B deck was similar.

As we looked over the area, a loose compartment panel floated past us. Two individuals in pursuit paused to stare at us. One waved. We pushed off the wall and floated over to them. The four of us held to the ceiling.

"Captain Easton, Jeff James. Do you remember me?"

"You mean shift two Chief Engineer James, usually called JJ, right?"

We shook hands. Descard reached out and hugged James.

"Looks like it's going as well as can be expected, JJ."

"I predict we'll have all these compartments put together in four hours."

"Everyone here seems to be holding up well."

"Yeah, there were a few who had to be taken upstairs. The crowd at the toilets was a bit of a problem. It's tricky; we can't have space sickness around the panels we're trying to mate."

"It looks like you're getting there."

"Yeah, we just have to be standing by with the vacuums."

"We're headed down to B to see how they're doing."

"Tell Prolen we are already joining panels up here, would you?"

"We'll do that. Keep up the great work, JJ."

We followed the ceiling to make our way to the ladderway. This time we pushed feet first down.

It was the same diverse crowd on B. The central showers and toilets were being guarded by security, many seats had been removed but they were just beginning to pull panels from the walls to assemble compartments. Again there were erratic groups of sick and semi-sick passengers circling the toilet entrances. I spotted Engineer Prolen as he headed our way.

"Doing well here, Captain. Where are they at on C?"

Descard answered, "How's it going Brian? They're assembling compartments on C but you're ahead on launch seats."

"JJ and I have a bet. He doesn't have a chance."

"Everyone here looks fairly okay. Any problems?"

"The bathroom crowd is not helping but otherwise we're good to go."

I nodded. "Let us know if you have any serious problems. We're heading down to Engineering. Keep up the good work."

"So we are green across the board then, Captain?"

"Flying perfect, Brian."

"Great, just great."

We pulled down to A deck. The place was heavily decorated with colored indicator lights and gauges that were alive with movement. A low chorus of equipment noise filled the air. Half a dozen people in green Engineering flight suits stopped and took notice of us. In the center of the room the main column for water recovery and solid waste processing were receiving the most attention. Several technicians were monitoring both processes. To our right an engineer was hovering in front of the two Cray computer stacks. On our left two others were putting security seals on the main engines console. Next to them a tech was staring at a checklist in front of the hydraulics control area and on the opposite side of the room two others were monitoring the main power station. The life support monitoring console next to it was also being scrutinized by engineers.

I made a point to take note of the main airlock directly across from us. The tags and seals were all still in place meaning the techs had not yet run the checklists. Descard's second in command saw us and pushed off in our direction.

"Engineer Hada, good to see you," I said.

Hada nodded to his boss Descard and replied, "Everything is on schedule, Captain. We still have quite a few checklists to go through but so far so good."

"Any problems with crew?"

"Not with these guys, Captain. They're all veterans."

Descard said, "Setup is going well upstairs, Kane. We should be able to split up into the three eight-hour shifts as soon as they finish the compartments. Roughly half are sick so they're busy up there. Are you seeing anything out of limits?"

Hada shook his head. "It's been surprising. So far it's all on the money. I know ground crew checked this stuff out a dozen times but it still surprises me that launch ops didn't shake anything down."

Descard said, "It's been like that all the way up, Kane. Let's hope our luck holds."

"And if it doesn't you guys will be the first to know," said Hada.

Descard smiled.

I tuned to Descard. "Well, I'll leave you to it. Let me know if you need anything."

Descard joined Hada and they pushed off the ceiling and glided back to the power station area. With a last wave he and his associate went back to work.

I floated all the way up without stopping or being stopped. Some took notice of my passing but were in no mood to intercept. Back on the Command deck the Bridge personnel were locked in their seats still running checkout procedures. Personnel Director Amanda Bishop had left. I assumed she had joined the B and C deck melee.

Pars noticed my arrival. "How was it down there?"

"Battle zone."

"Is it really that bad?"

"About half of them are sick but the setup is going quickly. We'll be just fine."

"Wow!" replied West. "Half? That's a little worse than they forecast."

"Nerves," added Pars. "People just facing the reality of it all. Mark, Dr. Bishop headed down to help coordinate."

"How about Engineering?" asked West.

"They are all okay. They are less than halfway through checkout but there are no alarms."

"Praise the Lord," replied West.

For the next three hours we continued to work the checklists, comparing notes with Ground Control. There were very few problems. As we completed the assigned checkouts it left Brent Shaw straggling behind on the communications and life support documentation. He signed off on the last tablet document and looked up with an expression of exasperation and victory only to find he was the last and we were all staring at him. Laughter broke out.

A call from C deck came through. "James to Easton."

"Go ahead JJ."

"We have completed twenty-six habitat modules. We've had to take time out to tag them with the assigned individual's name and number because some of our guests are trying to use other people's modules. I guess being sick in public is too embarrassing. We'll have all forty set up in about two hours. I thought I should keep you advised."

"Great job, JJ. Carry on. You might want to tie-in with Doctor Bishop. She can probably help with the rush."

"A few people are already inside their assigned module decorating, Captain. By the way, have you heard how B deck is doing?"

"Not yet but I will advise them of your progress."

"Great. James out."

"Easton to Descard."

"Go ahead, Captain."

"How's B-deck construction?"

"Sixteen more modules and we're done, Captain. We can't keep people out of them. You haven't heard from James, have you?"

"Rumor has it he also has some occupancy."

"I'll have to check on that."

"Any serious problems?"

"Not really except for occasional squatters in the wrong cubicle."

"Sounds hopeful to me, Paul."

"So far so good."

"Easton out."

I twisted in my seat in time to see Amanda Bishop float up through the ladderway. She was poking at her tablet. She grabbed the wall to steady herself and noticed me staring.

"Amanda, I believe you are Personnel Director, correct?"

"Uh-oh, I'm not sure I like where this is going, Mark."

I stifled a laugh. "Well, here on my directive it says as soon as all living modules are ready we are supposed to announce the beginning of the eight hour shift divisions."

Bishop narrowed her stare, "And doesn't it say the Captain announces that?"

I smiled. "Actually it says it's up to the Captain to appoint someone."

"And I'm the deer in the headlights."

"Think of it as another award, Doctor."

"Right. When do you want to do it?"

"The sooner the better. They are just about done with the cubicles. People are in a hurry to get into them. I don't expect anyone to sleep or begin their exercise routines, but it will be helpful if everyone has an assigned basic area to be in. It will spread out the masses and help everyone get orientated to a routine."

"Let me scribble down a few more talking points and I'll do it. To be honest, that's why I came up."

"Thanks, Amanda."

I turned to Brent Shaw, "So, Brent, the ship's intranet is up and running at max?"

"It is, Captain."

"And they can get television, radio, movies, talk shows, anything they want?"

"Captain, they can watch prerecorded TV twenty-four hours a day for six months and not see it all, compliments of Cray A."

"And Live-Delayed Earth transmissions?"

"Up and running. Recent news and science as it comes in."

"Good."

"Some are already using it, Captain. Just a thin bump in the bandwidth charts so far though."

Bishop interrupted, "Okay, I'm ready, Mark. No complaints allowed. You get what you get."

"Set her up, Brent. The shipwide address and video conferencing systems are yours, Doctor."

Bishop straightened up and gripped her tablet tightly.

Shaw nodded that he was ready.

"Attention, everyone. This is Personnel Director Amanda Bishop. We are pleased to announce nearly all habitats have now been assembled and are ready for use. Per our mission directives that means we will now be switching to standard eight-hour shifts. Obviously none of us are going to get any sleep for a while but if this period is scheduled to be a normal sleep shift for you, you may want to spend time setting up your compartment and trying to get some rest. Also, all of the news and entertainment is now available on your tablet or laptop via the ship's intranet. The same goes for those of you who happen to be on your daily exercise schedule. We would not expect anyone to immediately begin their routine, but if your gym requirements do fall in this time slot you might consider visiting that area and checking on the equipment and other services. In this first shift of our eight-hour cycles we should all begin mentally training ourselves to adapt to these assignments. If you find you are having any special problems please let someone in Medical know and we will do everything possible to assist you. As Captain Easton said in his earlier announcement, New Dawn is operating without any difficulties. We are on course and on schedule. So do your best to align yourself with yours and have a great new day."

We all looked at her and smiled. Pars clapped.

"We are now officially a society," said West with a smirk.

"May the bathrooms keep working," added Bishop.

I floated up from my seat and held to the seat back. "At this point only three people are required on the Bridge. If anyone would like to go check on their module or grab something to eat in the galley, go for it."

"I need to return to the habitat decks or I'll be accused of hiding out," said Bishop.

"I intend to try out the food dispensers," added Pars.

We watched Pars and Bishop meet, push away, and pause before dropping down the ladderway.

I thought for a moment and decided it's quite an odd thing to announce to a large group of people it is time to begin living a new life.

Chapter 4

Five days of understanding. New Dawn gave us a brilliant ride. Cabin air was always a constant seventy-three degrees Fahrenheit. The air smelled fresh and clean despite the fact the air handlers were being pushed to their max from sickness and loose personal articles. Surprisingly, waste management was up to the job even though there were cases of misuse by desperate personnel. Water reclamation filters had to be replaced and cleaned early but clear, pure water was still being produced. Our miniature nuclear cores hummed smooth, steady power all over the ship. Both Cray mainframes fed our systems and terminals without pause-feedback circles. All eighty-two active personal communicators seemed to be receiving and transmitting as needed. The black sky and stars beyond the many New Dawn portals watched over us. There had been many manned starship missions but none this complex or so heavily populated. I spent my shifts in the command seat or at the displays in my personal quarters watching the systems readouts and feeling like we were getting more than we deserved.

But there was of course the alternate perspective. Five days dominated by a carnival of social chaos. Most of the space sick had recovered but were still trying to reconcile where they were. There had been a furious effort to unpack duffel bags and decorate living compartments. Some trading and bartering had broken out.

There were a few arguments. Overcoming the dizziness and nausea along with the other effects of zero-G had left many people edgy, an aftereffect fully expected. Tranquilizers were passed out by Medical quite freely. Some of the most difficult people were now happy about everything but they had to be watched while awake. The Medical staff was putting in too many hours. Quite a few had worked twenty-four hour shifts during the worst of it.

Mr. and Mrs. Bisley, the couple who had decided just before trans-Mars injection they had changed their minds, were now trying to decide what they wanted to do.

We were also still faced with one kidney stone patient. The patient's attacks would come and go. Pain killers were administered as necessary. There was no way to set up for surgery yet so the staff was praying the thing would come out with urination even though it already had been too many days.

For the first two days there had been barely any use of the food and entertainment area. Veteran flyers had those facilities all to themselves. That changed quickly on day three. Suddenly people discovered they were starving.

Some were taking extra food packs and storing them in their habitat for later even though there was no need to do that. The primeval instinct for food survival had kicked in. Empty food packs would occasionally float by on the habitat decks, the contents having been consumed cold or even unmixed. Stores Manager Martha Higgins was caught hoarding food packets in her cubicle.

By day six people began to find the new normal. The three-shift social structure proved to be a blessing. Between work shifts, sleep periods, and free time in the habitats, there was never more than half the ship's complement spread out on D, E, and F decks with roughly a dozen people on each. Velcro card games went on almost continually. Email and text groups formed. Television and movies were always playing somewhere. There was talk of scheduling a regular movie night using a three-screen wrap around display setup. Electronic game tournaments were frequent. Mars education classes on D deck became well-attended. Except for people bumping into each other doing flips, traversing the decks was easy.

Our daily briefings were held at the beginning of first shift. One Bridge officer from third shift was designated to attend. Director of Personnel Amanda Bishop, Chief Engineer day shift Paul Descard and Chief Medical Officer Andrea Dumars also were required. Typically we sat at the small conference table in the Bridge conference room with armrests locked down so

42

we were all at eye level. The black star sky through the overhead windows made for a surreal meeting area. The people on duty at the Command Station could see us through the open entrance. There were frequent glances in our direction.

The Day 6 meeting was fully attended. When I had everyone's attention, I began, "So, ship's systems last shift?"

Descard replied, "No significant problems. We had an out of limits on the hydraulics monitor but when reset the problem did not come back. We unsealed the showers and thankfully there was not a mad rush to use them. There was a temperature advisory on the water reclamation but it cleared itself. That was probably the system adapting to the showers being used for the first time. Power systems have been a little slow to stabilize at shift change but the core has remained perfectly stable. All in all we could not ask for a better shift."

I asked, "How about the water cells around B and C decks, Paul?"

"Yeah, they have been very stable, line pressure right on the money. I forgot to mention them. We are perfectly ready to take cover during a solar storm. No problem there."

"Anyone else have any Engineering items?"

No takers.

I continued, "So it's on to you, Amanda."

Bishop smiled at everyone. "Well, first I was asked to sit in for the IT group so I'll start with the Crays. The report is they're operating at about half their processing capability with no errors. There have been no HAL 9000 issues so far."

A few of us stifled laughs.

Bishop continued, "It's a blessing that all of our entertainment and communications systems are running perfectly. Thank God. Have any of you experienced any delays or computer problems at all?"

No one responded.

Bishop continued, "So on to personnel. To be honest I believe Andrea should be speaking to this. Medical is managing the brunt of personnel problems and doing a remarkable job I might add. Most of our people problems are psychological. But things are quieting down now that everyone has a place to call home. The arguments we've had were not serious, in fact a few are downright hilarious. Jen Parry and her husband Gary somehow became aware that their living compartments are directly above the waste ejection system in Engineering. They have been complaining they can smell it, which is of course completely impossible. We took air samples in their habitats and showed them the air is far cleaner than that of Earth but they have a mind block. We have two

Engineering techs who are willing to change habitats with them so problem solved."

"Good God," commented Pars.

"That's the sort of thing we are dealing with. As I've said, things appear to be settling down."

I turned to Andrea Dumars, "So, Doctor, you're dealing more with that kind of thing than actual medical problems I take it?"

Dumars nodded, "Yes. It's a good thing there are few medical conditions to deal with. A few headaches, bumps and bruises, upset stomachs, and zero-G bathroom difficulties. Nothing too serious except we do still have a kidney stone patient."

"No chance of passing it, then?"

Dumars shook her head. "It's been too long. The damn thing must have lodged somehow that it won't come loose. We are going to have to do surgery."

"How unexpected is this, Doctor?" I asked.

"They were all screened for kidney disease but you get into a long-term weightless environment and anything that's been hiding in the kidney starts floating around like everything else and eventually something can find its way to the urinary tract."

"So what happens now?"

"We set up the X-ray equipment and evaluate. Surgery will need to be endoscopic."

"Every man's greatest fear," said Descard.

"How painful will this be?" I asked.

"There will be anesthesia."

"How is he?"

"He's feeling no pain but we're getting him ready while Paul's people unpack and set up surgery. We are sedating and hydrating him by intra and orally so he's in no pain."

Bishop added, "We should take note this will be the first surgery of its kind outside of Earth orbit. A weightless patient being operated on by a weightless doctor. That should make front page on Earth."

"Are we confident about this, Doctor?"

"I will be attached to the table with the patient. The VR helmet will keep me in 3D during the entire procedure."

"But you're expecting this to be pretty much routine?"

"I do not expect any complications with the procedure, but whenever anesthesia is called for that introduces an element of concern."

"When are you scheduled to do this, Doctor?"

"If Engineering is ready we will begin prepping as soon as I leave this meeting."

Bishop said, "We'll be clearing the deck before they begin so they will have quiet in the operating area. All personnel will be informed D deck is off limits until further notice. They'll be advised using text and audio on the comm units only. No public address announcement will be made for the sake of the patient. Also, we'll have Doctor Dumars and her staff on a private comm channel during the procedure. You can listen in, Captain, if you wish."

"Yes, I would like to be included. Thank you."

We paused and exchanged glances.

"Does anyone else have anything for this morning?" I asked.

When no one spoke, Pars snapped up her armrests and pushed out of her seat toward her private compartment. The others floated up and headed for the ladderway. I paused for any additional private comments then coasted back to the Bridge command seat.

There was a yellow caution icon at the bottom of my systems display. It was not flashing. I clicked it and got a message window saying, "Cell water pressure out of limits."

I called down to Engineering. "Easton to Engineering."

"Markus here, Captain. Go ahead."

"I'm seeing an out of limit caution in the water cell circuits."

"Yes, Captain. That's new. We've just cleared three of these. The system is barely out of limits on each caution so we think the parameters are just too stringent. We want to expand that range a tiny bit. That should stop the alarms."

"You have my approval. Go ahead and do it. Send me the email request and I'll sign off on it."

"Sounds good, Captain. Markus out."

I closed the message window and began going through the systems checks required at the beginning of each shift. Thirty minutes later my comm came alive with the sounds of Dr. Dumars setting up her surgical unit. I kept working and listened to the surgery unfold.

Dumars sounded completely relaxed but also completely in charge. At one point she made as statement full of medical jargon I did not understand except one word she used was "inserting" which made me cringe.

The process went on for forty-five minutes until I picked out the words "laser on." There was long pause after that. Next there was something about "extraction" followed by "wake him." The last audio I heard from her was, "That's it. Now it's wait and see."

Nearing the end of my morning checklist I finally got a call on a private channel. It was Dumars.

"Yes, Doctor."

"Well, it looks like we got it all. He should have no further symptoms. It was a very straightforward operation. No surprises."

"That's good to hear. How is he?"

"He's still groggy but overjoyed to hear of the stone's demise."

"So that's it?"

"There was some blood in his urine afterward but that's to be expected. He should be up and floating tomorrow."

"Congratulations, Doctor. First real surgery in space."

"The team is breaking down the surgical equipment and the X-ray. We should have all of our Med Lab space back later today. D deck is open for business again. Talk to you later. Dumars out."

I set my left display screen to randomly step through the decks and enjoyed the moment. D deck now busy setting back up after the surgery. No more kidney stone patient. Everyone reasonably healthy and adapting. On E deck a few people were now using the exercise equipment and sweating profusely. The required two-hour workout was making real men and women of us all. The video screen workout programs were also in full use, people dancing weightlessly or wearing VR helmets and performing physical feats like superheroes. On F deck there was more than a dozen seated at the tables or floating at the food and oven racks. Others were watching movies or talk shows. Engineering looked busy but calm and collected with tablets floating from one person to another. The views on B and C decks were now largely blocked. Twenty cubicles fastened to the deck floor circling the room with twenty more cubicles situated on top of those. Each protruded out from the wall, side by side, seven feet, four-point-five feet at the head by the wall, two-point-five feet at the accordion-door entrance facing the central toilet/shower area. With those toilets and showers taking up the room's center, very little was now visible from any of the deck's cameras. Nevertheless, there did seem to be a steady flow of people coming and going from their cubicles.

Someone tapped me on the shoulder. It was Janet Pars.

"We've got the one-o'clock briefing from Momma Earth coming up. You want to go get coffee and watch it?"

I looked over at Steve West on the Engineering station. He nodded his approval.

"You have the Con, Steve."

"I have the Con."

"Coffee where?"

"I believe we should take it on F deck like everybody else. It's good for them to see the Captain and XO in a casual setting, don't you think?"

"I do."

We coasted down to D deck, got quite a few looks from the visitors there, went and got our coffees and locked down at an empty table.

Nearby others had selected an old talk show interview with a New Dawn crew member. The interviewer was asking about living on Mars.

"But Mike, once you're settled on Mars you will not be able to go outside without a space suit. Don't you think you'll miss that? Won't you regret being locked in all the time?"

"It's a good question, Maureen. No, I do not think I will feel locked in on Mars. There are three supply starships already there on the surface at the landing site sent there two years ago in anticipation of our arrival. We also have three more supply starships on their way to Mars right now three weeks ahead of us. When we arrive, we will have literally tons of supplies and equipment there waiting for us. We will initially set up six large interconnected domes and several smaller ones. Those domes have large transparent segments that look out over the surface. They are treated with a radiation absorbent material developed from the coatings used on stealth aircraft and submarines."

The interviewer interrupted, "But still, Mike, you won't be able to go outside and touch the world out there like you can on Earth."

Mike cut back in, "Maureen, think about this. Many people live in the colder regions of Earth like Alaska, Canada, northern Russia. Even if they work outside they are usually heavily suited up and most people spend the majority of their time inside, especially in the winter months. We will be living and working in large domes that have transparency that is very much like being outdoors. So which of us will feel like they are outside more, the folks living in the northern hemispheres of Earth or those of us on Mars?"

The debate continued.

Pares sipped and smiled. "You know I actually still feel a little guilty about our luxurious living compartments on G deck. I mean we even have a workstation and all."

"They put the two of us up on the Bridge for a reason."

"Of course I know that, but every now and then I get reminded of the layout for the B and C cubicles for one reason or another."

"What of it?"

Pars stifled a laugh. "Well it's actually hilarious when you think about it, but Amanda has this idiosyncrasy about the foot of her compartment being narrower than the head. You know how the head space is fifty-four inches, which is kind of luxurious really, but the foot end is only thirty inches. So she says every time she wakes up still half asleep, it looks like her feet are a mile away."

"That's one I haven't heard before."

"Of course not, we being up in the Carlyle on G deck."

I sipped my coffee. "Now that *is* funny."

"Semiprivate adjoining toilet and all."

"There had to be a toilet on the Bridge, Jan."

"God knows."

"By the way, I've checked your daily logs. Any personnel problems on your shift you didn't mention?"

She nodded. "We've had a few arguments about stupid things that had to be

52

broken up. It's like that joke about a person complaining endlessly about the peanuts on an airliner flight. Somebody can't take it any longer so they stand up and remind the guy he's in a seat in the sky."

"Yeah, we've got that one beat I think."

"And you had the Bisleys bitching about changing their minds and wanting to be dropped off back at Boca. How'd that end up?"

I smiled deviously. "They have free first-class seat reservations on the next ship back to Earth."

"Don't tell me they bought into that?"

"Medical has been eavesdropping on their communications just in case they're planning a Bisley Mutiny on the Bounty or something. The two of them have been studying the chemistry of Mars soil as tested from the return samples that came in. They seem to be back into farming."

"The irony of it is we need those people. We had trouble getting Agronomists and Horticulturists for this trip."

I nodded. "Yeah, it's those four pesky absolutes; air, water, shelter, and food. We've got to have them to live. So, you have any other social warfare?"

"Not really. The three-shift division is working well. Even the all-nighters who don't retire to their caves have not been a problem."

I glanced at my watch. "Time for the transmission."

"Yep, let's go. Your place or mine?"

We coasted back up to my quarters. I offered Jan the keyboard seat and hooked into floor stirrups next to her. She typed in her credentials and passwords until we were at the *'Captain's Eyes only,'* icon. She clicked us in and the latest video file from Earth Command switched on.

It was a full-face image of Dr. Ben Epstone, Mission Director for the New Dawn program. He looked half asleep. His gray-red crew cut was thinning badly. He was overdue for a shave. He had tired lines in his tanned aged face. He raised his eyebrows and began.

"Captain Easton and XO Pars, greetings from Earth directorate. I am obligated to remind you these briefings are confidential, not to be shared with anyone. I've read through your latest reports. We are all in agreement here that things are proceeding even better than we'd hoped. Keep up the good work you two."

Epstone paused then continued, "I have several updates for you. Solar activity continues to be flat and the forecast is for no major eruptions any time soon. Our luck is holding. The solar-link chain of communication satellites that will give us faster two-way communication with Mars even during conjunction continue to be on track toward their assigned coordinates. And, Mission Control has now begun the process of waking the three cargo starships sent to Mars two years ago. They actually have the cargo hold main door open on one of them and have

54

exercised the crane. Very exciting. So, you should have several tons of equipment and supplies already there when you arrive. Also the three additional cargo starships presently on course for Mars are tracking perfectly and on schedule to arrive and land three weeks before you get there, as planned. You folks should have plenty of cargo waiting to be unpacked."

Epstone hesitated for a moment. "And, there's one last item. It's a little bit embarrassing. I hope to God it turns out to be nothing. We have been contacted by the mother of one of your passengers because she is concerned about her son's behavior aboard New Dawn. Bob Banabalas is the passenger. He's an IT type. I know this is all going to come as a shock to you, but apparently in his emails to his mother Bob claimed to have discovered New Dawn was off course. He further claimed he managed to reach Engineering and correct a thruster problem just before it was too late. He went on to tell her the entire affair is being kept secret to avoid alarming the passengers and their families on Earth. He is expecting a citation of merit and may be promoted to Bridge officer."

Half under her breath Pars moaned, "Oh-my-God."

Epstone shook his head in dismay. "So of course we have looked into this in great detail and it's a bit worse than you might expect. Apparently, Bob was treated over several years during his youth for being a compulsive liar. I don't mean a kid just trying to get away with misdeeds but rather the textbook definition of compulsive pathological liar where he lies just for the enjoyment of it. It is generally referred to as a personality disorder. Apparently for this type of patient the more they get away with a lie the greater the motivation to embellish it. We are consulting with several doctors to advise you of the best way to proceed on this. We are assuming you knew nothing about this and that there have not been any problems with Bob, otherwise we'd have seen something mentioned in your updates. I'm sure you're wondering how Bob got through the selection process. Apparently because he was still a juvenile during his treatment all his records were sealed. He chose not to mention any of this on his applications or paperwork and his family and friends were never asked about this specific condition so they just chose not to bring it up. According to the now unsealed records he was diagnosed as having been cured of the illness. Sorry to drop this in your laps, guys. Maybe it will not be an issue. At this point the advice from our medical staff is to monitor his communications and have your medical people do more frequent checkups. The only real danger we've been advised of is that this person could potentially start false rumors that could lead to panic in the population. Keep us posted and we'll be advising you further in the near future. That's all I have. Warmest regards. Epstone out."

Pars looked at me with a smirk. "It's like a bad joke."

I nodded. "We were bound to have some of these kinds of problems."

"Well maybe that's our glitch for this trip."

"Oh boy. You shouldn't say that. That's the same thing one of the Apollo 13 crew said after they had a premature engine cutoff on takeoff. If I remember correctly, he said, '*Looks like we've had our glitch for this mission.*'"

"And that was Apollo *13*?"

"Yep."

Chapter 5

Over the coming days we watched planet Earth grow smaller and smaller until it was reduced to the size of a large blue star. By week four life aboard New Dawn had become routine. Medical still bore the biggest burden of responsibilities. Quite few people were not fulfilling their daily two-hour exercise regiment, something that had to be done without fail. There were also instances of people consuming too many food packets while others were not eating enough. The Personnel Director also did not escape the occasional social faux pas' that took place. More than once she had to counsel couples on too physical and too vocal behavior when both were occupying the same privacy module. And at one point there was an instance of a small food fight on F deck, considered by most to be an extremely sinful waste of supplies on a spacecraft to Mars.

This day had the potential to be relaxed and collected. My own routine had settled into a required two-hour workout every day before lunch. With the conn turned over to Steve West I dropped down to E deck and scanned around the room for an open treadmill. Of the eight units installed around the gym area, one was available. I glided over to it, wrestled into the Glenn Harness and set the friction level and timer. I chose to leave the runner's video screen off. A slow start quickly brought me into sync with the other runners around the room. The gym area had become the busiest place aboard ship. Everyone was required; no one exempt. No one argued the need for it but quite a few had to be encouraged to maintain their schedule. All eight of the HULK lifting kit devices were also in use. I have no problem with the run but it takes some personal goading to get myself into the lifting kits. On the opposite side of the room a dozen people were hanging out, sitting around the refreshment-entertainment area. Most had just finished their workouts. They watched us sweating and grunting, ignoring the fact that sweat had provided some of the water in their coffee.

As I ran, I noticed a young woman in tights, her reddish-blond hair tied back, floating in my direction, wiping herself with a towel as she drifted along. As always, my mind raced to recall her name. Someday I would know them all.

"Captain Easton, can I ask you about something while you run? I don't mean to be a pest." She held to a wall strap and worked herself upright.

Whenever they say they don't want to be a pest that's always a bad sign. I managed to make out the name on her comm unit. Helmsly.

"Of course, Ms. Helmsly. How are you doing?"

"Patricia, Captain. I wanted to ask you to consider allowing shower time to be exchanged if both parties agree. My friend tends to shower only every other day. She would be willing to let me have her shower minutes on the unused days."

"Have you discussed this with the Personnel Director yet?"

"Yes, Dr. Bishop is kind of inflexible about this. She has a standing joke of sorts that shower minutes are not transferable. Personally I don't see the harm in it."

I gasped for air as I spoke, "Patricia, if I recall, there were specific reasons for that rule. Let me think. One was they did not want shower minutes to become bargaining chips or items put up for sale. They didn't want people becoming angry or envious that someone had a way to acquire more shower time than they could. But the most important reason was they wanted to reduce stress on the system. Unused shower minutes means the reclamation system and the purification systems do not need to work as hard. That's also less power usage, less heat generated and a bunch of other benefits. So I can see why they would not want to make exceptions to that rule."

"But it's such a simple idea, Captain. It just seems like common sense."

"Only if you ignore the details we just discussed, Patricia. And, to remove that rule would require approval from Earth Command, so that would not be an easy change to get approval for."

"Well please think about it, Captain. That's all I ask."

I nodded. She looked unswayed. She pushed off toward the food area.

A voice next me said, "I heard that, Mark. I'd call that a good sign."

I looked to see Chief Engineer Jeffery James strapping into a HULK next to me.

I grunted, "A good sign, JJ?"

"Yeah. When they start being worried about trivial crap it means they're no longer worried about traveling through space in a tin can."

We both smirked. James began his squats.

"Something I should mention to you, Mark."

I gasped, "I'm a captive audience, buddy."

"We've got a funny engine sensor in one of the fuel feed lines."

"What's funny about it?"

"Everything in that section is shut down of course. Oh man, my left knee is still acting up. Sorry. Everything is shut down in main engine systems but we look in on them from time to time just for fun."

"I know that."

"So all the family of sensors down there should be showing null, a steady null."

"Yep."

"Well we've got one that is talking to us. It's reading up and down, zero to three volts, erratic."

"All three shifts seeing this?"

"Yes. We've started discussing it."

"Ground been notified?"

"No, and they don't check for this like we do."

"So maybe an open circuit?"

"Could be. Or, a faulty sensor generating its own signals, or something in the fuel feed line causing a reading."

"What could cause a reading like that?"

"I don't know."

I looked around to be sure no one was listening. "Would I be correct in guessing you've already looked at the replacement procedure?"

"Oh yeah."

"Where is the thing?"

"Access through a skirt panel on port side aft. Close to the service handrail so the tether will reach easily. Easy trip there. Comfortable place to work."

"We'll have to report this."

"Yeah, we thought we'd leave that to you."

"I'm sure everyone knows this, but mum's the word. We'd prefer the general population did not know about this yet."

"Already been made clear to the Engineering group."

"Thanks, Jeff. I'll stop down."

I finished my run and pushed off toward the changing curtain I had used. Halfway there, an inquiring mind caught up to me.

"Captain Easton. Captain…."

A middle-aged lady in a baggy one-piece suit was after me. I had to catch the ceiling to stop myself. Her shoulder length hair was splayed out above and behind her. She was still learning accuracy with makeup application. She was smiling wider than seemed possible.

"Captain Easton, I wanted to ask you. We're forming a bridge club. I was wondering if you'd like to join us? Eventually there will be several teams that will compete."

I managed to focus on her communicator name. "That's a very nice invitation, Ms Browning. It will be awhile before I have time for something like that. Please carry on, though. Maybe at some point in the future."

"Well, just thought I'd ask, Captain. If you change your mind let us know."

She swam off toward the next candidate. I pulled my curtain around and stripped then pulled out one of the three-foot paper-cloth towels. One towel only per customer. It must be used strategically. When done drying off it is fed back into a slot that snaps it back in, rings it out, sprays it with a disinfectant, and dries it, ready for the next user. As with everything else, no water is lost.

I prefer the blue flight suits over anything else. Nothing under it other than jockey shorts. It saves greatly on laundry. I also prefer soft ankle boots rather than the thick socks many people wear. The boots are warmer in the constant seventy-three degrees we live in. On my way to the ladderway, I stopped at a dispenser and grabbed a fruit smoothie pack. They come with a very fat straw. They are particularly good.

I dove down toward Engineering, past the habitat decks both of which had quite a bit of coming and going activity. At the entrance to Engineering I had to paste my smoothie to Velcro on the wall. Food and drink not allowed in Engineering.

Descard was off shift but Engineer Luca Greco was with two other engineers, talking. I pushed over to them and held to the ceiling.

Greco came up next to me. "So James found you I take it."

"Yep, what do you think?"

"Well, in the grand scheme of things it's like nothing. But for those who are as fussy as us, it's something."

"It's not nothing, Luca. We have a midcourse correction coming up in a few weeks. Which Raptor does it belong to?"

"The number two. We were able to do a few line impedance checks. That sensor wiring is intact to its full length. That means if this is

64

an open circuit it has to be located right at the sensor."

"So it's either a loose connection or a defective sensor?"

"Those are the best guesses. Otherwise it would have to be some unintuitive type of signal induction but that's just extremely unlikely speculation."

"You know we're going to have to go fix it before the mid course."

"Have you notified Ground?"

"Not yet but the EVA is not open for debate."

"Who are you going to send if it does come to that?"

"Me and someone else."

"I volunteer. I'm propulsion but I also have electrical."

"Thanks. My other *will* be a propulsion specialist like you. This will be a chance to inspect those Raptor bells while we're out there."

"Oh, absolutely. Get some great snapshots of the thrust chambers and outriggers."

"Guess I'll go give Ground the bad news."

"How long to hear back?"

"It's a five-minute delay. Wanna bet it'll take them a lot longer than that?"

"Maybe they'll just decide not to use number two."

"Oh, I really doubt that."

"Me too."

"Try to keep everybody quiet about this, okay?"

"Yeah. So far so good."

I nodded appreciatively and headed for the Command deck. I made it all the way up in one pull with steering along the way. After a wave to Steve West, I coasted into my office, locked down in the seat, then used a stylus and tablet to sketch out what I wanted to say to Ground. No stuttering or stammering allowed. When I felt I had it cold and concise, I opened a private video channel and said my piece.

Approximately five minutes for the message to get there and another five for them to send one back. There was the sudden realization I was pumped at the thought of having a reason to go outside. I sat back and waited and thought. We could only keep this under wraps for just so long. There would be no way to keep a spacewalk secret and trying to would only make the rumor mill worse. As I waited there was a tap at the door.

"Yes?"

The door clicked open to reveal Doctor Bishop peering in at me.

"Got a minute?"

"Five or ten Amanda. What's up?"

She slinked in and shut the door. She hooked a foot in a floor strap and looked at me with folded arms and a narrow stare. "How long are you going to try to keep this from the general population?"

"What?"

"The sensor issue. How long will you conceal it?"

"What sensor issue?"

"Come on, Mark. You know Brian Prolen and I are engaged. You'll probably be marrying us on Mars! Of course he told me about it. I'm the Director of Personnel for God's sake. Who has more of a right to know than I do?"

"Engineer Prolen told you about a sensor problem?"

"It's a simple question, Captain. When does the general population get to know there's a problem with their spaceship?"

"Amanda, you will have to excuse me. I will discuss ship status with you as soon as I'm free. Please keep any rumors you hear to yourself. That is also part of your job. Now, some privacy please."

It set her back a few notches. She held to the corner of my tiny desk, gave me her best fearful frown and pushed off. She exited the door and closed it without looking back.

I selected a private comm channel. "Easton to Prolen."

It took a few seconds as unexpected calls often do.

"Ah, Prolen here, Captain."

"Would you please report to the Captain's office?"

Another unusual pause. "On my way, sir."

It took him a long ten minutes to arrive. He tapped at the door.

"Come in."

He had the inquisitive look of a man about to be sentenced to death. He wore brown work slacks and a blue New Dawn T-shirt. His dark hair was short. He had big blue eyes which had earned him sympathy in the past.

"Yes, Captain?"

"Latch that door behind you."

"Reporting as ordered, sir."

I kept my voice low. "You were directed to keep the sensor problem to yourself."

He wrinkled his brow worriedly.

"But you briefed Doctor Bishop about it."

"But sir, she's Director of Personnel. I thought she had a right to know about it."

"Who else have you decided has a right to know about it?"

"Well, no one."

"So *you* made the decision Doctor Bishop should know about the sensor issue?"

"I didn't see any harm in it."

"You didn't see any harm in disobeying a direct order to keep that issue quiet?"

"But it was Doctor Bishop."

"Let's try this again. When your Engineering lead tells you not to speak about something to anyone, what should you do?"

"Don't speak to anyone about it."

"Can you pick and choose exceptions to that order?"

"No."

"Can you tell Doctor Bishop all about it?"

"No."

"So will you discuss this conversation with her?"

"No."

"Mr. Prolen, you are not a child. I should not need to spend time on this kind of crap. If you breathe one more word about ship's status to anyone outside of Engineering, I will have you held in the Security office confinement area until the sensor problem is resolved. Just nod if you understand and close the door as you leave."

He gave a injured expression along with multiple nods and wasted no time in leaving.

There had been no answer from Mission Control. I could only imagine the conversations taking place there. It was time to get back on-shift. Steve West needed to hit the exercise area. On my way back to the command seat I stopped to heat up a coffee pack. At my seat, West gave me a knowing look as though he had taken note of Prolen's visit.

"I have the Con, Steve."

"You have the Con." He pushed up, gave a half-salute and headed off.

It took the rest of the day for Ground to respond to my message. As I was folding into my sleep sack a Ground transmission icon began flashing on the desk display. I stretched over to click on it.

"Sensor concern received. Expect evaluation and recommendations tomorrow."

Chapter 6

In the morning I emerged early from my zero-G cocoon and hung around the command deck coffee dispenser and food oven. The on-duty crew gave me tired smiles and nods. Coffee was not enough. I dropped down to F-deck and tabbed through a packet drawer to find scrambled eggs and bacon. Two minutes later I was forking the food out of the bag, in free drift, distracted by the pleasure of it. A hand on my shoulder brought me back.

"You were about to bump into someone, Mark." Amanda Bishop smiled at me while holding us to a wall strap.

"Oh, thanks. This stuff always tastes better than you'd expect."

"I'm glad I caught you. No pun intended."

"Yeah, I guess bacon and eggs in one hand and coffee in the other is too much. I should've pasted myself somewhere."

"I want to apologize for yesterday. I've discovered I was being a jerk."

I managed to hold both packets in one hand and grab a wall brace. "I wouldn't go that far."

"Oh ,no; it's the truth. Sometimes I am impulsively blunt. I'm working on it."

"Well, you know what you should have done, right?"

"Of course. First, I should have blasted Brian for not following orders. Then I should have come to you and explained the problem."

"I would have liked that a lot better."

"Since I now know what I'm not supposed to know, I'll start working on a plan to advise the population when you're ready."

"That would be helpful."

"Enjoy your ham and eggs, Captain. I'm already due at a counseling session with Patricia Helmsly who is dissatisfied with the shower water rationing system."

"I do not envy you that, Amanda."

"Thanks, Mark. Have a great G deck day."

She flew slowly away. There happened to be an empty table nearby. I coasted down to it, locked the armrests and finished breakfast.

On my way back to the Bridge, I met Mick Pacal, Chief of Security. "Hey, Mick! I haven't had time to touch base with you. How are we doing?"

"Captain, all is well. I've hung back at the staff meetings because the civilians are getting along pretty well. As you know after we got through the sick period things slowed way down. We have people on each deck twenty-four seven but the population barely notices. Except for a few minor arguments there's still been nothing to report. But give it another month. People may start getting ship weary. We'll see."

"By the way, Mick. I have a meeting down in Engineering later today I'll need you to attend. It's confidential. I'll give you a call when the time comes."

"Any time, Captain."

I nodded and pushed up. Back on the command deck Steve West had already taken his place at the Engineering station and turned the third shift crew loose. I coasted over to my seat and locked in. "No hand-offs, Steve?"

"They had nothing to report. Green across the board so I let them go."

I adjusted my position and read the display. All three screens were stepping through ship's systems. I went into the arms floating rest position and studied the data. As West had said, the ship was operating at near perfection. In fact the only glitch was the one not shown on the displays; the wandering fuel flow sensor. While the screens stepped through the data pages I opened a quarter percent window in the lower right-hand corner of my center screen and called up displays of the Raptor number two fuel flow schematics. I began memorizing the wire routing. There were also JPG photo files taken during assembly of New Dawn. With persistence I found the one relating to the Raptor in question. There were images showing the sensor installed and waiting for its wiring harness. Others showed the wiring attached and the backshell in place. From there the last of the images captured the insulation packed into the service port then the service hatch installed and sealed.

I stared at the images of the sensor for quite a while. I tried to image my spacesuit gloves holding tools to remove that sensor and replace it. The wiring would need to be reattached. It would mean a micro laser weld in the vacuum of space. Could I do it?

I had no doubt.

Communication from Ground came four hours later, a flashing blue icon on my center screen. Steve West had gone for his two hours of workout. Brent Shaw was floating behind the Life Support/Comm control station.

"Take the conn, would you, Brent?"

"I have the conn, Captain."

Closed in my compartment, I opened the transmission from Earth. It was Mission Director Ben Epstone.

"We've reviewed your sensor problem at length, Mark and we agree with your proposal. Our engineers are baffled by how this could have happened but they agree this is an open circuit problem of some kind. We'll be very interested to see the pictures of that sensor. So obviously we also agree with your plan to go out and fix it. This early in the mission is no time to lose a Raptor. The technical group feels micro laser welding of the contacts should work just fine. They advise you'll need multiple mag

74

lights and adhesion knee pads to steady you, along with a replacement backshell which we show as being located in the bar code 780201 storage area. Management also concurs with your choice of Luca Greco as your second. Your plan to inspect the Raptors while you're out there if you have the time is approved as well. Please advise us of your EVA schedule so that we can be on station for the operation. Let me know if you need anything else, Mark. We'll be standing by. Epstone out."

I keyed my comm unit. "Easton to Pacal."

"Pacal here, Captain."

"Can you meet us down in Engineering asap?"

"On my way, Captain. Pacal out."

"Easton to Bishop."

"I'm here, Captain."

"Would you meet us down in Engineering right away?"

"See you there."

I headed out, waved acknowledgement to Shaw and pulled down into the ladderwell. Somehow I managed to pass through all five decks without being stopped.

In Engineering, the staff on duty had gathered around Jeff James in a quiet discussion that stopped upon my arrival. Pacal was already with them. Bishop dropped in behind me a few seconds later. We grouped together, holding on to straps and each other.

There was no difficulty in getting everyone's attention.

"Ground has approved a trip outside to fix that sensor. We'll use today and tomorrow to put the repair kits together, set up the main airlock and rehearse the EVA. As you all know it will almost certainly be micro laser welding depending on what we find. Ground sent the location for the replacement connector backshell but I'm sure you guys already have that. I will be taking Luca as my backup. We'll be visiting the Raptors after the job is done to take some pictures. Anyone have any questions or suggestions?"

"You'll need the kneepads, Captain," said Brolin, one of the techs.

"Yeah, we got that. Anything else?"

No replies.

"Has anyone here ever used a micro laser in open space?"

No replies.

"Another New Dawn first," commented James.

"Not really, Chief. It's been done on orbit dozens of times," replied Brolin.

"Shouldn't be a problem, Mark," said James.

"Mick and Amanda, we don't want to do this without telling the crew. Have you got a plan for that?"

Amanda spoke, "I don't expect it to cause any problems, Mark. We keep it simple. We say you're making an EVA to do an inspection before our mid course correction and to fix a broken wire. That's self-explanatory enough not to cause any stress."

Mick added, "We'll pay close attention to the gossip."

"All inquiries can be directed to me," added Amanda. "When can I do this?"

"At your discretion, Amanda."

"Could you possibly place an extra magnetic camera or two out there so this could be televised? That would go a long way to show we're being open about this."

"Yes, we could do that."

"Great. I'll begin releasing all this as soon as I get back to my office. This could actually be a beneficial stimulus event for everyone."

"Okay, then, if no one has anything else would you guys get us set up? We'll be down here tomorrow, rehearsing. I'll see you all then."

There was a long pause and the group began breaking up. Pacal nodded to me and headed up. Amanda joined me at the ladderway.

"Beneficial stimulus event?" I asked.

"Some excitement during an otherwise routine trip."

"And that's supposed to be a good thing?"

"There won't be a person on board who isn't watching you out there."

"If you say so."

I pulled myself up to B-deck, wondering if I could make it all the way to G without being stopped. B and C decks were no problem, people coming and going to their cubicles or using the central showers. Made it through E deck, people busily putting in their exercise time. But on F deck she was waiting for me.

"Captain Easton, Captain?"

Her comm unit name tag said Dorser. She had one foot in a floor stirrup. She wore baggy shorts and a New Dawn T-shirt. Her dark blond hair was tied but floating behind her. Her red lipstick was slightly smeared on one side. She gave me a big smile with thin lips and a tiny nose below blue eyes. I held to a ladder rung.

"Hello, Ms. Dorser. How are you?"

"Angelena please, Captain. We just watched a wonderful old 1950's movie called Destination Moon. You must watch it if you haven't seen it. The spaceship is just like a starship and it even flies like we do."

"Isn't that the one where they had to lighten the load?"

"You have seen it! Wasn't it amazing for the 1950's?"

"I recall that it was, Angelena. You'll have to excuse me. I have some schematics I need to study."

"Nice talking to you, Captain."

"Angelena, try Forbidden Planet. That's my favorite."

"Okay. I will."

I escaped into the Command deck and breathed a sigh of relief. Shaw and West both took note. As I headed for my seat, Amanda Bishop came through and caught up to me.

"I've scribbled a draft of the announcement. I'm ready to do it if you approve."

It was short and to the point. I nodded and handed the tablet back to her.

"Shall we?" she asked, and she gestured toward Shaw at the communications console. We pushed over to it.

"Can you put me on shipwide announcements and on all comm units simultaneously?" she asked.

Shaw smiled. "Of course." He tapped a few controls on his touch screen and nodded to her.

Bishop gathered herself. "Attention all personnel. This is Doctor Bishop. I am pleased to announce that tomorrow we will all have an exciting event to watch live on the ship's local network. Captain Easton and Engineer Luca Greco will make an EVA to perform a standard inspection of the ship's engines as well as repair a minor sensor problem. We do not have an exact time yet. Watch your global emails for that announcement. Doctor Bishop out."

"How was that?" asked Bishop.

"I don't hear any screaming and hysteria down there," joked Shaw.

"Great, Amanda. I see what you mean about the entertainment value."

"And if it all goes well, there will be a shipwide feeling of satisfaction as well," added Bishop.

"Thanks, Amanda. Now I'm going to warm up some coffee and get back to my schematics."

She gave a final wave as she pulled into the ladderwell.

The next morning Luca and I met in Engineering and began our rehearsals. The Engineering group had assembled our tool packs and camera bags. We used the open space around the central water recovery system to physically practice our travel and positioning. An empty transfer container was used to represent the service hatch. Though we did not use spacesuits we had our wrist procedure displays attached to our arms just as they would be. We danced weightlessly around, learning what positions might be a hindrance and what might be helpful. We pretended to use each tool and photographed each step in the process. We pretended to laser weld loose wires back onto the suspect sensor along with replacing the sensor entirely. With breaks, the practice session took us four hours but we both felt we knew the job inside and out. We decided to make our excursion in the morning.

The following day began with us wearing breathing mixture masks. In Engineering we had almost too many staff helping us suit up.

We closed our visors to begin breathing pure oxygen and waited for the slow depressurization of our suits to get down to the prescribed internal pressure. Thanks to the Z-suit research along with O2 capabilities of the newer EVA spacesuits the boring process of dropping pressure and purging nitrogen from the bloodstream would not be so excruciatingly long.

They sealed us in the airlock and crowded together at the observation windows to watch. Luca settled in with his tablet, reading something technical. I hooked a foot in a strap, folded my arms, and began a half-nap. It was soon interrupted.

"Captain Easton, New Dawn calling."

I looked at the inner door window to see Amanda Bishop's smiling face.

"Yes, Amanda?"

"This is an interview. How is the isolation? Are you keeping sane?"

"Amanda, we've only been in here for twenty minutes."

"Just joking. I wanted to ask. We're getting a lot of requests for live coverage of the EVA preparations. Would you mind if we accessed the airlock cameras?"

I looked over at Luca. He shrugged. I nodded to Amanda. "I guess that would be all right. It will be so boring no one will watch anyway."

"Thanks, guys. But don't be too sure about not being watched. They want to leave it on the main recreation area monitor."

Her face disappeared from the window. I looked at Luca and winced. Luca smirked.

So we float-slept, read from our tablets and exercised arms and legs occasionally, all with the knowing eye of the airlock cameras studying us.

The suit pressure wake up chime finally brought me back to awareness of the open space waiting just outside the doors. It is a time when the mood become somber and silent, a time when all consciousness becomes focused on the task at hand. You suddenly feel the vacuum of space just beyond the airlock outer doors much more acutely and your suit becomes the thing most dear to your heart.

There was almost no space at all between the double outer doors of the airlock. There is a hard fast rule that a starship pressurized compartment can never be trusted to a single functioning outer door. So when the airlock is opened from inside those double outer doors satisfy that rule. We set up and waited for the airlock to finish depressurizing. Luca went to the first outer door and unlocked the handle. This would be the first time a New Dawn outer door would be unlocked and shifted aside while in space. There were more faces peering through the airlock windows than I would have thought possible.

But the big handle on the door turned correctly and Luca swung the oval hatch over and out of the way. Beyond, the seals of the second door could be studied and the hatch appeared to be correctly seated.

"Looks good," said Luca.

"Looks really good, Luca." I looked back at the nearest airlock window. "Any alarms, Paul?"

Descard answered. "All green, Captain. You are cleared to continue."

Greco began turning the wheel lock. It clicked into the open position. I pressed a spacesuit hand against his back as he pushed on the door. The oval hatch begrudgingly broke its seal and opened outward. Black sky and stars began to appear.

From the Bridge Brent Shaw called down. "External cameras are on and working. We see that hatch opening."

Luca turned to look at me. "I never asked. How many EVAs have you done?"

"Fifteen."

"Jeeez."

As planned, I maneuvered around Luca, positioned my pack and worked my way out the airlock. The main rail was within hands' reach. A quick clip onto it and I was ready to take Luca's satchels. I had to force myself not to stop to consider the view. Luca handed out the satchels and tool bag. He pulled himself out enough to clip onto the rail, then pulled the rest of the way clear. We maneuvered to get positioned and having gained positive control we both stopped and scanned the new star field.

It was the densest, widest blanket of stars I had ever seen. It was as though there was more starlight than black sky. The depth of it was much more apparent as well. No two stars were at the same distance. Many were clearly far behind most others. On our right, the sun had shrunk to about half its size yet it was still lighting up New Dawn clearly. The big blue star Earth was farther off to our right. We both held to the rail and stared at it with special affection.

"My God, it's only a big star now but it's still blue," said Luca.

"Yeah, and have a look forward and way off to starboard. You see it?"

"The big red one."

"That's the one. Getting bigger all the time."

"Are they all seeing this from our helmet cams?"

Amanda Bishop's voice cut in on the comm, "We certainly are, Luca."

"Wow!" added Luca.

"Mars, on its way to meet us up ahead," I added.

I studied our spacecraft forward to aft. It presented a special beauty of its own. The rocket body's snow white coating had dulled from frost. Although the starship cargo vehicles had all retained their factory silver appearance,

84

New Dawn had adopted this treated surface as a result of the Materials International Space Station Experiments program. The MISSE covering provided a variety of protection for the spacecraft and its occupants. Looking aft it almost seemed like the rocket body went on forever. Even the aft wings looked huge. Not far in front of us our telemetry and communications antennas had been deployed. They also looked frosty.

"Ready to translate, Luca?"

"After you, Captain."

Hand over hand we followed the gold-colored main rail back, towing satchels along behind us. The right shoulder of my suit kept catching in one spot but a few back and forth motions cleared it. We slid along the cold metal for fifteen minutes before reaching the port aft wing. The service compartment we needed was another twenty feet within the skirt section. We floated along and above the wing, nearing the dropoff at ship's end.

The compartment was easy to see. The service plate was large, with big Phillips head attachment fixtures. Luca swung around into position, pressed his knee pads to the hull and pulled out a magnetic camera. He snapped it in place nearby and pointed it to monitor the service hatch. Next came magnetic service lights. Finally he began digging in the tool bag for the pistol grip tool. We took turns loosening the cover plate screws. As Luca remove the cover and secured it, I carefully pulled out the insulation padding and stuffed it into a satchel. We pointed the work lights to shine down into the hole.

There before us was the errant sensor and its backup amid a ganglion of tubing. There was a six-wire cable bundle leading to them. Two wires were grounds and were still attached, but to our amazement, all four data wires were dangling free of both sensors.

"It seems impossible," said Luca.

"Can't get my head around it either," I replied.

"One wire, maybe. Four? Impossible."

"Looks like we'll be using the laser after all."

"Are you seeing this, Paul?" I asked.

"I'm at a loss to explain, Mark," he answered.

Luca worked himself around and began pulling tools from the tool sack. I took the micro laser welder from him and clipped its safety line to the rail while Luca attached the battery pack to the hull. We repositioned the lights and attached the front of our suits to the ship so we were bellied up against it looking down into the service compartment.

I said, "You know, if you can hold each wire in place, it would be a lot faster than trying to clip it."

"Yeah, I think we can both get our hands in there. You've got a green light on the laser power supply."

Luca braced one foot against the rail and performed the very fine job of lining the first sensor wire with its contact.

I said, "So why is the backshell cover for both of these sensors pulled way back from the connection?"

"You know it looks like the job didn't get finished somehow."

"This vehicle passed two static fires."

"The mystery deepens."

"That's it right there, Luca. Can you hold it steady?"

"Laser me, man. Laser me."

I squirmed into position, held the laser welder tip up to the joint and fired. We could only see a tiny bit of blue light but with the gun withdrawn the joint looked good.

"I believe you've done it, sir," said Luca.

Thirty minutes later we had both sensors reconnected with backshells in place.

"Okay, Paul. Run your tests," I said.

"Stand by. We're on it."

For five minutes of waiting we were able to study the blanket of stars around us and take in our piece of the Milky Way galaxy. Engineering interrupted all too soon.

"We've got two null sensors now, guys. Flatline steady, just like they should be. We are good to go."

"Closing the compartment," I replied.

We maneuvered ourselves around, got everything back in place and sealed up the service compartment.

"So much for the hard part," said Luca.

We left the satchels behind and headed aft with only cameras. The safety rail ended four feet from skirt edges. We checked our safety lines then one at a time caught the aft end of the ship with one hand and pulled ourselves over and down. The family of giant black Raptor thrust chambers came quickly into view. To me they were a thing of great beauty.

Jeff James watching from Engineering could not help but comment, "God they look good, Mark."

"We concur, Jeff," I replied.

Luca and I held to the skirt ends and circled the family of engine bells, our headlamps illuminating some of the interior areas above the exhaust manifolds. I could make out some turbopump casings and heat exchanger plumbing. Overall our thrust core looked intact and strong. Nothing was out of place, nothing appeared damaged.

Luca said, "It looks good Jeff. The manifold areas all look tight and right."

"Yeah, we got that too, Luca," replied Jeff. "Here in Engineering we're all elated."

"Very cool, Mark. Very cool," added Luca.

"We'll be home in time for dinner, Luca," I suggested.

Luca laughed. "After you, sir."

It took some acrobatics to pull and push ourselves back to the main rail. It was a chance to see the full length of the ship from the engine compartment forward. It was a beautiful sight. One hundred and sixty feet of smooth white spacecraft. We could not make out the many windows from our position. What we could see was a huge silver arrow pointed at a dense starfield. I could have held that position and stared at it for a day.

"It's beyond description," commented Luca.

"Mind expanding," I added.

We gathered up our packs and tools and went hand over hand along the rail back to the airlock outer doors. Luca swung in feet first and came halfway back out to take the packs. After a long last look around at where we had been, I pulled into the airlock and we set about resealing the doors.

Mission accomplished.

Chapter 7

Midcourse correction day arrived. It was yet another day of events never before done with a starship so heavily manned. The plan was for all crew members except those needed at their posts to take refuge and brace inside their private module where they could maintain a prone position on their sleeping bags for cushioning. The force of acceleration would not be great, two or three Gs at most, but it was the best posture possible for the maneuver. Using the habitats that way was also the perfect layout for mass distribution.

Preps and checkouts for the engine firing were expected to take about four hours. I was locked into my command seat watching the test procedures, anxious to approve the automatic sequencer's request to start countdown. The Bridge was crowded. All three Bridge shift crews had shown up to watch and ride out the firing on the deck floor. It was the same in Engineering, all three shifts floating around the deck anxious to watch the Raptors line us up with Mars' future coordinates.

To my surprise, I was interrupted by Doctor Bishop's hand on my shoulder.

"Mark, can you leave the seat for a few minutes?"

"Huh?"

"Yes I know it's a bad time."

Her expression told me I needed to oblige her.

"Will my quarters be okay?" I asked.

"Yes, please."

We coasted over to my office-habitat, pulled in and shut the door. We held to wall straps.

"What could possible bring you up here now? Aren't you supposed to be consoling nervous passengers?"

"We have an issue, Mark."

"I can't imagine."

"We can't seem to find someone."

"Oh for God's sake, you're kidding me!"

"No, Mark. I'm dead serious."

"Who? Who can't you find?"

"Harold. We can't find Harold."

"This is ridiculous. There's nowhere for anyone to go, Amanda!"

"Harold Bateman. He's an IT tech. We have conducted two searches so far and have not been able to locate him."

"A computer nerd? You can't find a computer nerd?"

"He's a PhD for God's sake, Mark! He's a code writer, an A.I. specialist. Don't call him a nerd. He's missing. What do you want me to do?"

"We can't stop this course correction burn for any reason, you know that."

"I doubt very much Harold is outside, so that really doesn't matter, Mark. I'm not saying we're leaving him behind."

I rubbed my forehead. "Are all the passengers in their quarters?"

"Pretty much. That's still going on but most are already in and have been checked. That's how we discovered Harold is missing."

"You've done searches?"

"Yes, two."

I rubbed my forehead. "But it's a madhouse around here with all three shifts up to watch the firing. It would be easy to miss someone, right?"

"Maybe."

"I didn't hear any announcement calling for this guy."

Bishop shook her head. "I don't think we should do that right now. I don't think we should start a controversy right before an engine firing."

I nodded. "Okay. I agree. Look, I've got to get back to my seat. Never mind about Harold right now. Proceed as if everything is normal. Even if Harold is somewhere out of position and he bangs his head or something from the acceleration, we'll take care of that then. Right now we need all our attention on this burn."

"I understand. I'll call off any searches and we'll all take our assigned positions until you give the all clear."

"Don't misunderstand, Amanda. I appreciate you coming to me. This is just the hours of sheer boredom with moments of stark terror thing."

"I understand."

We opened up and pushed out. I returned to my seat annoyed. The checkout screen on my main display was now scrolling the countdown checkpoints the automatic sequencer was qualifying for engine firing. I pushed Harold out of my mind.

We had all-go's from Earth Mission Control. They were of course about twelve minutes old. I listened to Flight Engineer Jeff James do his call outs to different stations. They all approved propulsion readiness. My only actual job was to give the sequencer permission to sync with the mission clock and begin the countdown. As I waited for that moment I suddenly realized how quiet the ship had become. I could hear air coming through the ventilators. Only the subtle hum of ship power underlined the cool air.

A tap of a large green 'ENGAGE' icon on the screen took all control away from me, and gave it to the ship's onboard computers. I was permitted a single red command icon; 'ABORT.'

It is times like these you can't help but consider everything that could possibly go wrong. If the engines did not fire that would be a huge can of worms. It would mean we would be off course until the problem was fixed and all new calculations were made, checked, and approved so the entire process could be attempted once more. If the problem could not be fixed we would be a ship of eighty-two flying to oblivion. There was also always the possibility the engines would fire improperly and send us farther off course instead of correcting it. That would be another comparable can of worms. The thought of being in a ship with that many people, off course with no hope of rescue was too mortifying to consider.

I watched the clock on my display step down through five seconds then down to zero. For a long fraction of a second there was nothing. It was not quite long enough to evoke sheer panic because before that could happen we were all socked back in our seats by a rumbling vibration and noise signaling we were going somewhere fast. It was the first sensation of gravity we had felt in weeks, pushed back in our seats, our bodies reacting to the unexpected weight from two or three G's. Personally, my only thought was "Thank-you God."

From far below deck I heard a faint, "Yahoo!" What also sounded like distant shrieks of laughter echoed up to us. We sat back in temporary artificial gravity and watched the ship talking to us on the screens. We were being thrust ahead into empty space. Had there been anyone considering turning around and going back, that was technologically impossible now. We were going to a point in space where we hoped Mars would be when we arrived there.

At engine shut down the pressure against the seats quickly bled off. All items that had been loose took to floating again, including us. Vibration and noise faded away. Silence and stillness again surrounded us. There was a long empty few minutes before Doctor Bishop came back on the shipwide announcement system.

"All personnel, course correction complete. You are free to resume your schedules. Bishop out."

My display already had our new course projections selected. According to it, we were right down the center of the barrel, dead on course for our future spot in space. Instrumentation readings were scrolling by all within limits. Engine temperatures had behaved exactly as expected. Fuel pressures had read correctly on all engines.

Steve West looked over at me. "Well, that was fun; what do you wanna do now?" he asked with a smirk.

"Anything else would be pale in comparison."

"What a flying machine."

"It's a babe."

"You're going to ask me to take the conn, right?"

"Steve, you have the conn."

"I have the conn."

"Brent, give me shipwide. All personnel, this is Captain Easton. All indications are we just executed a perfect course correction burn and are on course for rendezvous with the planet Mars. All ship's systems are operating in the green. There are no trouble reports. Everyone please feel free to resume your day. All department heads please report to the Bridge briefing room. Easton out."

I nodded to Steve and Brent and pushed out of my seat. A quick stop at the counter gave me hot coffee. In the briefing area, I grabbed my usual seat, adjusted down to it and locked the arms over my legs to wait for the others. Bishop was the first to arrive. She sat across from me sucking on a straw which looked like it was supplying fruit juice.

She looked up from her straw. "We now have another issue but it's minor compared to the one I've already told you about."

Dr. Andrea Dumars was next in, nodding to Bishop as she went. Mick Pacal, security chief, followed closely behind. Chief engineers Jeff James and Paul Descard arrived. Finally my counterpart Janet Pars came gliding in staring down at her tablet.

I held up one hand. "I think we have enough to start. So how'd it look down there, guys?"

James and Descard looked at each other. James motioned to Descard. He spoke, "Nav computer showed us right on the nose, Mark and now that we've had time to travel a few hundred thousand miles the green nav line confirms it. We are dead on course."

"Everything was so in limits it looked like a simulation," added James.

"So our fuel pressure sensors worked then?"

"On the money. They even agreed with each other," replied James.

"How about our leftovers?"

"Actually, slightly less fuel than was calculated was used. We're still figuring that. Thrust levels were right where they should have been, so it's a little puzzling," said Descard.

"That's okay, we'll take extra fuel anytime. Any fluctuations in life support or main power during the ride?"

"They didn't seem to be affected at all," replied James. "Steady power all the way."

I turned to Mick Pacal. "Any personnel problems, Mick?"

He cast a wary glance at Bishop but shook his head. "Not really. I hate to mention it but we did have two burn riders who snuck up to the gym and did not secure during the burn. We let them get away with it. They were fine."

"How about you, Amanda? Any burn riders?"

"They all stayed in their compartments pretty well except for heads sticking out. There were no bumps or bruises or any real problems at all."

I looked to Pars. "That's all I have for this group, Jan. You have anything?"

"Just that it was another great job by the New Dawn crew. Thank you all for keeping us on course inside and out."

"Okay, carry on everyone except I need Jan, Amanda and Mick to stick around a bit."

The others pushed up and out. We waited until we were alone.

I looked at Bishop but did not need to ask.

She nodded. "The new minor problem, I'll get that out of the way. Someone has filed a formal discrimination complaint. It will have to be recorded."

I rolled my eyes, "Someone is complaining about racism?"

"Not racism. This complaint has nothing to do with race."

"How can...."

"There are many kinds of minorities, Mark. Senior citizens are a minority. Gender groups are minorities. Every country on Earth forms one or more minority. Religious beliefs constitute a minority. So this one is not about race relations."

"So what minority are we talking about?"

"We are not supposed to discuss that to avoid calling attention to the group in question."

I waved my hands in frustration. "The sensitivity of our job prevents us from knowing what we're doing. Is that what you're saying?"

"It's no joke, Mark. It's like this; Everyone on New Dawn has to pitch in and help with maintenance, not just the maintenance people. The decks are assigned to squads for cleaning and other procedures. Each squad has a coordinator who assigns people to make sure everything gets done. We have one individual who feels his coordinator is unfairly assigning him the worst jobs because of his minority status."

"Your job is tougher than mine, Amanda."

"Tell me about it."

"So what will happen?"

"We will have a review of who in that squad has been assigned to which jobs, then the affected parties will be brought in to work out the complaint. I'm not allowed to express my own opinion about the complaint but in the end we will work out something that hopefully satisfies the complainant. I have to bring this to your attention since it will go on the daily report to Boca."

"Okay. Do I need to do anything?"

"Not unless it escalates."

"I will pray."

"Good idea."

I paused for comments, then went on, "Let's go on to the big problem. I assume you have not found Harold."

Pacal said, "There's a chance he was never actually on board."

Bishop snapped, "That's stretching it a bit, Mick."

"Hey, my guys did the check-offs before takeoff. If we mistakenly marked the guy off that will be on my head."

Bishop persisted, "His toiletries, comm unit and sleeping bag are in his compartment."

"But no pictures on the walls and no laptop or tablet," countered Pacal.

"That may just be his way. Keeps his lap with him."

Pacal sounded exasperated, "The man hasn't used any shower minutes since we left!"

I held up one hand. "Hasn't *anyone* seen him?"

"He's the reclusive type, Mark," said Bishop. "Kind of nonsocial. A trip to Mars would be a piece of cake for him. No family still alive. He's absorbed in code writing most of the time."

Pacal added, "So far one or two people believe they've seen him at the food dispensers but they're not sure. He's third shift. It's a little less busy then."

I shook my head. "I've got to tell you, I really don't want to call a general assembly to line everybody up to look for Harold. We must be able to solve this without that kind of dog and pony show."

Pacal looked like he wanted to laugh but didn't dare.

"We've completed two shipwide searches," replied Bishop. "We've been scanning the deck security cameras hour by hour."

"Where haven't we looked?"

Pacal tried to sound supportive. "Nowhere. I mean we've searched everywhere except storage compartments and service hatches but someone would need to reseal them after he went in. He couldn't hide in any of those places without help."

I asked, "What if this is some kind of joke? Maybe he is deliberately avoiding the search teams or someone *is* helping him. You know, big joke on everyone."

"Recluses hate that kind of attention, Mark," said Bishop.

"Well, before we start pulling deck plates and opening storage compartments see if Earth can verify he really did come aboard. They should have gantry elevator images of him."

Bishop nodded. "Already in the works, Mark. And I wish you could have seen me trying to send them a file explaining this."

"What did they say?"

Bishop laughed sarcastically. "They'll get back to us."

"So then, we will continue searching for this missing nerd until we hear back from Earth. If Earth can confirm he came aboard then that will be it. It will be time to start pulling floor plates and opening service compartments. There will be no choice. Have you searched the airlocks?"

Pacal answered, "We can see the entire airlock interiors through the observation windows. You and Luca were just in the main airlock and the emergency airlock seals are still intact which means no one could have gone in there."

"If Earth says Harold definitely came aboard, open both airlocks and search them anyway. That will be our plan going out. Anyone have anything else?"

We traded looks of concern but no one spoke. I unlocked, pushed up and nodded to them on my way back to the command seat.

West took note of my arrival. "Any news of interest?"

"Bingo on Fridays from now on. What did I miss?"

"That's funny but that's not a bad idea. What you see is what you missed."

As I locked in, out of the corner of my eye I saw Doctor Dumars coming up through. She headed right for me.

"Anything on our missing person?"

"We don't really want that public yet, Andrea."

"Forget it. So many people have been questioned there's betting going on already."

"We're still trying to prove he actually came aboard."

"Well, he or someone we thought was him was examined in the post launch medical checks."

"Is that why you're here?"

"Oh, no. I need to let you know there was a little mishap in the exercise area. Passenger Darlington didn't fasten his tread mill harness properly. He broke loose, spun forward, and whacked his head on the equipment. A nasty little cut on the forehead."

"How is he?"

"Well he's getting sewn up as we speak. Probably mild concussion. The pain meds will keep him happy. He'll be off cleanup duty for a couple days. No big deal."

"Okay. Thanks for letting me know."

"I'll give you a call if I run into Harold." She stifled a laugh and pushed away.

I let my arms float in the horizontal and focused on the navigation display. The tiny little New Dawn dot was inching along the green line toward the Mars' orbit line. The thought had never occurred to me that I might end up with a ship under perfect control and a population that was a challenge to manage. I gave a quick prayer of thanks that at least New Dawn was behaving well.

Chapter 8

I allowed them one more day to find Harold. If he was still missing by the morning briefing it would be time to start tearing the ship apart.

As I was leaving for breakfast a video communication icon appeared on my terminal. It was Ben Epstone. He had a partially suppressed look of curiosity on his face.

"Mark and Amanda, we have reviewed our flight prep videos. IT member Harold Bateman did attend suit up and we also have video of him coming down the ramp from the O&C on his way to the pad. We show him entering the gantry elevator. After that the images are a bit too crowded for positive identification, but no one in a launch suit came back down so we must assume that you do have a Harold Bateman aboard somewhere. This is not a problem we were expecting so I sympathize with your predicament. We will be standing by to hear you have found him and why this mystery has occurred. Epstone out."

I float-sat in the food court talking with Steve West over breakfast.

"Have you ever really wondered about the ship's complement, Mark?" asked West.

"I fret about it constantly."

"No, I mean why did they do it this way? Why not divide the passenger list in two and send two starships at the same time? Much bigger chance of at least half of us getting there if one ship runs into trouble."

"Oh yeah, about that. It's classified but I can tell you. Just don't pass it on. Think about who we have with us. We've got doctors, computer geniuses, propulsion specialists, agricultural specialists, chemists, a big group of construction people and a bunch of other important people. So say we're divided on two ships and one ship is lost for some reason. Which of those people would you say we didn't need?"

"Wow! I see your point."

"Mars is a two-year mission. A study was done and it was determined that were we to lose half our group we probably could not survive for two years. We could not make the next delivery from Earth. So it was decided to send one carefully supervised ship. That was the best chance."

"Guess that's why I wasn't in the planning group. You ready to go up? I saw the staff meeting people already pass by."

In the Bridge meeting room there were more staff than usual. Some off-shift leaders had decided to attend. It was easy to guess why.

We went through the usual routine of ship and personnel status. When there were no further comments I excused anyone who needed to go. No one went.

I checked the expressions of those involved in the search for Harold. They all seemed to want to speak.

I said, "So about Harold...."

"We do have significant news, Captain," said Pacal.

Bishop straightened up and focused intently on him.

"One of my security officers has located a friend of sorts of Harold Bateman. He has been playing chess with Bateman for several weeks on and off until recently. He said Bateman got sick of always being beaten and finally stopped playing."

"When was their most recent game?" I asked.

"We have the gentleman down in Security. They are going through his laptop to get the exact day and time of the last game."

"So that's it. We know he was here. Why can't we find him?"

"The last chess match will give us a good starting point. We should be able to back track and forward track him in time from that."

Bishop asked, "This witness is in Security? Can I talk to him?"

"Of course. We can stop in there as soon as we're done here."

"So who is it?" asked Bishop.

"It's a programmer. His name is Robert Banabalas."

I said, "This still doesn't explain why we haven't found Bateman. We're going to have to…."

"Wait! Wait a minute!" interrupted Bishop. "What was this person's name?"

Pacal looked taken back. "Robert Banabalas, IT programmer, hardware repair."

Bishop was beside herself. "Robert Banabalas? Bob Banabalas?"

"Yes. So what?"

I realized why Bishop was concerned. I rubbed my eyes and shook my head, then held up my hand for attention. "Would everyone please go back to their assignments except for Dr. Bishop, and Mr. Pacal." I had to look around to get them to do it. The crowd begrudgingly disbursed.

I continued, "This involves someone's personal medical information, so it is between just the three of us, okay? Amanda, continue."

Bishop moaned, "I don't believe it."

"What?" exclaimed Pacal.

"Banabalas is a pathological liar. He can't help himself. We've been alerted to him by Boca. He slipped through the cracks somehow. You can't believe anything he says. Ask him if he ever played quarterback in the Superbowl. See what he says."

"Oh cripes," replied Pacal.

Bishop added, "You can't mention this about Banabalas to anyone. We don't want anyone being socially blacklisted here. We have to keep this to ourselves, understand?"

Pacal replied, "The Captain has already made that clear. But, we should at least verify he's telling us a tall tale using the cameras," said Pacal. "It won't take long."

"And as soon as you prove he is lying, I regret to say it's time to start opening storage panels and every other place a man might fit into," I said.

"Right," said Pacal.

"Meeting adjourned."

I wasn't ready to lock into my command seat. I floated around the Bridge looking at everyone else's display, sucking coffee and peeking down into the entertainment deck below us. Harold had made me restless. I finally sat at my command seat and began looking at Harold Bateman's photos and record.

Two hours later, I got a call.

"Pacal, Captain. You'd better get down to D deck."

"What's up now?"

"Just come down, sir."

I did not like Pacal's tone. "Steve, I've gotta go."

"I have the conn."

On D-deck there was a gathering of six security people at the entrance to the emergency airlock, along with Doctor Dumars and an assistant. Passengers waiting at the entrance to medical had taken notice. People in the training section had stopped studying and were watching as well.

I swung down next to Pacal and Dumars.

Pacal spoke in a low tone. "Well, we found him. Emergency airlock. The seal looked as though it was intact but someone used a chemical or something to unstick one half of it without tearing it."

"His condition?"

"Deceased."

"He was in the airlock?"

"In the airlock in a sealed spacesuit locked into the suit docking bay. My guys weren't supposed to bother with the suits. I told them I'd have suit techs check them later. Luckily they didn't listen."

"You're saying he put on a spacesuit?"

Pacal gestured in frustration.

"Cause of death?"

Pacal winced. "We removed the helmet, gloves and were barely able to get the torso off. We were able to look under his T-shirt some. No marks on the body we could see. No head injuries. Doctor Dumars will have to figure this out."

"Have you been in there yet, Andrea?"

"No, and I've asked them to keep the secondary door sealed to protect the ship's atmosphere."

"Can we tell how long he's been dead?"

Pacal answered, "Long enough that the officer gagged as soon as he twisted open the helmet seal. Nobody wants to be in there. You need a mask to go in there."

"Andrea and I need to take a look."

Dumars assistant reached through the group and held out three respirator masks.

Pacal repeated, "You'll want them, believe me."

We held on to security people to reach the airlock door. Pacal looked around to be sure we were ready and pushed the secondary door open. We hurried inside and shut it behind us.

Pacal spoke through his respirator, "I'm using my guys to shield the airlock from view."

Harold was hard to miss. He was parked next to floating sections of a spacesuit. He was standing in spacesuit legs, leaning forward slightly, head erect, arms nearly at his side, frozen. His nearly bald head was staring straight ahead, eyes open. Death had highlighted the deep lines in his face. He looked as though he was about to say something. It gave me the creeps.

The morbid sight had no effect on Dumars. She pulled herself quickly over to him and stared close into his eyes. She grabbed his chin and turned his body from one side to the other. She lifted his plain blue T-shirt, felt his chest and searched him. She pulled out his stretch pants and looked down at his groin. Next was the fingertips. A close exam seemed to reveal nothing.

I came beside her. "A rough guess at how long, Andrea?"

"From the condition of the body, two weeks. I can't believe they got the suit torso off. They should have waited for medical. We'll need to do a complete autopsy, of course."

"Any idea of the cause?"

"My first impression is suffocation in the spacesuit. The bloodshot eyes would suggest that. But there's something else significant. We'll need to do some blood work."

"Could he have gotten into a spacesuit, sealed himself in, and died from lack of oxygen?"

She looked at me annoyed. "That's quite a bit of conjecture, don't you think?"

"Hey, I'm just asking."

She looked over at Pacal. "Did you isolate the airlock atmosphere immediately?"

"Oh, hell yes. As best we could. That was the first thing."

Dumars turned back to me. "Except for disturbing the body, Security did a great job. This could have been a virus, never mind contaminating the ship's air supply with cadaverine."

I nodded and cast a quick glance at Pacal. "We do have procedures for a death aboard ship, Mick. Are you up to speed?"

"Yeah. We have a dozen body bags in storage that use portable air conditioners to keep the body refrigerated. My guys are already opening that compartment to get one of those sets."

I added, "The procedure recommends not keeping the deceased aboard. It recommends ejecting the body out to space."

"Getting ahead of ourselves aren't we?" asked Dumars.

"Can I request that if the doctor has seen enough for now we resume this conversation outside?" asked Pacal.

We headed back to the secondary door, opened and hurried out to reseal it. We pulled off our respirators and wiped the sweat from our faces.

I spoke in a low tone, "Andrea, can you do the autopsy right in the airlock?"

"We just put away the surgery set up from the kidney stone, now we have to pull it back out and set up in an airlock. But yes, everything can fit in there for this type of exam. There will be some special planning for bio-containment and sterilization but yes, we can do that."

Someone bumped into me. I looked to find Amanda Bishop staring at me nervously. "How are we going to handle *this* one, Mark?"

Dumars answered, "No worry, Amanda. This is probably already all over the ship by now."

Bishop nodded at me. "She's right, of course. I was one of the last to find out."

I thought for a moment. "How about we don't make any grand public address announcements. Why don't you write up something that just says this is being investigated. Let's release it by email. Say there will be more info coming as we complete our investigation. Can you do something like that?"

"If you don't need anything else from me I'm going to round up my staff and start planning this out," said Dumars. "I'll need help from Engineering. Whose shift is it?" She pushed away toward her office.

Paul Discard arrived a moment later.

"You know what's going on, Paul?" I asked.

"Yeah, but when I sent one of my guys up here to open the airlock for Security I had no idea this was going to happen."

"Doctor Dumars needs your help to set up a surgery in there."

"Surgery? Oh, you mean postmortem. You need anything before I head for her office?"

"No. Just help her get going. I need answers."

"Right." He pulled away and headed for Medical.

With four guards covering the airlock and keeping people at bay I pushed back up to the Bridge. All eyes were staring at me as I entered.

Brent Shaw stopped typing at the communications panel as I approached. "Really?" he asked.

I shook my head. "Really."

"Anything we can do?"

"Just try to keep everyone calm while I go shock Earth. How's the board, Steve?"

West nodded. "Nothing to do here. On the green line."

I pushed off toward my office, pulled in and shut the door. Took a moment to gather myself. At the terminal I locked in and rubbed my chin trying to decide how to word the email.

To: Mission Director Ben Epstone
From: Captain Mark Easton
Subject: Fatality on New Dawn

Ben,

We have located missing passenger Harold Bateman. He was found deceased. The circumstances surrounding his disappearance and death remain under investigation. No cause of death has yet been determined. He was located inside EVA suit number six located in the emergency airlock. The airlock seal was somehow detached from the primary door

but it remained intact and gave the false impression of being in place. Doctor Andrea Dumars will be performing an autopsy to determine cause and time of death. We will advise you as soon as more information is available. All shipboard functions remain nominal at this time. Mission status remains green.

Mark

I rubbed my forehead and tried to imagine how Ben Epstone would react when he read that. It probably would feel like someone jamming on the brakes on a speeding car. For Capcom or a Mission Director there is no greater feeling of helplessness than when something goes wrong on a spacecraft. They are like prisoners forced to watch a tragedy unfolding. If they are lucky, they can assemble a team to formulate some devious method of escape for the space people they are charged to watch over.

As I float-sat considering Harold Bateman, an all-hands icon appeared on my screen, a tiny town-crier symbol.

All Hands;

Message from Director of Personnel, Dr. Amada Bishop

It is with great sadness and regret I must inform you of the passing of one of our New Dawn citizens. IT Programming Specialist Harold Bateman was found deceased early today. Although there were no signs of foul play, Dr. Dumars is currently conducting a full investigation. We will update everyone as new information is released. Harold Bateman was a well-respected A.I. specialist and programmer. He earned his PHD in Computer Technologies from Hyden University. He worked for several years for Neurotritan Industries and later for the Barden Institute of Science. Mr. Bateman did not have any immediate family on Earth but please join me in wishing his extended family and friends our deepest sympathies. Everyone will be invited to a memorial service for Mr. Bateman. I will advise you of the time and day once we have made those arrangements.

Warmest regards,
Amanda.

My comm unit beeped.
"Bishop to Easton."
"Go ahead, Amanda."
"How does that look? Have you read it?"
"It's outstanding Amanda, but in the future would you allow me to go over these before you send them out shipwide?"

"Oh, yes. Sorry. But you think it's okay?"

"It's perfect considering the circumstances."

"Have you heard anything from the doctor?"

"Amanda, it's all just happened."

"Yes, of course. Do you need anything, Captain?"

"I'll let you know."

"Bishop out."

Before I could try to put everything in focus there was a tapping at my door.

"Come in."

Janet Pars peeked through the door then closed herself in. Next to my tiny desk she caught a foot strap.

"Aren't you in a sleep period, ma'am?"

"Are you kidding? At a time like this?"

"Who got you up?"

"My comm officer. I don't know who got her up."

I shook my head. "Another New Dawn first."

"Cause of death?"

"Can't say for sure. Dumars said it's probably suffocation."

"How'd it happen?"

"Good question. Didn't look like he was in a fight or anything. It's possible he just decided to end it all."

Pars gave a curious look. "I brought someone in to take the Bridge for you. I was

117

guessing you'd need some space. So, you're off-duty too unless you object."

"You are a smart woman, you know that?"

"Yep."

To my surprise Pars pulled a small silver flask out from the inside pocket of her flight suit. She unscrewed the lid and took a sip and handed it out for me.

"You dared to bring that aboard?"

"Didn't you?"

"Hell, no. No way I was going to risk my command for a drink. You got a problem we don't know about XO?"

"Oh for God's sake, Mark. It's just a medicinal drink. God knows you've earned it. I'll bet there's a couple dozen more people aboard secretly doing the same thing."

"Can you imagine eighty people closed in and living together in a tin can and some of them tie one on? You know what could happen?"

"You want a drink or not, Captain? I don't think they'll recall the ship for that."

I reached out, took the flask and sucked in a mouthful. It was high grade whiskey. Pars laughed.

We took a few drinks in silence but Pars' gears were turning. "What's your best bet on this guy?" she asked and she sipped again.

"It's gotta be self-inflicted."

"Otherwise it's the unthinkable," said Pars.

I winced and accepted the flask and drank.

"Worst timing possible," added Pars. "I've been hearing people talking about reaching Mars. Like their hopes are up. I overheard one discussion in the dining area where people at the table had decided inflation of the recreation dome was the most important milestone. They were talking about one-third gravity ping pong, pool and one-quarter court basketball. I have to admit, that stuff ought to be a blast."

"Yeah, even the work will be all new. Every time we add a new dome to the atmosphere, every new tunnel, never mind the real Mars exploration excursions, it will be a city rising up around us. People think two years would be too long, but everything is too new there. I'm betting it will be Disneyland."

"Maybe we'll find out about the disclosure rumors finally."

"Which rumors?"

"As you know, there's strong evidence for artificial structures on Mars. I can't wait to go looking for artifacts."

"Yeah, I don't know much about that stuff. I'm trained to toe the company line."

"I'll bet you I will eventually find an artificial keepsake before I'm done. Like maybe a stone mouse or something."

"Do *you* have any guess about Harold?" I asked.

"Got to be suicide. Or, at least some kind of really weird accident."

"I'll settle for either of those."

"We'll find out. He can't hide from all the cameras."

"He has so far. The guy was a recluse in space."

Pars blinked. "My, my. I do believe the flask is doing its job. I gotta go-oh back to bed."

"Thanks for the break."

"You probably are gonna need it. You want me to leave the flask?"

"No ma'am. I've got to keep my wits about me. Don't let anyone see that, by the way."

Chapter 9

Using the D Deck cameras, I watched Security, Engineering and Medical setting up outside the airlock. It was an amazing thing to watch because both they and their equipment floated around the entrance in a game of catch and control. They were being prudent about opening the airlock door and quickly resealing it to prevent foul airlock atmosphere from escaping.

I called the Bridge comm officer. "Easton to Shaw."

"Go ahead, Captain."

"It's time to lock out all the D Deck cameras to everyone except Bridge-level personnel."

"I understand, Captain. I'm on it."

"Easton to James."

"Yes, Captain?"

"Jeff, is there any way we could set up a barrier around the airlock to block those operations off from the rest of the population?"

"You mean just visual, right?"

"Yes."

"Let me work on that."

"Thanks, Jeff."

Fifteen minutes later they began stringing equipment covers from floor to ceiling, enclosing the airlock and the people working outside it. I had to switch to the airlock cameras to watch the autopsy set up. Not surprisingly I was interrupted by a quick response to my Epstone email.

Mark,

Received and understood your very disturbing preliminary report on Bateman. Please make a point to transmit all of your raw investigative findings as quickly as possible. We will want the original blood chemistry readouts and Dr. Dumars voice recordings of the procedures. Please let us know in what ways we may assist. Standing by.

Epstone

"Easton to Pacal."

"Go ahead, Captain."

"How's it going down there, Mick?"

"They are still moving equipment into the airlock. They're deciding the best way to get Bateman out of the rest of the suit and to secure the table. Our Medical people are so good. It's impressive."

"Any problems with the rest of the population?"

"Not really. They are slowly dispersing. Once the rest of the blind is in place spectators will be a non-issue."

"Keep me posted. If you need anything let me know."

"Will do, Captain. Pacal out."

"Easton to Bishop."

"Yes, Mark?"

"How are you holding up?"

"Well, my email is overloaded and I had to ask Brent Shaw to block anything but high-level calls to my comm unit. I've had to talk to and disperse a crowd at my door three times so far. I'll be sending out new additional information emails every hour. They all know the situation but they can't help but ask, over and over. Do you have anything for me?"

"You know as much as I do, Amanda. I'm sorry you're going through this but I'm sure glad you're here."

"Yes, if I were you I would remain on the Bridge for the time being, Mark. You will have trouble going from point A to point B."

"I did receive an answer from Earth to my preliminary report. They are as concerned as everyone else. They are waiting for test results. That's about the only update I have for you."

"Well, that's something. I can send out an all-hands update that Earth has been informed and is waiting for additional information. It will be something to give them so they know we're being up front about it."

I thought for a moment. "You know there is one thing coming up that might help you and I through this. We are supposed to get a Mars update before the three supply ships land. I'll get that to you as soon as it comes in. It might help refocus people on where we are going."

"Great. That would be just great."

"You let me know if I can do anything else, Amanda."

"Thanks, Mark."

After a moment of reflection I called up New Dawn's systems panel overview and status. Once again, New Dawn was behaving like a dream. Then I noticed a yellow comm icon in the bottom-right hand side of the screen. I touched it. It was a message from one of the engineers.

To: Captain Easton
From: Engineer Douglas Shwindt
Subject: Sticky Antenna Platform

Captain, be advised our A-Link telemetry antenna has been acting up during reorientation sequences. The base targeting system either fails to complete its reorientation or hesitates as it is doing so. Sending a repeat command to the targeter usually corrects the misalignment.

We are now monitoring this antenna real time because of this problem. The problem has not affected communications with Earth. Chief Engineers Descard and James are in agreement the problem may eventually clear itself. They do not recommend corrective action at this time. The antenna in question is located above and close to the main airlock, so if repair becomes necessary it would not be a difficult EVA.

Douglas Shwindt

Another issue added. I switched my display back to the emergency airlock. The medical staff was floating around working diligently to fasten an examination table to the airlock floor. They had removed Bateman from the lower half of the space suit, removed his clothing, and attached his body to the far wall next to the outer doors. A naked man at attention. He still looked as though he wanted to make a comment.

They had reassembled Bateman's smelly spacesuit and removed both suits from the airlock to make more room. A silver case which I assumed contained surgical tools was attached to one wall. A few specimen jars were floating free around the room along with a vacuum hose. I switched back to ship's systems monitor page. The indicators were all green.

The waiting began. It turned into a long day of reflection between moments of communication with various staff, and periodic eavesdropping on the autopsy. I needed Dumars to tell me with certainty that Bateman had taken his own life. It was the most logical explanation. He had planned his exit carefully. He figured out a chemical mixture that would unstick the airlock seal without breaking the tape. He applied the mixture as discretely as possible so no one would notice. He waited for a moment on D Deck when no one was aware, opened the airlock door and slipped inside, canceling the door alarm from within probably in less than a second. There were warning lights both in Engineering and on the Bridge life support console but they would only have illuminated for a second or two. When Engineering finished scanning the records they'd probably find the momentary alert no one had noticed. Once in the airlock Bateman had it made. Maybe blind the cameras somehow as though it was accidental. No one would be monitoring them anyway. Suit up, keeping the helmet in easy reach. Maybe take a tranquilizer. Kiss the new world goodbye and twist on the helmet. Wait for the medication to kick in and the oxygen to die out. Avoid all possible embarrassment about the act of killing yourself. If he was lucky no one would find him maybe for months or even after we were on Mars. Disappearing man. The recluse who achieved the ultimate in reclusion.

Dumars surgery began very late. I allowed myself a sleep shift so I would be clear headed when the results came in.

The next morning a persistent twe-deep from my terminal awoke me. It took half a second to remember the deep crap we were in. I peeled off the previous day's dark blue flight suit and turned it inside out to prepare it for dry cleaning, then pulled on the light-blue flight suit, the only other one I was allowed.

No messages on the screen. Coffee. I looked at my door and for a brief moment considered locking myself in for the rest of the day. Aircraft and starships were a pleasure to manage, people not so much. I pulled on my boots and headed out.

Tired waves from the third shift Bridge crew. With a hot coffee packet in my hand, I pushed over to Tracy Shannon in my seat. She nodded hello.

"So what have I got coming up at the handoff meeting?"

"Absolutely nothing, Mark. It has been perfect and boring, all night."

"Nothing from medical? No rumors?"

"Dumars has been in there all night. But no info has come out."

"Any telemetry problems?"

"None. Should there have been?"

"There's an iffy antenna targeting platform. It's a non-issue so far."

"Haven't seen it on the screen."

"Thanks, Trace. Guess I'll go wait for the crew in the briefing area."

I coasted into the meeting room, took a center seat and switched on the wall monitor. Using my access code to select the emergency airlock camera, an image came up that surprised me. Dumars and her med staff were still in there, but Bateman's body was now sealed in a heavy blue body bag attached to a refrigeration unit. They were packing things up and putting tools away. The body was held to the examination table by large orange straps. Dumars and her associates had pulled back their headgear and were breathing airlock air.

Jeffery James floated into the room and stared at the screen as he pulled himself down. I switched it off.

Mick Pacal followed him in and float-sat. We remained silent as the others entered.

It was a very short hand-off meeting. There had been no problems with ship functions. Amanda Bishop had items but asked to hold them for a later meeting. I understood. When there were no more comments I let them all go. Pacal and Bishop were held back.

"Easton to Dumars."

"I'm on my way up, Mark. Be there in a minute."

We sat in silence until she entered. She gave us an ominous look and slid the seldom used accordion doors shut behind her. She seemed to need to sit even though in zero G that meant little.

"Take your time, Andrea. We know you've been up all night."

"It was suffocation in an airtight spacesuit as I originally thought. But that's the good news."

"That's the *good* news?" I repeated.

"He did not take his own life. Someone put him in there. The lab work shows that he was drugged and unconscious at the time of death."

I said, "But couldn't he have…."

"No. He could not have put himself in that spacesuit."

"Explain."

"I can't fully explain it yet. More lab work is being done. The body will have to remain in the airlock until I'm satisfied that we understand the chemistry."

"So he couldn't have taken some drug himself and just passed out in the suit?" I asked with irritation.

"No. There are several indicators at play here. We have to separate and understand them, but I can promise you he was unconscious for quite some time before he was put in the spacesuit. One eye was abnormally dilated. The other was not. He may even have been in a coma."

"What?"

"I can't give you anything else than that until we finish. Anything more would be conjecture."

I rubbed my eyes with one hand and held up the other for pause. "But you are guaranteeing me someone else was involved?"

"Yes."

I turned to Pacal. "Mick?"

"I have nothing, Captain. Dr. Dumars has provided this intel to us confirming someone else had to be involved so we have been concentrating our video search on the airlock cameras. It takes a long time to go through just one day of video file. You can only fast-forward so much without missing something. By all accounts we should find video of both subjects by the end of the day or sooner."

"You have kept a tight lid on this downstairs of course?"

"Only three of my people are searching the video files: Jenkins, Patterson and Robertson. I trust them. They are under strict orders not to talk about this to anyone. They understood the reasoning."

"And you understand Amanda, this can never be told to the general population, at least not until this person is caught and we understand why this happened."

"Yes, except that means they won't know they might need to protect themselves."

Dumars interrupted, "Amanda, I agree with the Captain on this. There is more danger from telling a population confined in a spacecraft that there is a murderer among them than there is from withholding that information."

I looked at each of them. "Okay, let's just keep our heads here and go about our business as though everything is as normal as possible. Andrea, please rush that lab work as much as possible."

"Of course."

"We'll reconvene as soon as Andrea's report is done. That will be all for now. Mick, please stay behind for a minute."

The others pushed up to leave looking understandably concerned. I waited for them to exit and slid the door shut.

I took a seat next to Pacal. "So, we're in deep crap here."

"I have to agree with you."

"What can we do?"

"For now, wait on the video feeds. See what we get from those. The bitch of it is we don't even have a motive. If we knew what was driving this person we might be able to set up a trap. Even if we had a suspect we could put them on twenty-four-hour surveillance, but we've got nothing."

"Someone wanted Bateman dead."

Pacal nodded. "But can we even be sure of that? Maybe it was some kind of weird accident someone wanted to cover up rather than get blamed."

"Man or woman?"

"Can't say. In zero G anyone could have moved the body. If you want a guess, I would bet the death occurred in the living modules somewhere probably on C deck right below the emergency airlock. Move the body probably around 05:00 when there is the least amount of activity going on. It's either that or the whole event took place in the airlock, which I doubt. Bishop has psyche degrees through the roof. Maybe she can put together a profile but she doesn't have much to work with."

"How do we protect the general population?"

"I'm thinking around the clock video surveillance; extra cameras installed in the living quarter areas. We can't have a camera in every module but we could set up to see every entrance."

"That sounds good. See how inconspicuous you can be installing those."

"Problem is, we're going to have to tell the people on duty what they're looking for."

"We'll have to hand pick them."

"Maybe we ought to add extra security on the Bridge and Engineering."

"Plain clothes."

"Yeah."

"Anything else we can do?" I asked.

"We could start going through everyone's private communications. What do you think about that? Is it legal?"

I shook my head. "If it's illegal on Earth, it's illegal here."

"Okay, but how about this; there is an A.I. surveillance program that monitors communications by listening for keywords so no one but the computer hears your communication. If the computer picks up a keyword like terrorism or assassination it notifies us of the subject, where it came from and where and when it was directed. We could scan all New Dawn communications from before today using that and look for Bateman being mentioned, or the word airlock, or whatever else might cue us."

"We'd still need to get a warrant from Earth to listen to that comm."

"Of course but desperate times call for desperate measures."

"See if you can quietly set that up. I'll get permission from Earth to try it. I'm sure they're going to be as panicky as we are."

"I'm on it."

I rubbed my forehead. "Let me know if you come up with anything else. I'll have the comm officer set up a private channel between us."

"There is one thing to our advantage."

"What's that?"

"The murderer can't get away."

Chapter 10

It was a full day before I heard from Dumars again. I had to stop myself from contacting and bothering her. She did not make the morning meeting.

"Any other Engineering items?" I asked.

James answered, "We're having water cell pressure out of limits again. You remember we widened the limits on that and it cured the alarms, but the pressure is just below the new limits again. It doesn't seem like a serious problem, but it's possible there's something developing there."

"But we still have protection on B and C decks, right?"

"Oh, absolutely. Any solar flare activity and B or C deck is the place to be. It's just that the water in those cells has to be kept slowly moving through the network of cells. We can't have it stagnant. The water pressure brings the water back to meet the water reclamation output before some is input back into the cells. The system is fine at the moment."

"Will you be putting a team on that pressure loss?"

"Kind of busy at the moment Captain, but we'll get to it."

"How about the A-Link antenna, Jeff?"

"Still sticking. Don't send us after it yet. We still think it will clear itself. Probably an ice fragment from something. It's bound to break free."

"If there's nothing else I need Mick and Amanda to stay behind. Keep up the good work everyone."

As the group was breaking up James pulled in next to me. "I'd better stay for this."

I nodded. When the room was clear we slid the doors shut.

"Has Andrea spoken to either of you?" I asked.

Negative expressions.

"She's taking a long time on this. Guess I'm going to visit her after this. How are we holding up, Amanda?"

"Life on board is reasonably normal. Everyone's keeping to their schedule. Quite a bit of rumor mill but nothing we can't control. There is some sense of loss even though most of them did not know Bateman at all. Maybe a touch of insecurity from all this. I'll send out an update this morning after you check it. We'll let them know Earth has been informed and is supporting us. I will not correct the previous email that indicated no signs of foul play. I'll just say we are still investigating. How does that sound?"

"That's good. You might add that we will be having a Mars update from Earth later today. I'll pass that on to you for dissemination."

"Great. That will be helpful."

"Mick, how are we on added security?"

"The A.I. comm monitoring is in the loop. Nothing from that yet. New battery powered cameras transmitting on secure channels installed in B and C decks. We can see all entrances to all modules. We also added a few in other places. I'll be sending you the link later this morning."

James added, "That's why we've been so busy, Mark. The techs have kept very stealthy putting those in. They wait for the right moment, stick them to a surface, make a quick aim, and then resume being general population personnel. I don't think we've attracted any attention at all."

I nodded appreciation. "Nice."

Pacal continued, "So I think we have good coverage now in places that were formerly camera blind. We will have three shifts of people selected to watch those cameras by the end of the day. Their comms will have an alert channel if they see anything not right. We'll have a two-man fast response team if anything comes up."

"I have to ask, how do we know none of our monitor people are suspects?" asked James.

Bishop answered, "I put together a profile for the person we're after. Not much to go on but obviously this person has some knowledge of chemistry since they were able to remove an airlock seal without damaging it and this person knew about spacesuit mechanics, along with a few other things. So Mick and I used that profile and our own gut instincts to select people for these positions. I think that's the best we can do."

Pacal said, "There is other news, Mark. But, you're not going to like it."

"Okay."

"We now have a time window for when this took place in the airlock so we should have been able to see video of Bateman and our suspect in there. We've reviewed all the airlock video files. Bateman is never in the airlock. All we ever see is the two spacesuits in their docking stations. Those video files must have been edited and I expect we will find the exterior camera files have been altered also."

"Oh, brother."

James squinted in disbelief. "You are saying this guy hacked into a Cray and changed the videos? Really?"

Bishop cut in, "Don't say *guy*, Jeff. We still don't know if this was a man or a woman. But now we do know this person is an expert at programming."

I shook my head and paused for moment. "Is there any other *good* news?"

Before anyone could speak the meeting room doors slid open and in coasted Doctor Dumars, looking exhausted but somehow uplifted. She pulled herself down, locked into a seat and floated in a mental fog.

"My God, Andrea, you look exhausted," declared Bishop.

"Toughest mystery I've ever had to solve. I loved it," she replied.

"You loved it?" asked James.

"Had to go back in for a second round."

"You had to resume the autopsy?" asked Bishop.

Dumars looked down at the dirty scrubs she was wearing and gave a guttural sound of dismay. "Sorry, I didn't want to take the time to change."

"Don't keep us in suspense, Andrea," said Bishop.

"He had two benzodiazepine class drugs in his system, administered through completely different media. He had a strong dose of Triazolam taken in tablet form still present in the stomach. I forget the exact level but it was too much to be using, an abusive type of amount. It's used as a sleep aid mostly for insomniacs so we can assume Bateman was an insomniac, except I had my staff search his module again and they found his stash in a flat pack in his sleeping gear. There was no prescription. They were sold as a street drug. We also checked his medical records; no mention of Triazolam or of any sleep disorder so

138

he kept that a secret when he applied for this trip then stashed himself some tablets when he came aboard."

"So that explains why he was unconscious in the airlock," said Pacal.

"No. Even with that much Triazolam in his system moving him into an airlock and into a spacesuit would almost certainly have awakened him to a very groggy state at least. There was another drug introduced after the Triazolam. Some form of Alprazolam, also a benzodiazepine, and as I've said it was introduced through the lungs well after the Triazolam was taken. Alprazolam is used for anxiety or panic attacks. It acts on the brain and central nervous system. We did not find any of that in Bateman's stash and it's not a popular street drug. Somehow Bateman inhaled Alprazolam, and that's a very bad thing when you're already on too much Triazolam. It will cause loss of coordination, loss of consciousness, even seizure. For Bateman it was a death sentence."

"You mean even without suffocation in a spacesuit?" asked Pacal.

Dumars continued, "Bateman's diet on Earth was poor. His cholesterol was through the roof. The Earth med team let that kind of thing slide because they knew a few months on space food would quickly cure that. But Bateman already had stenosis waiting to happen. When his BP fell off from those two drugs, intracranial stenosis took over. Bateman had a beauty of stroke. He would have died from *it* if the spacesuit hadn't got him first. And that, ladies and gentlemen, is the story of Harold Bateman."

Dumars looked at us as though she expected applause. We all stared back dumbfounded.

"What?" asked Dumars with a gesture of exasperation.

Pacal asked, "He breathed that second drug?"

"Inhaled it, yes. And, I doubt he was awake when he did."

"Someone sprayed it at him?" asked Pacal.

"Or just released it into his compartment somehow."

Pacal looked at me, "So that *had* to be done in his module while he was asleep."

Bishop interrupted, "Andrea, when did you last sleep?"

Dumars looked confused. "When did we start the autopsy?"

Bishop continued, "Andrea, you need to go down and go to bed."

I added, "Please, Andrea, go to bed. We appreciate all you've done here. Please get out of those surgical clothes and sleep."

Dumars looked woozy.

Bishop said, "Perhaps I will accompany her."

Dumars gave an inquisitive look as Bishop rose and put a hand on her shoulder. Together they coasted gently out. Pacal closed the door.

Pacal spoke, "We now know Bateman was gassed in his module and it OD'd him. Somebody was robbing him or wanted something from him for some reason. Maybe the guy didn't know Bateman was on sleeping pills. He gassed him just to knock him out but something went wrong. Dumars said there might have been seizures. The guy probably figured out that he'd screwed up and Bateman was going to die even though he didn't understand why. He needed to cover his tracks. He needed to get rid of the body. When the coast was clear he got him into the airlock and hid the body. Then he went back and took Bateman's laptop and tablet. Maybe they were all he was after to begin with. There must have been evidence in them. He used a terminal somewhere to hack the camera files and mask what he did. Then he disappeared into the population. That's the scenario I'm coming up with."

"You think this wasn't intentional murder?"

"I don't think so."

"Why, exactly?"

"Dumars said it was the combination of drugs that OD'd Bateman. The aerosol Bateman inhaled by itself wasn't lethal. Our suspect wasn't trying to kill Bateman, just sedate him."

I said, "It was still murder. Bateman was still breathing when he was put in that spacesuit."

Pacal shook his head. "From what Dumars just said there was no saving Bateman. We know the guy wasn't trying to kill Bateman so I'll bet he thought Bateman was already dead when he put him in that suit."

The three of us sat in thought.

Pacal added, "Right now, searching for that laptop and tablet would cause too much attention."

"We can continue searching his communications," said James.

"Yeah, and Earth will be doing a deep background check on him now. There must be some previous association between Bateman and his killer," suggested Pacal.

"Anything to add, Mark?" asked James.

"So we're looking for someone who knows hacking files and how to take off and put on a space suit."

"God, it almost sounds like someone from the astronauts corps," said James.

Pacal added, "You know, our guy was probably gambling Bateman would not be found for a very long time. Think about it, if we had not done the midcourse correction setup and noticed Bateman missing, when would we have ever checked inside the spacesuits in the emergency airlock? We'd all be distracted with the approach to Mars, the setup for orbit and descent and all that. We might not have realized Bateman was missing until the emergency airlock spacesuits were needed for the Mars surface set up."

"But what did this guy want from Bateman?" asked James.

"I'd sure like a look at that missing laptop," replied Pacal.

"What do you think, Mark?"

"I'll have to consider all this further. Jeff, what is the status of the emergency airlock now?"

"After Dumars made her second trip inside, we rebagged Bateman's body, resealed the airlock, and purged the atmosphere into space. The airlock has now been refilled with fresh air."

"New seals on the door?"

"Multiple new seals on the primary inner door."

"So where do we go from here, Mark?" asked Pacal.

"Let's keep up the surveillance and watch for *anything* out of the ordinary. I need to go write all this up for Epstone. That ought to be fun. I'll get permission to access private communications where we think there might be evidence. You can be sure Ground will be doing stuff far beyond what we do. You guys keep me posted up to the minute. Earth needs to know about this right away so I've got to go send them the bad news."

They nodded. I pushed out of my seat and opened the door. The three of us went our separate ways.

My command seat was empty. West looked at me and gave a flat smile.

"You have the Con, Steve?"

"I have the Con, Captain. Nothing to report. Any news?"

"Maybe later."

The rest of the Bridge crew looked on but made no comments.

In my office I pulled down to the keyboard and did my best to tell the sordid tale of Harold Bateman along with the adventures of Doctor Andrea Dumars. Earth's death notification was bad enough. This latest news was bound to put them in panic mode. So many people working for years to make this mission possible and somehow one person suddenly becomes a threat to everything. It is an irony of free will that a single perverse individual can destroy the good work of millions.

As I clicked SEND on the finished work of tragedy, Bishop's email icon appeared. It was her update to the crew.

All Hands

Message from Director of Personnel, Dr. Amada Bishop

Be advised we are anticipating a short memorial service for Harold Bateman

144

sometime next week. Although it has been determined that he took an excessive amount of sleeping pills, the investigation is continuing. We will post the time and date of the memorial service in the next few days.

Also upcoming, an update on Mars status, including remote power up operations and robotic placement of dome equipment along with the approach to orbit of the next three supply starships. We look forward to sharing that report with you as soon as it comes in.

Warmest regards,
Amanda.

"Bishop to Easton."

"Go ahead, Amanda."

"How does it look?"

"Great as always. Send it on."

"Will do."

"Pacal to Easton."

"Go ahead, Mick."

"We've had an incident in the exercise area."

"An incident? A security issue? I'm listening."

"A disagreement over a treadmill came to blows."

"A fistfight? You had a fistfight on E Deck? How is that even possible?"

"Men find a way, Mark. One of them had to be taken to medical. Possible broken jaw. Doctor Davies is handling it. Dumars is sleeping. I'll send you the video file as soon as it's extracted."

"What have you done with the other guy?"

"He is being held in detention in the Security Office."

"What are you going to do with him?"

"Well, that's just it. By law in these situations you are the judge and jury. Of course I know you really don't need this right now."

"Call Bishop and bring her into this. Have her do an evaluation of both of them. Did either of them finish their required workout?"

"No."

"Take the healthy one escorted by a security officer and make him finish his routine then put him back in detention. No contact with anyone but your officers."

"Bread and water only?" I heard Pacal laugh to himself.

"When Bishop has evaluated them we'll decide how to proceed. Okay?"

"Sounds good to me. I'll send you the video file. It should be good for a laugh."

"Easton out."

"Easton to Doctor Davies."

No answer.

"Easton to Davies."

"Sorry, Captain. I had my hands full. Davies here. Go ahead."

"Is it really broken?"

"We're still setting up the x-ray equipment. It was put back in storage after the kidney stone. But yes, I'm certain there is a fracture of the lower jaw. How about I call you as soon as we're finished?"

"Yes, please do. Thanks Doctor. Easton out."

"Bishop to Easton."

"Hi Amanda. Has Mick contacted you yet?"

"Oh yeah. I heard the story."

"I'll kind of need you to tell me how to handle this."

"I'm really not surprised this has happened. There is a certain degree of subconscious stress in the crew left behind from the Bateman affair. This is probably an expression of that. We'll need to take that into consideration."

"Okay, just let me know what you think."

"There's one other thing. I probably shouldn't bring it up right now but since we're talking."

"It's okay. I'm listening."

"I was approached by three people who would like to start a New Dawn online newspaper, or news channel. They want permission to do that. They're trying to go about this the right way so we have to respect that. I know with everything else that's going on we don't need this but remember we're trying to contain what is happening right now. This might be a good distraction."

"I've got too much on my plate to think about something like that. All I can say is you would have to approve any shipwide publications before they went out. How does that sound?"

"Maybe we should both approve anything that goes out."

"You are wise, Amanda. I'll leave the rest of it in your hands."

"Bishop out."

An Earth transmission icon flashed on my screen.

BC Mars Mission Control
Mars Base Alpha Update
Resource Delivery and Deployment Group
Dr. Hans Beltram Reporting
Phase Status and Projections

Starship Cargo One

As previously reported the landing of Cargo One almost two years ago was successful. The Lander Vision System using the Map Relative Localization algorithms combined with starship IMU data proved successful in isolating an adequately flat terrain with a minimum incidence of natural debris. The Active Landing Leg System was invoked at touchdown

correcting a four-degree off-vertical orientation. Over the past few weeks in anticipation of the arrival of New Dawn, Cargo One was commanded to power up by MBA Team One, after which telemetry from onboard lighting, cameras, and sensory data was received. Opening of the level one cargo hatch and exercising of the primary crane were also both successful. Load testing revealed the robotic earthmover vehicle batteries had not been affected appreciably by their twenty-two-month hibernation on Mars. Consequently vehicle one and two were lowered successfully to the Martian surface and commanded to initiate their standup and startup sequence and deployment of masts and antennas. Link up with the MBA Positioning System satellite was established soon after. Both autonomous vehicles were then commanded to begin assignments to clear roadways from each Cargo Starship unloading zone to the central MBA hub. Offloading of the two Carry-Deck Autonomous Cranes will begin as soon as those inroads are accomplished. In-Situ Resource Utilization modules are to begin next with translation of water mining and CO_2 collection equipment to the Martian surface. Off-loading of the three Central Power Stations will follow.

Starship Cargo Two

As previously reported Cargo Two landed with a nominal orientation. MBA Team Two has sent power up commands to Starship Cargo Two. Telemetry from onboard lighting, cameras, and sensory data was received. All Habitat and Support Modules appear intact and ready for placement, deployment, and inflation. Off-loading of Solar Shield Habitat Interface Tunnels and power conduit will follow.

Starship Cargo Three

As previously reported, Cargo three landed with a two-degree off-vertical orientation. That deviation was corrected by the Active Landing Leg System. Over a period of ten months however, Cargo Three experienced a slow deviation at the ninety-four-degree mark and is now three degrees off-vertical. That deviation has stabilized and remains constant. MBA Team Three has sent power up commands to Starship Cargo Three. Telemetry from onboard lighting, cameras, and sensory data was received. All materials containers appear intact and ready for deployment and unpacking.

Starships Cargo Four, Five, and Six.

All three starships are on course and preparing for orbital insertion prior to entry and landing. Earthmovers are scheduled to clear three landing pads and place beacons at the appropriate coordinates.

End of Update
Dr. Hans Beltram

The report pumped me up pretty good. It made me forget all about broken jaws, dead IT Specialists, space newspapers and everything else. It was like a bucket of cold water in the face to remind me of what we actually were trying to do.

"Davies to Easton."

"Go ahead, Doctor."

"We do have an uncomplicated jaw fracture. It probably wouldn't have happened on Earth but after weeks of zero G…."

"I understand Doctor. How long?"

"There will be surgery. Probably two months of recovery under the circumstances. We'll brace the jaw so his mouth is slightly open. That will make it easier to eat and speak, but it will be a real nuisance for the patient."

"Is Pacal still there?"

"Yes, hang on a second. Mick, can you click on, he wants you. He's here, Captain."

"Mick, once Doctor Davies has the jaw all set, bring the other one in to show him what he's done, then throw him back in detention, okay?"

"I understand, Captain. Will do."

"Thank you, Doctor. Easton out."

Despite all that was going on, it was time to start thinking about our Mars arrival.

Chapter 11

Over the next several days our morning meetings became aggravating, a mindset I was required to conceal. Harold Bateman remained at rest in the emergency airlock, sealed in his air-conditioned shroud. But not one clue as to the identity of the second person involved in his death had been uncovered. The added security monitors also had shown nothing unusual.

"We're going to have to make a decision about the body," said Bishop. "The written procedure is to follow the burial at sea protocols."

"You think we should go ahead and do that now?" I asked.

"Yes, in this our winter of discontent," replied Bishop.

"It would mean opening the emergency airlock outer doors," added James. "That is, unless you want to move the body downstairs to the main airlock."

"We don't want to parade Bateman's body around," I answered.

"So one person in an EVA suit in the airlock to open and push him out?" asked James.

153

"Can someone in a suit fit in there with Bateman in a shroud?" I asked.

"They'd position the body in a spacesuit docking station," replied James. "Then it would just be a question of maneuvering the body into position at the door."

"And Amanda, you'll have to do your best to say something for the general population to feel okay about this. Do you agree with all of this, Andrea?" I looked at the doctor with raised eyebrows.

"There's nothing more I can get from the body. There is no reason to keep him onboard except for sentimental reasons."

"How long will the body remain near us out there?" asked Bishop.

"You're wondering if he'll be floating along with us to Mars?" asked James.

"Very definitely a concern," replied Bishop. "We don't want the body being visible out the windows."

"That won't be an issue, Amanda. There is most definitely a big difference in mass. With a strong push out, Bateman will fall behind and away fairly quickly," I answered.

"Then if there's nothing else Captain, I'll go try to figure out how to write this up," said Bishop.

"You all try to have a good day. Mick, would you hang behind a minute?"

When the others had gone Pacal and I looked at each other with frustration.

"You want a coffee, Mick?"

"Cream and sugar packet, please."

I left and returned with hot coffee. We sipped at the straws and tried to think of something positive to say.

I fidgeted with my armrests. "We have to wonder why this mystery guy is really onboard."

"You really thinking guy as opposed to girl?"

"My gut feeling says it's a man."

Pacal nodded, "I agree with you. To be honest, of all the crap that could go wrong none of this ever came to mind."

"And we still have nothing new to go on?"

"Not a thing. Haven't found the laptop, the tablet, flash drives, or anything else. There is some video of Bateman in the gym and food areas, but nothing to give a clue as to friends or enemies. There is still nothing from Earth?"

I shook my head. "They are working it like crazy. They found a possible connection to Bateman with one of those conspiracy theory groups, but no names or direct associations."

"And he passed all the psyche and historical reviews?"

"His record was clean. I guess because there wasn't anything but school and work to be found. What did someone want from him?"

"I don't know what we can do, Mark. Just go on and hope this individual doesn't have any other bad intentions."

"I'd just like to know what his real motive is."

"You're worried about sabotage?"

"There are other governments that would love to see us fail."

"If it was a suicide mission he probably could already have done something."

"Not really. He'd wait for the maximum distance from Earth to make any real investigation impossible. All Earth would be left with would be a sudden loss of telemetry."

"We really don't have anything to suggest something like that."

"Entry and descent would be the perfect time to stage an accident. There would be almost nothing left to find. It could be that all he needed to do was conceal Bateman's body until then."

"I don't think that's it, Mark."

"The other option would be to sabotage the Mars orbit insertion burn. We'd continue away from Earth forever."

"We can monitor ship's systems closely to be sure nothing like that happens, Mark."

"We have to consider this stuff, Mick. It's our job. We need to be one step ahead of this guy, whatever he's up to."

"We're watching twenty-four-seven. He'd have trouble doing anything at all right now. We can be fully prepared by the time we start taking down modules and setting up the seats for landing."

"Yeah. We have to be ready before any of that starts. The insertion burn is just three days before the landing. Bridge and Engineering will be busy as hell."

"So let's both spend some time dreaming up ways to prevent sabotage."

"Discuss it in person only, Mick. We know this guy is a hacker."

"Yeah, right."

In my mind I became a starship saboteur and went over every possible way to misdirect or destroy a starship. It became a game of sorts. How would I catch myself to prevent a catastrophic event? Three days later an email from Bishop interrupted my game; the announcement for Bateman's burial.

All Hands
Message from Director of Personnel, Dr. Amada Bishop

This is to announce a brief memorial service followed by burial for IT Specialist Harold Bateman, to take place tomorrow morning at 08:00. In keeping with the traditions of maritime customs and law and Mr. Bateman will be laid to rest in the ocean of space, his journey with us now concluded. It is not necessary to attend the service on Deck D, it will be broadcast on all monitors and displays. During the service we would ask everyone to stay

where they are and share our prayer quietly

to yourselves.

Warmest regards,
Amanda

With great misgivings I replied to Bishop she could release the notice. I escaped back to the blessed diversion of the command chair. The A-link antenna was still sticking. We were going to need to send someone out to fix it. The B and C Deck water cell bladder system was still giving pressure alarms. Engineering was searching cell by cell for a leak. Broken Jaw had been released to his cubicle on home confinement. His nemesis was placed on supervised work detail and home confinement. The New Dawn Times was being written and compiled. That one worried me. Gen Parry and her husband Gary had switched living compartments with someone else so they wouldn't smell the non-existent aroma from the waste management equipment below their deck. Patricia Helmsly had stopped complaining about sharing shower minutes. I received a somewhat unauthorized email from Angelena Dorser saying she'd watched Forbidden Planet and loved it. I should try Prometheus by Ridley Scott next.

By the end of the day my office-cabin was a wonderful place to take refuge in. I even considered inviting Pars and her flask to join me, something I'd normally never do. I eyed my sleeping apparel, decided it was too soon, locked myself into the desk seat and just sat staring at the blue screen with the New Dawn icon in the center of it.

There was a tap at the door.

"Come on in."

Dr. Dumars slipped in and shut the door behind her. She seemed irate. She was wearing sheer light-blue night clothes that billowed out around her. She had to keep collecting parts of it. It was transparent but no private areas were visible. Her long hair was loose and splayed behind her.

"God you must have looked like an angel coming up here. I hope you didn't scare anyone."

Dumars' tone was indeed irate. "I wasn't going to change just to come up here to complain about the Home Office's screw up."

"Well, we all need visits from angels now and then."

"Is that a come-on, Captain? I wouldn't have expected that from you."

"Just trying to lighten the mood. What do you mean the Home Office's screw-up?"

"I forwarded it to you but I needed to make sure you read it before you started snoring."

"How do you know I snore? I don't by the way."

"The point is…. Well look, just read it."

She pulled in and held to the desk and leaned next to me. I was taken for a moment by the smell of jasmine. A section of her nightwear pressed against the side of my face. It too smelled like jasmine. She tapped at my keyboard, found her forwarded email and opened it. It was the Earth report on Harold Bateman.

**Department of Internal Affairs
Off-World Investigative Group
Final Report on Incident 86743
Dr. Charles Bacon Reporting
Subject: Harold Bateman**

A thorough investigation of Harold Bateman's background activity and previous associations has revealed no unusual behavior that would suggest any illegal or unethical activity. When taken in context with the circumstances of his death it is likely that death was the result of an ill-advised act of personal recreation combined with the misuse of prescription medication and an existing medical condition. All evidence in this unfortunate loss of life indicates death by accident and misadventure. This case will be classified as suspended pending submission of any additional evidence.
Dr. Charles Bacon

I looked up at Andrea's puffy sleep face and smeared red lipstick. "Odd that this should come out on the very day we announce his memorial service."

Dumars' unleashed hair drifted in front of her face so that she had to wipe it away. "Odd that they are trying to cover this up, never mind that I have to bring you this report when no one should have seen it except you."

Dumars pushed her blond hair out of the way again and lost her hold so that her legs came up behind me. Her left hip bumped the back of my head. In turning and placing my hand on it to steady her, little male notification bells went off in my head telling me she wasn't wearing anything under that thin material.

She ignored the touch and held onto me to right herself. "What if this went out to someone else and not just me? It might be forwarded all over the ship."

"Well it doesn't suggest anything other than an accident."

The jasmine was really distracting. Dumars tried to bend at the waist to bring her legs back around which put her chest against the side of my head for just a moment. The male notification alarms instantly pointed out to me that there was no elastic of any kind between me and her unusually warm soft upper body. I again reached around through the veil and placed one hand on her waist to help her stabilize. At least that's what I was telling myself.

"That's another thing. You see what they're doing here? They're declaring Bateman's death to be an accident. That was no accident."

"Not so loud, Ann. These are thin walls."

Dumars got partial control and held on in a kneeling position next to my seat with an arm around the back of my chair. I was now looking down into the waves of sheer transparent fabric as it formed a blue haze around me. It floated up between our faces and became mixed with her long blond hair so that I could not see anything at all except that wonderfully aromatic mist of blue. I felt her moving next to me trying to get it under control, her free hand sweeping gently at the fabric. I started to laugh but somehow, suddenly her face was directly in front of mine, a single layer of shear blue haze between us. There was a long-suspended moment, the two of us staring at each other through the blue fog.

Reality instantly changed. Our lips suddenly were together though I could not recall it actually happening. My brain was nearly paralyzed trying to understand exactly what *was* happening but my body didn't care. That shear blue netting was still between us. I had a brief moment to consider breaking off the kiss. That option never stood a chance. We seemed to be held together with the greatest of resolve. Her lower body began to float up. She grabbed my upper thigh to hang on but got more than that. I reached up blindly and placed a hand on that warm hip. The sensation of hot, smooth doctor spiked through me once again. It was a long massaging kiss. A hand fumbled around to find the zipper on my flight suit and pulled it open. She became impatient and unsnapped my armrests, setting us both into freefall. We began a slow drift upward, turning in midair as the transparent lace enveloped us. Passion was in complete control. We turned slowly in the air, out of control, wrestling with desire. She had found her way through the veil and was holding me and trying to meet me with her bare thighs. I'd lost track of where we were. We bonded and in the shifting, slapping of us together I managed to bump my head on the floor to which she uttered a breathless, half-irate, "Shhh," which meant nothing at all to me. In our struggle she accidentally caught one foot in a restraint resulting in our erotic dance suddenly becoming momentarily controlled, but she quickly lost her catch and we circled away into my sleeping bag fastened to the wall. Our breathing was becoming labored but it did not diminish the effort. As we worked the bonding I managed to find an opening of bare skin on her neck and locked my lips onto it. Her nails dug into my back. The exchange went on and on. When the lust of it finally began to release us, we drifted together in silence, just holding on to each other not caring where weightlessness took us. We had wound ourselves together in blue veil.

After a time she whispered, "If I could just sleep right here just like this for the rest of the night it would be the best sleep I've had in years."

"You want to?"

"Nice of you to ask, but you know we can't. You know we're already both in enough trouble."

"Maybe."

"The Bridge crew is out there and these walls are too thin."

"What did just happen?"

"I have no idea. Do you?"

"We'll have to think about it."

"Help me try to look respectable."

She found a foot strap and the two of us pulled at her flowing nightwear. It had been wrinkled and ruffled in a very telltale way. We tried to straighten it. I even tried taping it here and there. My hairbrush recovered her golden locks fairly adequately. She dabbed at her makeup with water.

A few deep breaths at the door and she said, "We'll have to talk more about this cover up."

"Okay."

She dashed out giving the Bridge crew only a second or two to appraise her appearance as she swirled down the ladderway.

I slipped into my sleeping bag and fell asleep adrift in the center of my compartment.

Morning came a moment later. As I pulled on my flight suit I tried to make sense of the night before but a sudden pang of concern reminded me this was shove Bateman out the door day. On the Bridge I checked on the staff and headed for Pars' quarters. A tap at the door brought a "Come."

Pars had chosen a dark violet flight suit. Her hair was tied back. She was typing at her laptop and gestured me to enter. "Got any news?" she asked.

"We got the follow up on Bateman from Earth. They're covering it up."

"Wow! That's a little spooky. What are they saying?"

"They're inferring it was just a weird accident; Bateman playing around. They're calling it death by misadventure."

Pars turned her seat toward me. "You know, in all fairness I'm not sure what they could do. They can't let everyone know there is probably a murderer on board so what *can* they say?"

"Yeah, I suppose."

"So you still going to push him out the airlock this morning?"

"You're the XO. I'm open to suggestions."

"What are you going to do about that report?"

"Not publicize it, but I'll tuck it so deep into the computer's general access reporting system that if anybody is hell bent to read it they can find it but only if they work hard enough at searching."

"I agree with that. Does Andrea know about the cover up yet?"

"Let's not refer to it in those terms anymore. She does. I think she's still trying to sort out her feelings. I know I am."

"Hey, it's out of your hands. Sometimes things just happen you don't have any control over."

"Yeah, don't I know."

"Can you stomach some breakfast on the way to the ceremony?"

I nodded. "I can if you can."

We gathered at the emergency airlock, Dumars, Bishop, James, Descard and Pacal. As planned, only one person in an EVA suit was needed to open the outer doors and guide Bateman out which made the whole process much easier. A GoPro was used to better cover the ceremony.

When the doors to space were finally opened, Bishop read her dedication and prayer.

"Friends, we are gathered here to honor the life and passing of Specialist Harold Bateman, a man of vision and courage. We did not know him well but he was one of us, a man willing to venture into space to build a new world. Harold, we all hope you rest in peace. May your journey be one of enlightenment. We now commit your body to God's ocean."

With a nod through the window, Bateman was smoothly ushered out the door and into black space. I looked up to see a sizable crowd gathered at the windows, watching the body drift away. The hatches were sealed; the airlock pressurized. And that was the end of Harold Bateman.

Chapter 12

BC Mars Mission Control
Mars Base Alpha Update
Resource Delivery and Deployment
Group
Dr. Hans Beltram Reporting
Phase Status and Projections

Starship Cargo One, Two, and Three
Unloading of ground support
equipment aboard Cargo one has been
completed and it awaits human access for
the remaining cargo distribution. The three
power stations have been offloaded from
Cargo Two and have been placed at the
MBA central coordinates along with
conduit/cables by the Carry-Deck
Autonomous Cranes. The three main
habitat domes are presently being
stationed on the surface pads created for
them by the two robotic earthmover
vehicles. They will be ready for inflation
upon arrival of New Dawn. The two In-Situ
Resource Utilization Mobile Drilling
Transport Rigs have been offloaded from
Cargo Three and are undergoing power up
tests before being sent to the SWIM sites

found during subsurface water ice mapping performed previously near the area's Lobate Debris Apron. The transfer cases housing the heated water collection bladders await the arrival of New Dawn. Also, all three SuperMOXIES have also been offloaded from Cargo Three and are in preliminary tests prior to being powered up. They are expected to begin extracting oxygen from the Mars atmosphere by the end of the week. Starships Cargo four, five, and six remain on course and expected to make orbital insertion on schedule. At this time all critical Mars systems are condition green or expected to be condition green by the time New Dawn arrives.

> **End of update,**
> **Dr. Hans Beltram**

It took me about thirty seconds to send that report out to everyone. It was exactly what we needed after the Bateman affair. I decided to celebrate with breakfast in the food area. I flew down there headfirst, grabbed coffee and pastry and spotted an empty seat next to Paul Descard. He was studying a small tablet.

"Sure you're not making all this up?" he said as I locked into the seat.

"Hey, that's Earth reporting, not me! Checkout the telemetry stream, Paul. You can see it for yourself."

"Yeah, it must drive Ground nuts that we'll be watching the next three ships land before they get the telemetry."

"We will all be very puckered up I'm sure."

"I'm not worried. You know what the landing success rate for this vehicle is?"

"You're asking me?"

Descard laughed. "Actually the recreation dome is on one of the next three. That *is* something to worry about."

"That's right, you're a free throw champion if I remember, right?"

"Eastern States High School champion."

"It's not going to be the same, buddy. A toddler could slam dunk in that gravity."

"Yeah, but I'll be the first. Everything I do will be a new record."

"I see your point."

"So what was the deal with Bateman? Did he do himself in?"

"The final finding was death by misadventure. They're saying it was just a strange accident. But don't pass that on to anyone."

"It's classified?"

"No, but I want to keep it low key. I don't want to set off any conspiracy nuts we might have."

Descard held back a laugh. "Those conspiracy guys are not really nuts, you know. I've seen photos of a slab on the moon that would have made Arthur C. Clark sit up and take notice. You've been to the moon, haven't you ever seen anything that didn't look right?"

"Nope."

"Did they tell you not to talk about it if you did?"

"No. I was there for a rescue mission. A seam split on a habitat module. They were running out of O2. We were in and out."

"Some people say they've already started the process of Disclosure. Others say a lot of that stuff is intentionally leaked. It's kind of funny, you know; once they announce a microbe has been found on another planet or moon that's the end of it. If there is biological life anywhere else, then there must be biological life everywhere else and after billions of years of universe some of it must have gotten smart."

"Personally I don't have a problem with that."

"Well, yeah, you're Flash Gordon. But society is full of narrow view people. They want to believe they have a good bead on things and they don't want anything screwing with that."

"They did lock Galileo up, didn't they?"

"Damn right."

Descard tucked his empty packets in his breast pocket and straightened up his flight suit. "Mark, you know we've got to go outside and fix that damn A-link antenna mount, right?"

"Yep."

"Who you gonna send? I want to go."

"Okay. Who do you want with you?"

"Williams. He's got a lot of EVAs. He can nursemaid me along."

I laughed.

"I'm just joking. You know that right?"

"Yes."

"When can we go?"

"Whenever you're ready. It will be another good event to take people's minds off things. Good news from Earth and another spacewalk. What more could I ask for?"

"Great! I will go set up the logistics."

Descard hurried off excitedly. He pulled down feet first through the ladderway. I sipped the last of my coffee and thought about Andrea. There was still time to visit her before my shift started. I wondered if it would be too noticeable. I decided to risk it.

The exercise area was full on E Deck. People were waiting for machines. Small groups gathered around those putting in their time. Cute comments being made. I passed by without being stopped.

D Deck was also unusually busy. Some kind of regular checkup. In the training area a Mars EVA class was going on. It was well attended.

I floated past the group waiting outside the medical exam room and made it all the way to Dumars' office. Her door was slid open. She was upside down with a foot in a ceiling loop, tapping at a tablet. She was all in white with her hair tied back. It stuck straight down toward the floor. She did not notice me enter.

I rotated to the same upside-down position and held to her desk to get into her range of vision. We met face to face.

"So this is your idea of reality?" I asked.

She stifled a laugh. "You know, yes. Sometimes this is my vision of reality."

"We were going to talk about the report from Ground."

"I've decided it's a lose-lose argument. But in the shower I keep hearing the soundtrack from Alfred Hitchcock's movie Psycho."

"That must make it an interesting two minutes."

"Wouldn't you like to know."

"I believe I would, now that you mention it."

There was a long pause. She searched my eyes for sincerity. I had nothing but.

Finally she looked back at her tablet. "You know you may be making us more of an item by coming down here."

"Well, no more than you coming up to my office late looking like an angel."

"I was mad, though. You don't look mad."

"I have a perfectly good reason for coming down. We're sending out an EVA team to fix that A-link antenna. You need to set up and be ready for it."

"You could have sent me an email."

"Hold still, you have a little smudge of something next to your mouth." I gently reached out and wiped away the nothing that was not there.

"Thank you. How embarrassing. What was it?"

"Nothing. Nothing at all." I pushed back, gave a wave and exited her office, still upside down. There were gawkers. I made as businesslike and dignified a departure as was possible. Someone laughed.

Dove down through the habitat levels and past the Engineering Authorized Personnel Only sign. In Engineering they already had the airlock inner doors open and techs pulling apart the EVA suits. Descard was nearby with a group discussing the repair. I pulled over, nodded to him, and listened.

"If it is just ice, the laser will clear it in a second," said Marcus Williams, Descard's choice for EVA partner.

"But if it doesn't, you'll be removing fasteners and replacing that motor mount," suggested another engineer.

"No problem. Pistol Grip Tool to the rescue," replied Williams.

"There's a little more to it than that," answered the engineer.

Descard asked, "What concerns do you have, Scott?"

"They're all three-eighth inch fasteners, supposed to be eighty-seven inch-pounds to back out. If you get one that doesn't want to back out it could be a real problem," replied the engineer.

"Let's just cross that bridge when and if we come to it. Are we ready to get dressed?" asked Descard.

"The lock is ours, Paul," answered Williams.

"Okay. Let's go start our breathing."

I tapped my communicator. "Easton to Bishop."

It took half a minute for her to answer. "Go ahead, Captain."

"We are setting up for an EVA to fix a sticky antenna. Could you come down to cover it or send someone?"

"When did this all come about?"

"We've been putting it off but we decided to just go do it and get it over with. It's a short walk outside."

I could hear Bishop breathe a sigh of fatigue. "I'll send an associate down and I'll write something up for immediate release to the general population. You want broadcast coverage, right?"

"Yeah but I'll pass that on to Shaw. I know you have enough to do."

"Thanks. Bishop out."

With a hand ahead for guard I flew up through the decks and headed for my empty command seat.

Steve West smiled at me and said, "You have the conn."

"I have the conn. Sorry we are about to…."

"We know. We got the email from Dr. Bishop."

"Already?"

"Yeah, who would have thought the lead psychologist on a space mission would be the busiest person on board."

I nodded. "I've come to believe we all need one."

"You can give us live from the scene, Brent?"

"Coming up available on all monitors now, Captain."

I locked down and called up the airlock camera on my left side monitor along with the external airlock outer door camera on my right. The guys were busy setting up. Descard and Williams had breathing masks on. I went back to scrolling performance numbers for New Dawn, one system at a time.

It took several hours for them to prepare and suit up. With duffel bags packed and visors down, the airlock depressurization began. We watched with great interest as the primary outer door was unsealed and slid aside.

There are usually glitches on every mission. It's not a reflection of the engineering or implementation, it's just the way it is. For Descard and Williams their glitch began almost immediately.

The secondary outer door latch lever would not swing around to the unlocked position. We were all patched in to the suit comms. I could hear Descard grunting with effort trying to push the lever down. Williams gave him a good ten minutes then floated in as close as possible to add what he could to the effort. Another fifteen minutes brought no joy.

Descard sounded annoyed. "Jeff, can we bang on this thing with something without hurting anything?"

It took James a couple minutes to answer. "We feel you could tap on it with the bar extension we'll give you through the airlock exchange compartment."

"Okay, let's try it 'cause it's not budging."

A few minutes later the two spacesuit figures got into position with one person bracing the other and they began tapping at the lever with a shiny chrome bar.

"You can go harder than that Paul," said Williams.

Descard raised the bar high and struck down at the uncooperative lever. It broke loose and swung around. The airlock door seals split slightly from their frame. There was cheering to be heard over the comm.

With both doors open to deep black space and stars, the duffel bags were gathered out, safety lines attached, and out the two spacemen floated. We picked them up on the exterior cameras.

"So that must've been the hard part, Paul," said Williams.

"I hope so."

"My God, will you look at this. Nothing but stars in every direction," added Williams.

"Yeah, no beach to walk on as they say," replied Descard.

"Desolate emptiness in every direction."

"We'd better focus. Did you clip on over here?"

"I'm secure."

I watched with envy as they circled the antenna and began setting up. They magnetically attached the replacement antenna mount and tool bags to the hull and began unpacking.

"I've got the laser. You got the scanner?" asked Descard.

"Got it and am on it."

Williams swung himself around and began scanning the seam in the base of the antenna mount, searching for ice or other interference. It took him a full thirty minutes.

"I got nothing, Paul. You want to try it?"

"I'd better. Any chance not to have to replace the thing?"

Descard took another twenty minutes of close proximity scanning.

"Well that's it. I'll be damned if I can find anything either. It's got to go."

"It's just eight fasteners to separate the antenna and eight more for the turnstile. Maybe it will be quick. You've got the pistol grip tools in yours," said Williams.

Descard began digging in his tool bag. He pulled out a shiny chrome pistol grip tool and held it up to check the settings.

"No, it's all set at ninety inch-pounds, Paul. It's ready to go."

Descard maneuvered for the first fastener. He held the PGT upright and squeezed the trigger. The fastener backed out obediently.

"That's one," said Williams.

Thirty minutes later Williams was set to refasten the antenna to the hull.

"Piece of cake, Paul."

"So far so good," agreed Descard.

Descard placed the PGT against the first base mount fastener. He squeezed the trigger. There was a brief rotation of the tool bit but the tool suddenly jerked to a stop.

"Did it turn at all?" asked Williams.

"I think so. I think I got maybe five degrees. Let me give it another shot."

Descard tried again and again there was a brief rotation of the fastener followed by a jerking stop. Several more attempts yielded the same result.

"It's turning, but just a few degrees at a time. We've got to up the torque on the tool. You hearing this Jeff?"

"We're with you guys, Paul. We see no reason you can't set that thing up to one hundred inch-pounds."

Descard held the tool up for a closer look. He twisted the control on the back end of the tool to set the new higher limit.

"Keep your fingers crossed, guys," said Descard.

Descard tried again. Again the same abrupt stop happened.

"I don't believe it," said Williams.

"Time to switch tools," said James.

Williams dug in the satchel and came out with the backup PGT. He handed it to Descard who went ahead and increased the settings.

With a deep breath for luck, Descard tried again. Once more the tool jerked to a stop.

A long pause of comm silence followed.

James said, "Paul, try a different fastener."

Descard took the advice but the result was the same.

"They are all that way, Jeff," said Descard.

Williams tried to be optimistic. "We've turned the first one almost one full turn so far. Maybe we should just keep going if this is the best we can get."

"What do you guys think, Jeff?" asked Descard.

"We've only got two choices. Try reinstalling the bad base or use the Scott Williams method. Maybe we'd better go for it. See how long it takes to get that first one in."

Descard went back to work. After nearly an hour he had the first fastener in place.

"So that's it. Probably seven hours to install the rest."

"Captain are you on?" asked James.

"Easton here. Go ahead."

"How do you want to do this? Go back to the old antenna mount, or take the time to replace it?"

"We can't take a chance losing the A-link completely. If you have the suit time, let's keep going. Even if you don't get them all in you can stow everything and we'll send out a second team to finish up."

"Sounds like a plan, guys," said James.

Descard went on to fastener two. Seven hours and twenty minutes later the last of the fasteners were seated in place.

"You guys have an hour and fifteen left in your suits. Time to pack it in," said James.

"Twisted my arm," replied Williams.

With everything stowed, they made their way to the airlock outer doors. Inside the airlock, Williams pulled the outer door shut.

He began to struggle with it but the door refused to seat.

Williams continued wrestling with it. "What the…?"

Descard took note and joined him. "What's keeping it?"

"It won't seat. It's like the damn hatch is warped or something."

"Let's brace against the wall with our feet and both bring it closed. Okay, 1, 2, 3!"

"Nope. That's not working."

Descard said, "Jeff, are you seeing this?"

"Yes, we see you. What's the problem with it?"

"It seems like something's not lining up correctly," replied Williams.

"Okay, but that's impossible," answered James.

"You got any suggestions?" asked Descard.

"We're showing forty-five minutes on your suit time. James to Easton."

"I'm with you, Paul."

"We're going to have to bring them in with the secondary outer door only. It will be a protocol violation to have only one pressure door protecting the ship's atmosphere, but I don't see we have a choice. We can just be quick about it."

"I agree. You are approved for a single door seal just long enough to vacate the airlock."

"You guys got that?" asked James.

"We are closing the secondary door," answered Descard.

There was a long wait as the two worked to close the inner door. To my surprise, I heard one of them cursing beneath his breath.

Descard turned to face the camera and airlock window. "This one won't seal either."

"What's the problem this time?" asked James in disbelief.

"It's the same thing. It won't seat," replied Williams.

Another long silence on the comm system.

James asked, "Captain are you still getting this?"

"Easton here. Paul, Scott, stop working on the doors, plug into the life support panel and take on O2."

Everyone understood.

The private channel tone sounded on my communicator. It was James. "Go ahead, Jeff."

"The O2 isn't a problem, Mark. They can pump up all right. But with their suits running, the batteries *are* a problem. They can't recharge those power packs while they're using them. They've got to be cooled down before recharge."

"I know."

"Even if they plug into the service panel there will be a drain on the power packs. We can't have them so low on suit power that they can't unplug from the service panel."

"I know."

"We're going to have to get them into the emergency airlock and figure out those doors later."

"I agree. Get someone up to the emergency airlock right now and start depressurization."

"Okay. We're on it."

I switched back to the EVA channel. "This is Easton. Time for you guys to head over to the emergency airlock and come in that way. Do you copy?"

There was a long pause.

Descard answered, "We understand. On our way."

James added, "You'll need the pistol grip tool and the three-eight, right? It will be eighteen turns counterclockwise to open the outside door."

Descard answered, "Got that. We know. Bringing both PGTs just in case."

We watched on the cameras as the pair made their way over the top of New Dawn and then forward to the emergency airlock door. I had their suit's power monitor on my left screen, watching the available ampere-hour meters counting down.

Descard was hurrying. Williams handed him the first tool. It was inserted into the opening for external airlock access. Descard pulled the trigger for counterclockwise rotation of the door lock.

"What the!?" Descard sounded shocked.

Descard removed the tool inspected the bit end and tried again. "Give me the other PGT Paul," he said.

With the backup tool in place the trigger was pulled. There was a sound of exasperation from Descard.

"Well guys, the emergency airlock door will not unlock. The tool freezes at all torque settings."

I clicked on the comm. "Paul, Scott get back to the main airlock and plug back in. Be quick about it."

I watched their suit power levels approaching red. They understood completely. They jammed their tools back in the bag and started hand over hand back to the main airlock. By the time they arrived suit power was well in the red. With some fumbling at the service panel they managed to get their suit OSCU cables plugged in. On my screen the suit display switched to suit external power.

"Easton to James."

"Go ahead, Mark."

"Tell your man he doesn't need to depress the emergency airlock."

"Got that. But what are we going to do?"

Descard said, "Put somebody in a suit and have them open the emergency airlock outer doors from inside."

I countered, "We know there's a problem with that door, Paul. We don't know that it *will* open. That's not an option."

Williams suggested, "Could we pull a backup power unit from stores and jury-rig an attachment to it that we could plug into?"

I asked, "Jeff, will a suit power pack fit through the airlock transfer tube?"

James replied, "Definitely not."

Descard added, "We just ran out of options."

I answered, "No, we didn't. Standby."

"Easton to Pacal."

"Here, Captain."

"Join us on channel four alpha."

"Four alpha."

"Easton to Bishop."

"What is happening, Mark?"

"Join us on channel four alpha."

"Okay."

"Jeff, you have all your staff on this private channel?"

"That's affirm, Mark."

"Easton to Shaw."

"Go ahead, Captain."

"Switch the spacesuit comms, Engineering, and the rest of us to private four alpha."

"Got it."

"Okay everybody. Let's review where we're at. They can't close the outer doors in the main airlock so we can't repressurize the airlock to let them back in. They can't open the outer doors on the emergency airlock, so they can't get into it. Everybody with me so far?"

A chorus of concerned affirmatives came through the comm.

"Anyone have an idea how a problem as exotic as this could have happened?"

There was a long silent pause.

James said, "Both airlocks' outer doors? It's impossible."

"No ideas at all what could be wrong with those doors?" I asked again.

Suddenly a new, younger voice come over the comm. "There is one possibility, Captain."

"Who is speaking?"

"That's Laurel Collins, Mark," said James. "You think you have something Laurel?"

Collins stuttered at first, not accustomed to leading a high-level conversation. "We opened the main airlock for the sensor replacement. Then not long after that we opened the emergency airlock. Not long after that we opened the main airlock again. The main airlock secondary outer door did not want to open. We had to bang on it pretty hard to get the lever to drop. Next, the fasteners in the antenna base mount did not want to go back in. It took hours. Now the main airlock doors won't seal, and the emergency doors won't open. It could be that the ship's superstructure has expanded or contracted slightly or flexed somehow. It would only take a millimeter or two to do this. We see it on Earth all the time. A house shifts on its foundation and suddenly the doors are slightly out of alignment. The ship's body has flexed very slightly, just enough to put the doors out of alignment."

Another long silent pause.

"Wow," commented Descard.

"Jeff?" I asked.

"I can't argue the theory Mark, given what has happened. If she's right then we'll just need to do a realignment on those doors and they should be all right. It's a three-to-four-hour job. But that doesn't help us right now. How do we get our people out of that airlock?"

"We're going to depressurize Engineering, Jeff."

Another long pause.

"Do you agree?" I asked.

"I'm thinking, I'm thinking," he replied.

I added, "We have the emergency ladderway plates to seal off the individual decks."

"Yes, yes, but we'd have to shut down the water recovery system. The water might freeze. And the 02 scrubbers would need to be temporarily shut down as well," said James. "You know that old joke; it's hard to heat a vacuum."

Someone else added, "The Crays have fluid cooling. They might not like the cold either."

"Yes, but it would only be for a few minutes. Just long enough to open the airlock inner doors to bring them out," I said. "Then the airlock gets closed up and we repressurize immediately."

Pacal jumped in, "We might want to evacuate B deck also just for safety's sake; seal it as well for an extra margin of safety."

"I understand your concern, Mick, but I don't want to do that. I don't want to wake up the B Deck people in their sleep shift and add them to the confusion that will be going on. There could be more danger trying to do that than just sealing off Engineering only. That pressure plate will be bolted down to frame, no chance of it failing."

"I see your point."

"Anyone else?" I asked.

"The deck emergency ladderway plate is under the floor panels. It will take about twenty minutes to bolt it in place," said James.

I added, "Jeff, you need to pull a spacesuit out of the emergency airlock and put someone in it to stay in Engineering while we do this in case they need help with the airlock or some other issue pops up."

"Okay, that would be me," replied James.

"Amanda, and Mick, let's *not* make a shipwide announcement about this, okay?"

"Everyone's watching the airlock operation on their monitors already, Mark," said Amanda.

"Yes, that's okay. Here's what is going to happen. We prep Engineering for vacuum. We bring everyone in Engineering up to B deck. We send Jeff James down in a spacesuit. We seal off the ladderway. Then from the Bridge Brent Shaw will override the airlock and Engineering safety protocols, isolate Engineering from life support and vent the Engineering deck's atmosphere out into space through the airlock. Jeff will open those airlock inner doors and get Scott and Paul out, then reseal both doors. Up here, Brent will verify good seals and command Engineering to repressurize. Anyone see any problems with all that?"

"Wow!" said Descard.

"You got something to add, Paul?" I asked.

"No, just wow."

"Then Ladies and Gentlemen, let's get going."

I unlocked from my seat and pushed over to Janet Pars office. I tapped on the door. She didn't respond.

I slid open the door to find her pasted to the wall in her sleeping bag, sound asleep. I pulled in and put one hand on her floating arm. She awoke with fluttering eyes.

"Oh, this can't be good," she said, squinting to wake up.

"Sorry. I need you to take the Bridge. We have a situation."

With no thought for dignity, she pushed down her sleeping bag revealing only bra and panties. On any other occasion it was a figure I would have paused to secretly admire.

"What are we into this time?" she asked as she pulled on a tan flight suit. "Do I have time for coffee?"

"I'll have someone bring it to you. We are depressurizing Engineering."

"What?!"

"Shaw and West will fill you in. I need to get down there."

"I'll bet."

I went down headfirst. People watched me pass by their deck with stares of curiosity. On E deck most were still working out on their machines, sweating as they watched the wall monitors. D deck personnel were also still unaware of the emergency, which reassured me. With luck it would be over by the time they found out. Two Engineering types were working on the emergency airlock to open it for a space suit. On B deck Engineering staff had already raised floor panels and were unfastening the deck's pressure plate from beneath. I nodded as I passed.

The mood in Engineering was one of controlled panic. Engineers and technicians were working at every system's control console. They ignored me as I flew past to the airlock.

Inside the airlock Descard and Williams were holding to equipment beside the service panel. I nodded to them and Descard gave a quick wave.

A voice behind me said, "Here comes my suit."

I turned to find James beside me. The torso section of a space suit was being brought down through the ladderway, followed by legs and then a helmet.

"Don't bring that suit pressure down too fast, Jeff."

"You know I know that, right, Captain?" James replied.

"Yeah, it's just that I've been in a rescue situation where the suit was still so rigid from pressure I couldn't turn the valve I needed to. It's a tempting situation."

"Have no fear. I shall leave the suit on automatic."

"Okay, then. Come on, I'll help suit you up."

James paused as a technician helped him get his feet into the spacesuit legs.

James continued, "We're only keeping one power station on active. The others will be on standby. There shouldn't be any power interruptions. Battery backup will give us thirty minutes to recover if we do lose power. They're shutting down water reclamation right now. We're going to catch some people in showers, you know that. The Crays are going to be left as they are. Everything else is being protected as much as possible."

James paused again as they fit the suit torso over his head and sealed it. "You know the unspoken problem we may face?"

189

"Yes."

"If those airlock inner doors also won't open, we'll be in a bad way."

"I'm betting that being internal to the ship, they'll be okay."

A technician fussing over James switched on suit power for him, and used a handheld scanner to check suit readouts.

"So what do I do if they don't open?" asked James as he slipped the helmet over his head and twisted it in place.

I though perhaps it was a rhetorical question, but James stared at me through his open visor waiting for an answer.

"I'll let you know."

He gave somber smile and began checking his suit.

"Pars to Easton."

"Go ahead, Jan,"

"They are ready to seal off Engineering."

I scanned the room. "Ladies and gentlemen, let's get upstairs so we can do this. Anybody not ready?"

The exodus began. A few stragglers made their last adjustments and headed up. I looked at James. His visor was down.

He smiled at me. His voice came through my comm unit, "See that, Mark. I'm already at twelve pounds and dropping. Piece of cake."

I gave him a warning stare. He laughed.

As the last engineers and techs floated up through the ladderway I took a last look around and headed there myself. Holding beneath the passageway I stopped to look back again to see James maneuver in his suit to face me. I could also see Descard and Williams through the airlock window. Not knowing what else to do I gave them a thumbs up and pushed up to B deck.

Two techs were holding to the floor ready to set the pressure panel in place. I nodded and they quickly guided the floating platform down into the stairway opening. There came the loud sound of two ratchets sinking fasteners into place to seal the opening.

A crowd had gathered around us. There were no wall monitors here to observe Engineering and the airlock. A few people had tablets and were watching those cameras. Others had pushed in around them to watch also.

A third tech with a scanner worked his way to the floor and scanned the seal all around. He looked at me and nodded.

"Easton to James."

"Go ahead, Mark."

"You ready?"

"Go for it."

"Easton to Shaw."

"Standing by Captain."

"Begin depressurization of main Engineering."

"Engaging that program, Captain."

I suddenly realized there was no procedure for overriding safety protocols and depressurizing Engineering. Brent Shaw had obviously written a program himself without having been told to.

"It's working, Captain. I'm seeing the incremental pressure drop."

"Very good, Brent. Continue."

I carefully worked my way out of the crowd and pulled up through the upper decks. Everything had stopped now. People were no longer exercising. In the food court everyone was glued to monitors. I made it all the way to the Bridge without being stopped. People understood.

At Shaw's console we watched the pressure numbers drop. He had already brought up Descard and William's space suit life support readouts. They were both running on panel power.

"Come on, baby," said Shaw to himself.

On Shaw's left-hand monitor James seemed to have gained enough mobility in his suit. He had moved over to the airlock doors and was watching a pressure gauge, waiting for a chance to unlock.

It was an excruciating ten minutes.

Finally I couldn't stand it any longer. "Jeff, it's point three and point three, that's got to be good enough."

"Okay, here goes," he replied.

James turned the necessary locks and grabbed the door lever. He pushed down and to our relief the thing swung hard down against its stop. He pulled on the door and it swung open.

"Primary door open. Standby, guys. I'm almost in."

"We do seem to be losing heat. Not a problem," replied Descard.

James raced to unlock the secondary door. He tested the wheel to unbolt it and the thing turned obediently. With a final effort he pulled the thing open.

Williams unplugged and floated out first with Descard following. Descard pulled himself out with James helping to guide him upright. There was still no time to lose.

"Sealing secondary," said James and he pulled the first door shut and sealed it.

"Sealing primary."

A moment later both doors were shut and locked.

Shaw said, "Reading good seals. Repressurizing A deck."

Descard said, "Guys, we've already brought our suits up to atmospheric pressure. We had to in case we lost power."

"Six pounds plus, Paul. Should only be a few more minutes."

We watched the Engineering deck pressure bar indicator slowly rise. As it neared fourteen pounds per square inch I started to relax. "Gentlemen, you may open your visors."

In Engineering the three of them looked up at the nearest camera and waved.

I asked, "Is it stable, Brent?"

Shaw replied, "Atmosphere shows completely stable, Captain."

When the two rescued spacemen finally began unsealing and removing their helmets a chorus of clapping and cheering could be heard coming up through the ladderway.

A technician's voice come over the comm. "Captain, permission to remove the B deck pressure seal plate?"

"Granted. Very nice job everyone."

I turned and looked over at Pars in the command seat. She returned a big smile.

I floated over to her. "You want to go back to bed?"

"Are you kidding? Who can sleep now?"

"Right."

"Besides, don't you have a hellacious report to write now and send to Earth? I'll love reading that one. We're a multimillion-dollar spacecraft on its way to Mars with two outer doors flapping open to space and two others that won't open at all. They ought to love that."

"We can fix that."

"Do you think there's any connection to the Bateman thing?"

"What?"

"Oh, come on; don't you see it? We find Bateman deceased in the emergency airlock. We know someone else was involved. A short time later those very same airlock doors malfunction along with the main airlock doors. You think that was just a coincidence?"

I looked around to be sure no one was listening then took a moment to consider it. "I don't see any way someone could do something to cause those doors to fail."

"What do you mean? You go in the airlock, offset the alignment pins, and that's it. The doors don't work right."

"Engineering is a busy place twenty-four–seven. How could anyone sneak into that airlock with tools to offset those doors?"

"What if it was supposed to be a routine inspection? They could get in then."

"There's no way, Jan. Those procedures are done by two people. Even if there were procedures scheduled recently, both techs would have to be involved. There's just no way."

"Okay, but it sure is a coincidence."

"I'll pass your concerns onto Mick Pacal but this door problem is something completely different, believe me."

"Have fun writing your report."

"Right."

Chapter 13

It took two days to get Engineering back up and running normally. Both airlocks remained out of service which was a very bad thing. I had time before the morning meeting to get coffee. In the food court I found a seat next to Bishop and locked in.

"Have you seen it?" she asked.

"What's that?"

"Take a look." She pointed up at a nearby wall display.

THE NEW DAWN TIMES WEEKLY

FIRST EDITION

EVA TEAM RESCUED AFTER AIRLOCK FAILURES

The story described the harrowing mission to repair the A-Link antenna base. It was reasonably accurate but embellished for excitement. The article ended with a reassuring note that everything was under control even though the airlocks were still out of service. The next story was a tribute to the Harold Bateman Memorial. Several other articles followed, including the Starship Cargo update and the "Ask Amy" advice column.

"Oh, God," I said.

"I warned you it was coming," chuckled Bishop.

"Are we losing control of our all-hands advisories?"

"Society is a living breathing independent organism," said Bishop.

"But you warned them there could be censorship, right?"

"Yeah, how dangerous is that?"

I opened my mouth to reply.

"It was rhetorical, Mark. There is no answer."

I raised an eyebrow. "We're late for the meeting."

The briefing area was full from extra off-shift attendees. There was floating room only.

I brought the room to attention by asking, "What's our plan for the doors, Jeff?"

"I'm sure you've already guessed. We suit up, depress the emergency airlock, go in and do the alignment procedures on those doors. If we get them open, we go outside and close them, then cross over to the main airlock, go in and adjust *those* doors and close them. The EVA team then exits into Engineering."

"Are we believing the ship superstructure flex theory?"

James nodded. Descard floating behind him nodded also. "We did some pretty thorough examinations using the helmet camera videos. We see nothing at all wrong with any of the doors. No damage of any kind to the frames or panels. It has to be that the fit changed somehow. The flex is the only thing we can come up with."

"So junior officer Laurel Collins was probably correct?"

James nodded again.

"Is she certified for EVA repairs?" I asked.

"She's not an airlock specialist but she is an MIT Brass Rat so she's qualified. She is certified for EVA."

"Can we pair her up with an airlock specialist for this job? I want to reward people who aren't afraid to speak up. That is if she wants to go."

"Oh, she'll want to go, no doubt about that. I had intended to use airlock specialist Samantha Ansuri. You have any reservations about an all-female EVA, Captain?" James gave a devious smile.

"You trying to get me in trouble, Jeff?" I asked.

A few laughs broke out.

"When can you start?"

James replied, "This afternoon. We need to move some gear up to the emergency airlock. We'll suit them up there of course."

"This afternoon would be a good time. Amanda, you want to notify the population and The New Dawn Times Weekly, I suppose."

There were a few chuckles.

"No problem, Captain," she answered.

I looked back at James and Descard. "Is the damned A Link antenna tracking again, at least?"

James gave a short laugh. "Actually, it is. There's a chance the flex problem had something to do with that too."

"Okay, on to the deck B and C water cells. We're still getting pressure alarms, I see."

Descard answered. "Yes, and we keep raising the limits in the software to get rid of them. We have scanned every inch of those areas and there is no water leakage anywhere. It must be sensor drift. The pressure loss readings are still too small to be significant."

"Makes me uncomfortable, Paul."

"I understand but there is nothing to fix. Maybe that has something to do with the flex theory as well."

"Anyone have anything else for this tie-in?"

No one did.

"Okay, everyone; have a great New Dawn day. Just need you, Mick and you, Amanda."

We waited for everyone to drift out. Dumars pulled down into the seat next to me even though I hadn't asked her to stay.

"Try to get rid of me. Just try," she said as she locked into the seat.

I wanted to answer with some personal remark about wanting her near me always but I noticed the other two were watching closely. "Yes, this could affect you too, Andrea. Please stay."

When we were alone I began, "So, Mick, still nothing new on Bateman?"

"I believe there was absolutely nothing left for us *to* find, Mark. I've received no additional updates from Earth. I don't think we're going to get any more help from them. They must be just keeping their fingers crossed."

I folded my arms and thought for a moment. "It's possible we might still see something from Earth. I don't believe they've stopped digging into Bateman's past."

"We have no choice but to keep up the added surveillance, do you agree?"

I nodded. "I agree but it's taking people away from the normal work routines. I don't think we should keep that up indefinitely. Amanda, what's the situation with everyone on board?"

"I would say the Bateman affair has mostly blown over. There's been enough distractions to help with that. Those who have persisted in thinking about it have spent time in the search engines and seen the Earth report of misadventure. So, overall I think we're past this as long as no new problems pop up."

"Okay, any other suggestions?"

Bishop replied, "It's time to start talking about landing, guys. There's nothing more important to the population now."

I nodded to her. "Andrea, you haven't given me an update on Broken Jaw for a while. How's he doing?"

Dumars winced. "I wish I could say he was healing quickly but in this zero G it's a long slow process. I hope we can unlock his jaw before landing, but I can't even guarantee that. He understands what is going on with his recovery. He's being good about it. Bones just heal very slowly here."

We all took pause at Dumars' update. I broke the moment. "Anyone have anything else for today?"

Bishop answered, "As for the upcoming landing, we're setting up for refresher training for the advance teams as well as the general population, not only for orbital insertion and landing but for post landing procedures. That will be keeping everyone busy enough to be maybe a little less apprehensive during our approach."

"Sounds good. Anyone else?"

Pacal said, "Don't forget about Cargo ships four, five and six, Mark. Cargo six has all the frozen food. Real, solid food. Can you imagine?"

"I think we're all imagining that, Mick," I replied. "So that's it. Let's head for our work areas."

We smiled at each other as I unlocked and pushed up from my seat. We coasted out and went our separate ways.

Pars had already left the command seat. Steve West nodded to me as I took to it. I obliged him by saying, "I have the conn."

"Mars is getting pretty big in the viewer," he said.

"Gonna be a lot bigger really soon," I answered.

Brent Shaw laughed.

At 11:35A.M. NDT, New Dawn Time, the airlock repair EVA extravaganza began with Laurel Collins and Samantha Ansuri. It appeared on every display screen everywhere except the Bridge and Engineering. I watched it on my right-side display. It was strange to see two people in EVA suits near Sickbay and the Security offices on D deck. The support techs were making a real project of them. Once inside the airlock they immediately went into depress mode as the door alignment was intended to be done with equal pressures on both sides of the outer doors. They had the access panels off quickly but from there on the scanning and adjusting slowed down into a long boring wait.

The two women worked well together. The tone of their voices assured us of that.

One hour, ten minutes to get the first exterior door open. For me seeing it swing aside was a huge relief. Another two hours and they pushed the secondary door open to outer space. I heard cheering come up through the ladderway.

I then became the nervous doting mother as they went out to shut the airlock and cross over the top of the ship. We had camera views all the way which completely distracted me from the conn. But the two spacewalkers were very, very good. We watched them enter the main airlock and go right to work unpacking tools. This time it was about two hours to close and seal both doors. I could hear satisfaction in their voices as the main airlock began to pressurize. I was impressed. Once again, I had a tight ship.

It became an easy morning watching data from the command seat and listening in on Engineering operations. Calibrations on the powers systems and water reclamation system. All standard stuff. The tone in Engineering sounded upbeat. They were still celebrating the airlock recoveries.

At lunch I lucked out and found Andrea sitting with an associate. Before I could ask, the assistant insisted I join them. She was just leaving.

"Was she really just leaving?"

"Nope."

"So does that mean we're…."

"An item in medical? We are a suspicion."

I kept my voice low, "I haven't noticed anything upstairs. No innuendos or anything."

"They're being cautious. We haven't quite given them enough to be sure."

"Plus I haven't had time to even see you for days."

"Are you implying we actually are something?"

"Wow, is that a loaded question! I'm not sure there's a safe answer."

"Thank God we didn't make the New Dawn Times Weekly!"

"Now there's a minefield if ever there was one."

She smiled provocatively. "You didn't answer my question."

"Doesn't the woman decide if there really is a thing?"

"Oh my God, playing the chauvinist card."

"I think I also need my jaw locked."

"That could be arranged."

"Okay, you really want an answer? I have definite feelings. Your turn."

"The jury is still out. I need to gather more intel."

"Okay?"

She gave a devilish half smile. "Which would you say is less conspicuous, the doctor coming to the Bridge late at night or the Captain coming to Medical?"

"I don't think it's the visit that's conspicuous. It's the long stay."

"And it *will* be a long stay, I can assure you of that."

"It may not be possible to remain out of the New Dawn Times Weekly."

"How would that affect your crew do you think?"

"To be honest, it concerns me."

She held back a laugh. "Your lunch packet is getting cold. What is it?"

"Macaroni and cheese."

"I have an appointment in the exam room. We should discuss this again very soon."

"Okay."

"That is unless some unexpected opportunity happens to pop up."

"We can only hope."

She pushed up and pulled away toward the ladderway. I had to force myself not to stare. It reminded me again of the old Kirk line mentioned by one of the spacewalkers, "No beach to walk on." I quickly decided, the hell with that.

Chapter 14

To: Captain Mark Easton
From: Mission Director Ben Epstone
Subject: Airlock Anomaly

Mark,

The Incident Evaluation Team has run several dozen simulations in an attempt to recreate the airlock door problem. They are of the opinion that Engineer Collins' theory that a minute shift in the vehicle body was indeed the cause of the misalignments you experienced. They have formally named the anomaly the Collins Flex Event. They feel certain that with time they can develop a formula that will predict when CFAs can occur. They believe New Dawn's dynamic mass of moving people and equipment, along with temperature, pressure and time all are involved in this phenomenon. Obviously, this is another new condition we are learning about as the mission continues. Congratulations on a great job managing the problem. Please advise us of any follow-on problems that might arise from the depressurization. I will keep you updated as the study continues.

Ben

A day we had all been waiting for soon arrived. Starship Cargo 4, 5 and 6 insertion, descent and landing day. If we got away with three more automated landings it would be like Christmas. Cargo 5 had the huge recreation dome packed away. Cargo 6 was stocked with frozen foods. Cargo 4 had twelve more Mars space suits that would allow twice as many people to work outside. All were extremely important.

The spacesuit Bateman had died in had been decommissioned by unanimous vote and stored and replaced by a spare EVA suit. That meant we now had a total of six Mars EVA and five Space EVA suits for when we landed. The other dozen Mars EVA suits on Starship Cargo 5 were packed away with eighty lightweight emergency suits intended to be lifeboats in the event of a Mars Base failure of titanic proportions. But this loss of just one of our New Dawn EVA suits bothered the hell out of me. Those first twelve suits were planned so the specialists could set up the domes, power and water systems quickly so we could move everyone out of New Dawn. There would be no privacy and a great loss of personal dignity until that happened.

As orbital insertion time for Cargo 4, 5 and 6 neared, Mars images began coming up on nearly every monitor in the ship. We had the privilege of tracking those ships more than fifteen minutes sooner than Earth. There would be numerous camera views of the landings. There were cameras on the three starships already parked on Mars, along with cameras on some of the autonomous machines there. Plus there would be onboard cameras for all three starships. The landing pads for all three had been carefully carved out by the earthmovers so targeting with each camera was easy. We were guaranteed a front row uncensored show. Whatever happened would affect our lives for years to come.

"Pacal to Easton."

"Go ahead, Mick."

"A cubicle exodus has begun."

"What's your estimate?"

"They all seem to want to watch this on screens bigger than a tablet so we may not have a single person left in their habitat for the landings."

"How's the distribution going?"

"No problem. As long as we don't separate friends nobody's complaining about being directed to a different level. F deck appears to be the favorite destination. They want food with their entertainment. That deck is pretty much already full."

"How about E Deck?"

"We can forget about the exercise schedule for today. It will be too crowded."

"So will the Med Lab be able to function?"

"We'll keep the population there down to about twenty. If there's a bad landing, though, Bishop's office may be overrun with hand-wringers."

"But it's peaceful so far, right?"

"Well, one thing I should mention, my officers have caught glimpses of flasks being passed around and believe it or not, the F Deck officers have reported smelling marijuana."

"You're kidding."

"Not at all. To be honest I expect that to spread. What do you want us to do?"

"Nothing. I think I'd prefer that to stress. If everything goes right they'll all get a good night's sleep. Tell Bishop not to worry about it."

"You got it."

I looked around the Bridge. West and Shaw were staring at me smirking. Their left and right monitors already had camera images of the Mars landing sites.

"Dumars to Easton."

"Yes, Andrea?"

"It's getting crowded down here."

"I know. Is everything all right?"

"Believe it or not we've had to prescribe sedatives to a few who were so worried they just couldn't stand it."

"I'll let you know if I need one."

"Very funny."

"You want to come up here for the landings?"

"Can't. We may have people passing out."

"I'll check in with you after Cargo 6 is down."

"There's fifty gallons of ice cream on that one, you know. That one's got to make it."

"I'll come down when I can get away."

"Okay, fingers crossed."

As I clicked off the comm I heard cheering erupt through the ladderway.

Shaw called to me. "Ground Control has switched on the external cameras for Cargo 4."

On his left screen there was an image of the nose of Cargo 4. Half of Mars was visible in front of it, back dropped by empty black sky. I called up the image on my left screen and sat staring at what we would soon be seeing first-hand. The approach speed was difficult to detect but you could feel the planet drawing closer.

I switched through the Mars Mission camera channels and found that more of the Mars surface cameras had also been turned on. The three parked starships were there in all their glory waiting for the humans to arrive. One of the earthmover cameras had been set to auto rotation and was scanning the colony area from left to right and back again. There were cleared roads leading to each of the starships now, along with the uninflated habitat domes. Their interconnect access tubes were in place waiting to be attached. The three power core stations were situated central to the colony with conduit running to the approximate connection locations. The place was coming alive in celebration of our coming arrival.

Four hours later Cargo 4 dropped onto orbit. More cheering from below. From the aft facing onboard camera we could see the thrusters firing for attitude. There was now red planet surface beneath the ship. Cargo 4 did not wait for its companions. It was designed to be single orbit to entry. There were interruptions to the camera feed as Cargo 4 maneuvered to slow itself at just the right time. We were visually slung around with sky and planet flashing in and out of view. On the aft camera the first engine burn was like a halo of white light and jets. The ground was visible and we were heading downward for it. I had no doubt that in everyone's mind they were seeing what would soon be happening to us. It made the hope for success even more desperate.

Down we went, falling through the feeble Martian atmosphere, thrusters reassuring us that everything was under control. Long periods of falling and falling, ground threatening to smite us all the while.

But ground targets came into view. On the ground we saw the deployed equipment and the three available landing pads. Then rockets a-blazing again, our death dive slowing. Almost all at once dust and visual quiet, no movement at all. And as the dust cleared, we were welcomed to the surface of Mars. One down, two to go. Then us.

Steve West looked at me. "I don't think I can watch the next one. My BP must be through the roof."

It took me a moment to catch my breath. "Do I look ten years older?"

He laughed.

Over the next two days we watched in earnest as two more ships of supreme importance arrived at Mars Base. Dumars joined me on the Bridge for Cargo 6 saying she couldn't bear to be alone if the ice cream didn't make it, which caused me to secretly wince at the thought of the other tons of food that would be lost as well. Cargo 6 was a multilevel food freezer designed to remain as such even on the surface. It was to be our giant food freezer patched into our power systems in the event the onboard power failed for any reason.

But both starships landed with the precision we had become so accustomed to. They sat on their pads waiting for us to show up and open our first Mars' Christmas presents.

And with that last touchdown a new stark reality set in. We were going down next.

Mars Base Alpha Update
Resource Delivery and Deployment Group
Dr. Hans Beltram Reporting
Phase Status and Projections

Starship Cargo 4, 5, and 6 have landed nominally and all have achieved true vertical after corrections by the dynamic landing leg systems. Commands for internal power-up on Cargos 4, and 6 were transmitted and power-up was confirmed. All shipping containers and stowed equipment appears intact and serviceable. Internal camera video can be access on channels 22A and 22B and 22C.

A problem has been encountered with Starship Cargo 5. Commands for internal power-up were acknowledged and the cargo area power did activate. Onboard cameras verified all shipping containers and equipment in place and deployable. However, commands to open the ship's main cargo door failed to unlock that door. Subsequent attempts were also unsuccessful. The Engineering group is researching this problem. This may be symptomatic of the same CFE rocket body flex problem encountered by New Dawn. Failure to access this main cargo door prevents use of the ship's onboard crane. Therefore unless this issue is resolved

access to the vehicle can only be made using an external man lift. Expect further updates on this problem as developments occur.

Transfer of materials and equipment from the cargo holds to the surface is on schedule and too extensive to list in this format. For detailed deployment information consult the scheduling information for each deployment group. The SITU water and air efforts are proceeding with better than expected results. The three SuperMoxie units have surpassed their expected extraction of 02 from the Martian atmosphere. The ISRU water mining systems are also running at full capacity.

We expect our next update to be received after the colony is on the surface. Good luck and Godspeed.

Dr. Hans Beltram
RDDG

I sat in my command seat mulling over the implications of the report. I looked over at Steve West. The report was up on one of his screens also.

"Who's he kidding?" said West. "Access Cargo 5 using someone in a spacesuit on a cherry picker?"

Brent Shaw suggested, "There's no way to open a cargo door from outside, never mind being more than a hundred feet up in spacesuit in a man lift."

"Damn, the huge recreation dome is in 5," added West.

"Gentlemen, do you really believe we won't get into that thing?" I said. "There's always the hard way."

"A torch?" exclaimed West. "You mean send someone in a spacesuit up there with a torch? Burn a hole in the side of that ship?"

"Hey, that's not impossible," said Shaw. "They've done welding and cutting on the new space station framework. Why not on Mars? They do it all the time deep sea diving."

"Big hole in the side of the cargo section? That would be the end of repressurizing the cargo area," said West.

"Duct tape," suggested Shaw, and they both laughed.

I tried to sound positive, "Guys, odds are they'll remotely get that cargo door open eventually."

"We should start a pool," said Shaw.

"I'm down for it not getting opened. I saw what it took the EVA girls to get ours open," suggested West.

"Yeah, but the vehicle is resting on its dynamic landing legs now. That's a whole different stress profile," said Shaw.

"Pacal to Easton."

"Go ahead, Mick."

"Could you stop down to my office when you get a chance?"

"Something come up?"

"I just need your opinion on a post landing procedure."

"I'm due for a break. I'll head your way after a quick stop in the mess hall."

"Thanks. Pacal out."

"Steve?"

"I have the conn, Captain."

I headed down the hatch to the food area. It was busy but everyone was upbeat. I acknowledged a bunch of greetings and waves, got my coffee and was trying to make the ladderway when a couple floated up alongside me. It was the infamous Mr. and Mrs. Bisley, the reluctant horticulturists.

"Captain, we've been hoping to catch you. We just had one question," said Mrs. Bisley.

I found a ceiling hold and stopped to face them. "Yes?" I worried it was a question about their catching a flight back to Earth.

Mr. Bisley put on his most endearing look. "The landings were perfect. Our compost is on Cargo 5. We were hoping we could get access to that sooner than is listed on the setup schedule. It would mean we could have Mars grown food all that much sooner."

"Well, I think I can promise you two Cargo 5 will get special attention and I'll see if we can offload your compost as soon as we're in that vehicle."

"Thank you so much, Captain. We are just dying to get to work in the greenhouse dome," added Mrs. Bisley.

"And everyone is looking forward to that with you, I assure you."

"Thank you again, Captain."

They pulled away and began talking privately. I headed quickly for the ladderway, a villain of misleading tall tales. Maybe I could get Bishop to run interference if they read the Mars update.

The exercise area was in full swing. As usual quite a few people were hanging around the refreshment area making comical remarks about those working out. On D deck the place seemed unusually quiet, just a few waiting in the Medical area and a small class in the HR room. I floated briskly by them and ducked into the Med lab. Andrea was in her office, holding onto the desk, her legs horizontal to the floor. She was tapping at her laptop.

"Oh! Hello, Captain."

"Should I slide the door closed?"

She answered without looking up, "You'd better not. You might be here a while."

"Wow, you're in a mood. I just wanted to stop in and see you."

"For what?"

I looked around to be sure no one was in listening distance. "Just to see you."

"Yes, for what?"

"Just to see you."

"Oh! Sorry. I'm distracted. We had to do a brain scan on someone but it turned out to be just a sinus issue. No gravity, no downward path for the mucus. They forget to take the meds and here they come."

"Mick called me down. I'd better get going."

"Did I turn you off with the mucus thing?"

"Nope. I'd better get going."

"Stop in again soon."

"Yeah, we should."

I turned in place and pulled out under her watchful stare. Pushing over to Security I pulled into Pacal's office. He looked up from his tiny laptop position.

"Thanks for coming down, Mark."

"Hey, a pre-landing procedure opinion is easy compared to some of the stuff we've had."

"That's not really why I called you down."

"Oh? What have you got?"

Pacal locked the arms on his seat and held up a tablet. "This was Bateman's."

"You found it?"

"One of my guys did. It was hidden away in the Human resources training area, mixed in with all their training tablets. It looks just like all the others, of course."

"How did you spot it?"

"It was locking up every now and then. It went to the computer geeks for repair and they found the hard drive had been swapped out. The new hard drive thought it was in a different version tablet so the thing would periodically lock up when the hardware was incompatible."

"Did you…."

"Did we look for prints and DNA on the bogus hard drive? As fast as I could make it to the IT area. The thing had been wiped clean of everything."

"Where'd the new drive come from?"

"It was nuked then the operating system reloaded. There's nothing to be recovered. The serial numbers say it previously belonged to a unit that was turned in for repair but was found to be unrepairable. We've checked out the previous owner. She says her tablet just suddenly quit. They gave her a replacement. She did not know Bateman. There's no way she was involved with him."

"So a dead end."

"Except we already knew this mystery person was very good with computers and we now know there's a faint trail of him leading to this woman's tablet and to his placing Bateman's tablet in the HR stock."

I nodded. "So he was hoping this tablet would never be recognized as Bateman's but made a slight mistake again. He's not infallible."

"He's pretty good though, if he's actually a he."

"I really don't thing the airlock problems were related to the Bateman thing, do you?"

"No, but Pars had some concerns."

"Yes, she told me." I shook my head. "It doesn't hold up. No way anyone could intentionally misalign those doors."

"I agree."

"So we will proceed with landing normally. We'll be watching closely for sabotage."

"Yes, and as I've said before, even after we land there's no way he can get away."

"Yeah, first murderer on Mars."

Pacal wrinkled his brow. "Another thing: what the hell will you do if we catch him?"

Chapter 15

We spent days rehearsing for the landing, the same ones we'd done on the ground on Earth. But it was very different this time. I remembered the sage advice a famous astronaut by the name of Hurley had once given his colleagues; *"Just make sure you stay ahead of it."*

We went over every procedure enough times that they were automatic; a Bridge crew who didn't actually need to speak to each other to complete the process. We were like one person in different bodies. It was exhilarating and rewarding, driven by the threat of a long fall.

The population was kept busy with sometimes unnecessary training and checkups, along with setup and inflation of the launch-landing seats that now filled Decks B and C where habitat cubicles had been for the past many months. As insertion time approached a silence fell over the ship I'd never felt before.

We had moments of gravity-feel as the ship slowed and aligned its attitude for orbit. We were momentarily pushed left and right or up and down as thrusters fired. The minor pushing and pulling was like a notification to get ready for the big swings to come.

We slipped onto orbit without any problems. Mars was now alive on all our displays. The red desert below beckoned us. I found myself keeping an eye on the airlock doors and the sensors we had replaced as I listened in on Engineering. Steve West was comparing data readouts with the guys downstairs, making sure the numbers agreed. For me, this was the best of times. Even though I was something of a Captain Dunsel as I followed along it felt like I was commanding every single automated move myself. In a way I was since I could override any of them at any time.

Our seventy-minute ride around Mars felt like ten or fifteen. And when New Dawn decided it was time to really slow down, our roller coaster ride began. Someone else once said orbital descent is like being inside a living machine and that's exactly how it was. Starship knew what it needed to do and we were just along for the ride. The images on the video display screens became blurs of black and orange motion.

As the turning and twisting faded, we could feel ourselves falling, though the monitors gave us only fading black sky. Somehow Brent Shaw had enough composure that he switched the main feed to a down facing camera which showed distant Mars landscapes rising upward. He went on to switch the secondary feed to a surface camera but I do not know which. It showed an empty landing pad waiting for us.

We fell and fell. Our stomachs told us so. It was that point in the landing so many had been dreading: the point where we were waiting to see if New Dawn would right herself and slow before impact. The silence in the cabin had become heavy. I was surprised there was no shrieking. Suddenly we were pushed up hard against our seat belts then immediately slammed back into the seat and pressed hard against it. I managed to spot a display showing New Dawn lowering itself to the pad, then a moderate jolt and the sound of engines cutting off. An ominous silence and stillness took over.

We had *landed* on Mars.

It was a full fifteen seconds before the cheering broke out over the sounds of venting. In about twenty minutes the same cheering would break out on Earth.

Engineering began calling out shutdown procedures. I had to scramble a bit to get my screens up to answer my call outs. We all hurried through the post landing checks and procedures and as soon as I was done with mine I motioned to Brent Shaw to put me on shipwide announcements.

"Ladies and Gentlemen, this is Captain Easton. We have landed on Mars."

There was an interruption of new cheering and applause. I waited for a second opening.

"Let me advise you all that the landing was picture perfect. We are in the true vertical and all systems functioned as planned. We have shut down main engines support systems and are currently safeing all other entry and landing systems. Our power levels and life support appear to be nominal. You may all remove your hoods and when you feel up to it, your flight suits. Please do not rush getting up and walking around. As you know dizziness is a symptom of acclimating to gravity. Dr. Bishop and Dr. Dumars will be attending to you shortly. Congratulations to us all on a great landing and a new future on Mars. Easton out."

I barely had time to breathe when the comm squawked back on.

"Greetings everyone. This is Dr. Bishop. My staff and Medical will be coming around to check on you and assist in any needs you may have. Please do not rush your activity until you've had a few hours to adjust to Mars gravity. My staff can answer any new questions you may have. Please be patient. We will be broadcasting all the Mars surface camera images while we all re-acclimate to gravity. Bishop out."

"Attention all personnel, this is Dr. Dumars. Please, please stay in your seats until a member of my staff has a chance to attend to you. We are administering the gravity acclimation medications already. Someone will be with you very shortly. It is important that you do not move about until you've had time to adjust. You risk personal injury from a fall and you could injure someone else. Please just remain in your seats. Enjoy the videos and we will be with you shortly. Congratulations to us all. Dumars out."

I began to be surprised at my own condition. I had returned to Earth's gravity many times and went through the two-week process for recovery, but now, it was nothing. I felt like I could hit the exercise area, at least briefly. The one-third gravity seemed less than it was. There *was* no dizziness. The blanket of weight on me was almost similar to waking up after an all-night party binge. I pushed up and stood and started to reach for a ceiling handhold then realized those were not needed any longer.

West laughed, "Uh-oh, you're gonna get in trouble."

"Even breathing is easy," I replied.

Both West and Shaw sat up in their seats.

Shaw said, "My God, we've got orange sky in the windows."

"Captain, some of the thruster bleeds are a bit slow," said West.

I held to one of my screens for balance and called up that system. "Easton to Engineering."

"James here, Captain."

"Any anomalies on your end?"

"Not really. Some of the thruster bleeds are slow but they're just about inert now."

"Sounds good to me. How are you guys?"

"We are shipshape, Captain. Could you stop down? We'd like to discuss the EVA schedule."

"Will do. Easton out."

"God, they're already chomping at the bit to go outside," said Shaw.

"I need to go down and make an appearance on the decks. You guys have the Bridge."

"We have the Bridge, Captain. You know that may be the last time we say that."

I nodded and thought to dive toward the ladderway but caught myself. With cautious initial steps I carefully balanced my way to the ladderway. At the big, deep hole in the floor I exercised my grip a few times, leaned over the opening and grabbed a handrail. With the greatest of care, I stepped onto a ladder rung and pulled myself over the hole. My strength was fully adequate though my agility was slightly in question. With slow patience I started down the ladder. At times it felt like I was wearing a heavy backpack, but nothing too heavy. I made the floor of F deck and turned to look around.

For the first time no one was using the food court. People were still in the seats that had been installed here. Most of them smiled and gave short waves.

"Everyone okay?" I asked sympathetically.

"Glad to be here," answered one person.

"Let's go back to weightless," said another.

I laughed and shook my head and started down again. My ladder work was becoming more confident. On E deck the exercise equipment was silent. There were only a few landing seats installed. Most people were sitting up already. As I stood and waved and nodded hello a very slow-moving person in white emerged up the ladderway next to me, one of Dumars' nurse practitioners. She gave a tired smile and headed for the group, digging in her belt pack for a syringe and medication, her BP unit dangling around her neck. I resumed my downward journey.

There were again few seats on D deck, there for doctors and nurse practitioners, security personnel and HR. Most of them were up and around. Dumars was at the opposite end giving one of her people an injection. I caught her eye and waved. She blew me a kiss which caught me off guard.

She called out, "Thanks for the good landing."

Others paused to look, wave and nod.

I continued down to what was formally the habitat sections where the majority of the population had ridden out the landing. Both decks were noisy with low moans and conversation while shots were being administered. All but a few were too distracted to notice me. I continued down.

As I stepped to the floor of Engineering I was shocked. At least twenty people in coveralls were milling around working. They had already pulled up floor plates and were removing Mars EVA suits. Others were monitoring consoles. There was so much going on no one noticed my arrival until Paul Descard happened to look over. He left the group he was speaking with and headed my way with half a dozen others following along.

"Captain, welcome to Mars Engineering."

I laughed despite the extra effort it took. "Paul, some of these people came down the ladders already?"

"I plead the fifth, Captain, or I didn't see a thing."

Someone behind Descard called out. "Captain, we're ready to go. Why wait?"

Someone else said, "Captain, the number two manlift has already been offloaded down there. We could at least go to work on Cargo 5 to get that hatch open. Then we could resume the planned unloading schedule."

A technician standing next to Descard tried to whisper something to him, "Paul, the crane."

Descard laughed, shook his head and pointed at the man. "See what I'm up against down here, Mark? The crane guys are ready to go up and deploy the crane and man-cage. They've already pulled up the procedure and are ready."

I held up one hand, smiled and shook my head. "Now you guys just hold your horses. None of us are allowed to work or even climb the ladder until one of Dumars' doctors examines you and certifies you for light duty, although I have a feeling the terms light duty are meaningless around here. So just hold on." I clicked my comm unit. "Easton to Dumars."

There was a ten second wait.

"Kind of busy here, Mark."

"I know, Andrea. Believe me I know. But listen, could you spare one doctor for say twenty minutes for the sake of inflating habitat domes early?"

"You drive a hard bargain, Captain. I'll send one down right now."

"What about Cargo 5, Captain?" someone asked.

"Okay, I agree with you about Cargo 5 but right now our only concern is to get these people off the ship and into those habitat domes. So inflation, oxygen, and water down there is all we care about. Oh yeah, except toilets. The waste management people are as important as the water and air groups. We can't have people coming up here to use the toilets. You all with me on this?"

There was a mass of head shaking and grunts of approval. Behind and above me a white suited person had started down the ladder. I moved out of the way.

I called out, "Can we have the crane people over here?" A disruption in the crowd brought three engineers and techs to the front as the doctor stepped down. I pointed her to the three and she nodded and began scanning.

Descard pulled me aside as Jeff James joined us.

"About Cargo 5, have you heard any more from Ground?" Dumars asked.

"Not a thing. I take it neither of you has received anything?"

They shook their heads.

Descard said, "You know it's beginning to look like it's up to us to get into that thing."

James added, "Our guys are thinking cutting into that cargo section will be a walk in the park, but it won't be."

Descard said, "It wouldn't be so urgent but the other twelve Mars EVA suits are stored in Cargo 5. God knows we need them for the setup."

"That has crossed my mind but I'm still thinking that getting our people off the ship and into the domes is our first priority. So if we can do that faster without first using resources to cut into 5 that would be the way to go. Who was it that said, *long is wrong, tight is right*? Do you both agree?"

They nodded agreement.

James said, "Still, we'll be pulling one guy out of a suit and putting someone else right into it while it's being recharged. Almost continuous use of the suits. Plus the EVA space suits aren't so easy to work in on the surface especially with people who are still getting used to gravity. We need Mars suits. It's going to be a challenge."

"So at what point do we send people up on a cherry picker with cutting equipment?" asked Descard.

"We need the structural engineers to study the problem and tell us where and how to make the cuts," replied James.

"Once we're in, the crane and airlock people will need to go up and get that hatch open from inside and get the crane to deploy."

I nodded. "So one of you set this up with our structural Engineering types and let me know when they have a plan. Then we'll decide when to break three suits away to get into 5."

James asked, "Mark, you're slated as part of the first group outside for electrical. You want a Mars suit or a spacesuit?"

"If I recall the EVA spacesuits are to be used by people moving gear around. I'll need a Mars suit. I'll probably be plugging in wiring."

James rubbed his mouth in thought. "Okay, that'll leave me to assign five others to the easy suits."

Dumars asked, "How did they come up with a total of twenty-four EVA suits anyway?"

I answered, "We'll still be on three shifts when we're set up on the surface. So roughly twenty-seven people per shift, twenty-four suits to cover their work schedules as needed."

The doctor tapped me on the shoulder. "These three are okay for light duty. I've advised them to work for ten minutes and then sit for ten minutes. If they start to get dizzy they're going to have to stop altogether."

One of the engineers straightened up and said, "I'll get the tool bag."

The others headed for the ladder without waiting.

Descard said, "I have a feeling we're going to have our elevator really quick," and he laughed.

"Remind me about the crane deployment," I said.

Descard answered, "The crane and folded up man basket are under the floor on E deck in their own pressurized compartment. Those guys will lift a couple floor plates to get to the control panel. They will fire explosive bolts to blow off the exterior panel housing the crane boom and basket. I expect them to call down for permission before they actually do that. There will be a noticeable bang we'll need to announce ahead of time. They will extend the boom and it will drag the basket out. The basket will unfold as it falls free. It should end up hovering outside the main airlock doors. We'll need to exercise the system several times all the way to ground level of course before signing it off as ready for use."

"Yeah, and that will mean the first boots on Mars next. Who's that going to be Captain?" asked James.

"Most people are expecting it to be you, Mark," said Descard.

It suddenly occurred to me I had not given the matter any thought at all. It stirred strong feelings of achievement. Thoughts of Armstrong and Aldrin.

"You know what guys, I don't think it should be me. We need to symbolize we're all in this together. We all took equal risk and made equal sacrifice to be here. You guys give me a list of the first eleven out for work and I'll pick one of them to represent us all."

"Wow! You are wise," said Descard.

"Somebody's going to go down in history," said James.

"Jeff, you'd better narrow down the first team out while you still have the doctor here," I said.

"Oh, yeah!" He started to dash off but quickly realized his body wasn't quite up to it. He walked gingerly toward his office and waved back as he went.

As the crane crew gathered at the ladder, I held up my hand. "No heroes, guys. Take one deck at a time. You all wait for each other. Okay?"

They laughed and nodded. One held out a hand to offer the first of them the ladder. Up he went, slowly.

Descard said, "So when it's starting to look like the manlift is healthy, you'll need to get down here early. We still have to pre-breathe. Don't forget."

"Don't worry. Stepping onto Mars will be stuck in my head. Is there anything down here I can help out with?"

"Not really. As you can see we've got all three shifts of people squeezed into Engineering deck. Everything we do is going to be like a G-job, a government job. One person working, three people watching and telling them how to do it."

"So you're saying I've got to climb back up there."

Descard laughed and shrugged. I put one hand and one foot on ladder rungs and looked back at him, rolling my eyes.

One floor wasn't a bad climb but it made me realize I had been standing too long. B deck was full of people, half sitting in the landing seats, the other half milling about trying to get their land legs back. I found an empty seat near the ladderway and sat sideways on it. An attractive blond woman in a pink flight suit came up beside me.

"You are most welcome to borrow my seat, Captain."

Her comm unit name was Borrows. "Thank you, ma'am. You are an angel to a weary soul."

She smiled and sat next to me. "So we are good, Captain?"

"We are very, very good, Ms. Borrows."

"Please call me Christina, sir."

"Then you must call me Mark, Christina."

"You're the second VIP I've spoken with this morning. My luck must be running."

"Not really a VIP Christina. We are all now equal on this trip. Who else did you speak with?"

"The engineer who solved the airlock door problems. Robert Banabalas. He is apparently quite a guy."

"Bob Banabalas? He told you that?"

"Yes. It was one of his many impressive achievements I might add."

"Christina, take anything Mr. Banabalas says with a grain of salt. You know what I mean?"

"You're saying he did not solve the airlock problem?"

I shook my head.

"Oh, for Pete's sake. He had me hook line and sinker. So I suppose he also does not hold the world's record for deep sea diving in a diving bell."

I broke out laughing. I couldn't help it.

"Am I a dumb blonde Mark, and just realizing it?"

"No, Christina. You are very nice. I'm sorry, what is your specialty?"

"Chemistry, Martian and Materials Science, but I also spent quite a bit of time researching the extraction of oxygen from lunar regolith."

"Every time I ask someone what they do around here, they sound smarter than me."

She laughed. "Wow, it still takes effort to laugh."

"Go talk to Bob some more. You'll laugh."

She laughed again, longer this time.

"Guess it's time for the next deck level. Nice talking with you Christina."

"Me too, Mark. See you down there." She pointed down.

The next level seemed easier but I realize rest was going to be badly needed before suiting up so I made the effort and went two levels this time. As I sat on D deck I was tempted to visit Andrea, but decided to conserve my strength.

It took twenty minutes to reach the Bridge. For the first time there was only one other person there, Steve West.

"Did I miss anything?"

"Only that there seems to be a downward trend in the population dispersal."

"Descard to Easton."

"Go ahead, Paul."

"Believe it or not, they say they're ready to blow the cover on the crane compartment."

"Okay, stand by. Let me make the announcement."

I looked over at West. "I don't dare ask Bishop. She's got her hands full."

I went to the communications station and selected shipwide address. "Attention all hands. This is Easton. We are in the process of deploying the manlift that will take us all to the surface. There will be a loud bang as the explosive bolts are fired to open that hatch. Please do not be alarmed."

As I switched off I thought I heard a smattering of cheering from below.

"Easton to Descard. You can give them the green light, Paul."

"Copy that."

I switched off and listened. It took another five minutes before the dull bang reverberated through the ship. There was more cheering. If memory served me, the crane extension process was very slow; as much as an hour. I had time to take a look at readouts and check for congratulatory messages from Earth. On my main screen there was an Engineering email icon. It was James' list of the first eleven people to set foot on the planet Mars. I read through the list and suddenly realized the selection for the first person to step onto Mars would be an easy one.

Chapter 16

We gathered in Engineering and had to ask some of the off-shift people to watch the emergence elsewhere. The crane and man basket had deployed perfectly. Six trips to the surface and back was enough to pre certify the lift. All that was left was one descent using weight. We were the weight.

"So it's to be Laurel Collins?" asked James with a dozen people gathered around him. "I'm sure you have very good reasons. Care to share them with us?"

I nodded and smiled. "Well, first remind me why you included her in the first eleven to go outside and work."

James understood. "Besides her engineering expertise she he now has airlock experience and that's exactly what we need to get into those domes and attach interconnect tunnels between them."

I nodded agreement. "So why Laurel as the first to step off? What you just said is one reason. Second, it should not be a high-ranking person because we need to show that all of us shared equal risk and determination to get here. Third, Armstrong got the moon. It should be a woman to represent us on Mars. And last, she is one of the youngest people aboard, so Mars and Earth will have her as a multi planet hero for a long time to come."

I even got a smattering of applause from some of them.

"So just the two of you on this first trip down?" asked James, though he already knew that was the written procedure.

"I promise we'll send the basket right back up."

"In twenty minutes you'll be on every TV and computer screen on Earth," said Descard.

I looked over the crowd and spotted Collins being suited up. She looked up and caught my stare. She jerked her head forward in an exclamation that said, "Is this really happening?"

I shook my head, "Yes."

When helmets were on and suit pressures had come up, Collins and I walked between two lines of engineers and techs to the airlock. We stepped in and they sealed the doors behind us. It seemed like a quick depressurization. We opened the two outer doors and found the man basket hovering just outside. I stepped in first to test it and clipped on to the safety rail. There was no breeze to push the basket. I had only a glimpse of the open Martian landscape before turning to beckon Collins out. She climbed out, clipped on, and together we stood for a moment to scan the Martian geology. It was breathtaking. But many were waiting on us. At the basket control panel, I lifted the plastic guard and pressed the down button. The crane obeyed and with a slight jerk began lowering us down the dusty white side of New Dawn.

It was a quiet ride down. Not a sound on the comm and no comments from either of us. We knew the two worlds would be listening. The horizon drifted upward. A glance down showed us approaching the Martian surface between two of the dynamic landing legs. There were no rocks to be seen at all. The earthmovers had cleared them all away. Nothing but ash red sand and as we settled down onto it, there was a slight rocking as the man basket cables slackened. We paused for a moment to get our bearings. Martian terrain surrounded us as far as we could see. We were part of a red world, totally silent and still. To our left, the central area of Mars Base alpha was strewn with equipment, modules, and pipe and conduit laying within.

I looked at Collins. She was wide-eyed. I unhitched the basket outer gate and swung it open. The blanket of red dust beyond waited.

"Whenever you're ready, Laurel."

She went to the opening, placed a hand on either side and stood for moment. She said, "It's not a single person stepping onto Mars for the first time today. It's the thousands of people who have worked so hard to make this trip possible. So together we all take this step."

Collins put out one foot and made her mark in the Martian soil. Carefully she followed with a second step then moved away from the basket and looked at me. "Care to join me on Mars, Captain?"

For some reason I laughed. I had just witnessed a dramatic change in a young person. The tone of her voice had suddenly matured. It was as though she had become almost a different person from the one in the man basket. It was more a feeling than anything else, but that one giant step had somehow affected her in a soulful life changing way. I nodded to her and stepped off, moved around to the side of the basket to slide the door shut, and pressed the up button. Immediately the basket lifted up and left us.

The comm could not contain the excitement aboard ship. The squelch kept cutting in and out letting cheering and shouting leak through. Finally Descard's voice came in. "Sending down the next three, Captain."

Collins said, "Captain, my mind has gone blank. What do we do now?"

"We have our choice, Laurel. There are two Mars open rovers waiting over at Cargo 3. We can head that way and ride in them, or we can just walk to Base Alpha from here."

"I think I'd prefer to just walk to get the feel of this place, Captain."

"Me too." I clicked the comm, "Paul, designate two Martians to walk over and fetch the rovers, will you?"

"Will do, Captain. They're almost on their way."

We shuffled through the sand feeling both heavy and light. The gravity was a blanket, but it was obvious we could take very long steps very easily. The adrenaline was still flowing.

"Dumars to Easton."

"Go ahead, Andrea."

"You have not made your required environmental check in. We are standing by."

"Sorry, Andrea. It is kind of exhilarating down here."

"I can confirm that," added Collins

"I'm sure it is, you two, but I'd like suit temperature and pressure and outside conditions," answered Dumars. "My telemetry says you're just fine."

"Suit pressure down to 6.4, temps a balmy 72 degrees. Mars temp minus 55C, pressure 6.2 Mb. There is no wind today that we can perceive."

"We concur with your readings, Captain. And your BP, pulse rate and body temps are in the acceptable range. You are cleared to continue your EVA duties," said Dumars.

"You are invited to join us out here, Doctor," said Collins.

"Count on it," was the only reply.

It was a long trek to the center of the Base Alpha. We began passing piping, conduit and storage cases that contained special tools. Ahead, the three main habitat domes were placed in their assigned positions, as yet unfolded and waiting hookup for inflation. Beyond them was my first target; the three main power stations. They too had been placed central to the Base and were dormant, waiting for a wakeup call.

As I approached Base Central I stopped and looked at Collins. "Laurel, my first job is to wake up those power stations. What's first on your list?"

Collins replied, "Look!" and she pointed toward the ship.

Three more Martian spacesuits were in the man basket and nearing the surface.

"What a sight," said Collins.

"Never before seen," I added.

"Oh, sorry. I am to inspect the SuperMoxies. Those tanks should be full of O2 by now if we're lucky."

"Okay, then. Let me know if you have any problems or need any help."

"Will do, Captain and thanks for choosing me by the way." Collins trudged off toward her oxygen generators. I pushed on to the three huge power stations. All three had their control panels already exposed. I chose the central unit and began.

If all went as expected, battery power would let me wake up the controls and telemetry transmitters. I opened a circuit breaker panel and flipped all the breakers. A red power available light came on which excited the electrical me. Holding my breath, I lifted the power-apply switch cover and pressed the big green button. Lights came on everywhere and a readout screen began scrolling startup data.

"Easton to Descard."

"Go ahead, Captain."

"Are you getting telemetry from power station 2?"

"Already? Wait a second."

I waited.

"My gosh, we *are* seeing data from power station 2. We are monitoring and are ready for startup."

I waited for the display screen to stop scrolling. It finally ran down to a line that read, **"Engage power generator**?"

There was a simple **Y** and **N** for me to choose from. I highlighted the **Y** and hit **Enter**.

I could not hear the noise being made but I could feel the vibration in the unit. On my screen several graphs appeared showing voltage and current. On the Power-Available graph the line was slowly ramping upward.

"Yes! We are seeing that, Captain. Alpha Base power is available!" exclaimed Descard.

"Collins to Captain."

"Go ahead, Laurel."

"Our tanks are full of oxygen! The readouts were correct."

"Great to hear, Laurel. What is your next procedure?"

"I'm to start setting up the O2 infusion lines to the center dome in preparation for inflation. The rovers are here, Captain."

I turned to search the area and found two space-suited people driving up in the rovers.

"Anders here, Captain."

"Petterson also, Captain."

I gave a wave. "I see three more coming down already. You guys should probably go give them a ride. Save their energy for work."

Collins came back on the comm, "Stevens has joined me, Captain. We're going to begin setting the infusion lines."

"All of you remember to stop and rest. Don't waste anyone's time by passing out and making us stop to take you back to the ship."

"No way," said one voice.

"Roger wilco," said another.

There were now already eight of us on the surface with three more coming. We went to work to make Mars Base Alpha livable for humans. All three power stations came up without a hitch. I had to dig in the Martian sand to find the first main feed line leading to the center habitat dome. The end connector was a twist lock. It was packed with red sand. I need a brush. As I knelt considering it, a hand tapped my shoulder.

"Bartlet, Captain. I have the tool pouch."

I twisted my shoulders to look at him. He smiled through his visor.

"I'm glad at least one of us is thinking, Mr. Bartlet. I need a brush."

He dug in the pouch and handed me one. I cleaned off the male connector, wiped away sand from the base of the power unit and plugged in the cable. We both looked back at the center habitat dome, still folded into a tall, multilayer square.

"On to power unit two, Captain?" asked Bartlet.

"I was just trying to imagine the first dome inflating, Mr. Bartlet."

"I wouldn't want to be anywhere near it when it does, Captain. They say the unfolding floors will bash you and if that doesn't kill you the weight of the structure will, even on Mars."

"You are correct, Mr. Bartlet. But the site of that dome rising will warm my heart."

"My name is Brennon, Captain. If that's okay."

"Power station two, Bren. Let's go."

Mars Base Alpha became a busy construction site. Periodically someone would overdo it and have to be escorted back to New Dawn for a replacement but the work never really stopped. As hoped, we had arrived early, so this was our first Martian morning. By afternoon, we were ready to inflate the first habitat dome. The glory I had been feeling all morning quickly became apprehension. This operation had been tested many times on Earth but never on Mars.

Descard, now on the surface with us, walk-hopped the perimeter to make sure everyone was clear. He sounded an alarm tone on the comm. He said, "All clear guys. You are authorized to blow up the balloon."

Subconsciously, I held my breath. It was still a silent scene but I could see the fat hoses leading to the dome suddenly become rigid and twisting in the sand. It took so long for the first panel to flip, I thought it wasn't working. Finally, panel one stood up on its side like a giant monolith then flopped over, pushed away by the next panel.

It was to be a three-hour inflation. I watched the giant card game opening up until I felt guilty. Then I realized I was six hours into my suit time. It would take me probably an hour to get a ride back to New Dawn, take the elevator and get into the airlock for suit pressurization. I also realized I was more than exhausted. Excitement and adrenaline had driven me.

A construction engineer drove me back. During the ride up the elevator I got a good look at Mars Base Alpha. It had already changed radically. There were people in space suits everywhere, working. There was a huge tent partially risen. A rover was speeding across the plain toward one of the cargo ships. A few hours earlier this place had been an empty red desert. Humanity had arrived. Mars was no longer loved from afar. It was now up close and personal.

Chapter 17

I awoke in my sleeping bag on the floor of my office not knowing where I was or how long I'd been there. It took a moment even to remember *who* I was. For a split second there was a scary, eerie question in my mind, "Who am I this time?"

I pushed up on one elbow and quickly remembered gravity. There was sliver of light from my door, someone slipping in. In the darkness, hands fumbled with my sleeping bag and a warm body forced itself in with me. There was the smell of jasmine. I had to blink myself the rest of the way awake.

Andrea purred, "Oh, just a few seconds of bliss. They'll never suspect. I've been back and forth up here monitoring you the whole time. I forbade anyone to wake you."

"Have I been damaged somehow?"

"Nope. Just sleeping. You needed it. You way overdid it. Everyone is." She wrapped an arm around me and pulled tight. "Really, it's been too long."

"That I've slept?"

"No."

"You shouldn't have stopped them from waking me."

"You have Pars. She's taking care of everything just fine."

"Is the first dome up?"

"Yes. It's so beautiful. Those plastic windows are just like glass now. The second one is half inflated."

"Andrea, I've got to get up."

"I know, damn it."

"Did you give me a sleeping pill or something?"

"Are you kidding? You were so knocked out a sleeping pill would have put you in a coma."

"You mean I just overdid it a little?"

"You and quite a few others. My staff has had to IV some of them. The idiots just wouldn't stop working. The excitement is contagious."

"You know, actually this would be a nice time to debrief you."

"Oh, please do."

Forty-five minutes later I slipped out of the sleeping bag, eased into the fortuitously empty bathroom, then pulled on a brown flight suit. I left her there sleeping, knowing I could use the same excuse she did.

The Bridge was deserted. For a second I considered being angry about that but realized they were all down in Engineering still monitoring life support and other systems and taking shifts outside.

The climb down the ladderway was much easier this time. I made it to D deck before stopping to look around. The place was still busy with gravity-heavy patrons. I headed back down past the multitude of launch-landing seats and people on C and B.

Engineering was busy as expected. There was a distinct atmosphere of great excitement. I finally thought to look at a wall monitor. It nearly took my breath away. There in all its glory was a fully deployed gray central habitat dome, windows glistening in the light. I did not see James, but Descard was gesturing and giving orders to a man and a woman in space suits. As I approached, they lifted their helmets into place, snap locked them, and headed for the airlock.

Descard saw me and laughed. "You know you shut your eyes around here for five minutes and the whole world had changed."

Before I could answer Janet Pars approached, saw me and laughed. Her hair was a mess, makeup smeared a bit, both as though she'd been too busy to care. "Well, well, finally decided to join our planet," she joked.

"Why'd you let me sleep like that, XO?"

"Hey, blame Dumars, not me. Her associates wanted to IV you, but Dumars said she'd take personal care of you instead. What'd she mean by that anyway, Mark?"

"Very funny. I see we have one beautiful Dome."

"And there will be a second in exactly eighty-two minutes," said Descard.

I gave a thumbs up. "What's status on this first one?"

"It's all good," said Pars. "All thirty of the rooms erected correctly. The fabric walls are very rigid. The inflatable couch-sleepers are in place ready to be blown up along with the guest seats. They've tested one countertop and it lifted into place and the legs unfolded nicely. They may only be the size of a small hotel room, but compared to the cubicles we've been living in they are the Ritz."

"And the toilets?"

Descard said, "The waste management and water recovery people are bringing in equipment through the central airlock as we speak. They've already begun setting some of it up. It won't be long for shower stalls and toilets."

"Heat?"

Pars answered, "It's minus 50 F in there right now. The air handlers are attached. They're going to run them at twenty-five percent power for the first hour. If all goes well with the power system, they'll switch them to op mode. It should warm up fast."

"Have either of you been in there?"

Pars looked at Descard and shook her head. Descard replied. "No, but we've had a complete tour, compliments of the structural engineer's head cam. Which brings us to the next subject."

"You have my full attention."

Pars said, "We've got to get those suits out of Cargo Five, Mark. The structural guys studied the plans and have already gone up in the manlift and marked out the cut lines. We have two mechanics going back up now with the cutting equipment."

"Pressure differential?"

Descard said, "We can't open that damn cargo hatch but we do have telemetry and control inside the ship. We've already commanded it to vent its atmosphere. There will be no pressure differential from Mars atmosphere to the ship's internal pressure level."

Pars added, "We don't want to wait while they to try to fix that hatch from inside. We plan to remove the suit containers and hand them out the new hole. We can decide about the rest of 5's cargo later."

They looked at me for indications of disapproval.

"Sounds good to me. How dangerous will the cut edges be to the people wearing suits?"

Descard said, "There will be some danger of suit cuts but they know that. As long as they're careful it shouldn't happen."

"So when will the first dome be ready for residents?"

Pars replied, "We assume you do not want to wait until all three domes are certified before moving people. So, if everything passes the certification testing the central dome might be ready in four hours."

I raised an eyebrow. "You need the emergency suits in there before you can let people in."

Descard replied, "Those will be the first offloads once we're in 5."

Pars added, "Yes. And, once we get people moved in we'll have a small army to continue the set-up work in there. They are ready to move food and water supplies in there but they're waiting for the heat. They are picking up the Wi-Fi we're sending, too."

"Have you looked at the list of names assigned to that dome?"

Descard said, "Yes, and they've already been notified that's happening."

"Are you two assigned there?"

"Yes, as are you," answered Pars. "But I'm thinking we will be the last to report in since we're needed here."

I nodded agreement, "Right."

"It's going to be a pain moving those people unless we get those other suits," said Pars.

"Do you guys have me scheduled for electrical work any time soon?"

Descard answered. "You have three hours, then I have you down to assist electrical hookup for Dome 3 air handlers. Is that okay?"

"Are you kidding? I can't wait."

"That seems to be the general attitude around here," said Pars.

"You'd better go get something to eat," added Descard. "I recommend high protein."

"Yeah, I need to check on Bishop too. I'll bet she's still got a tiger by the tail."

Pars said, "Yep. People either itching to get down to the surface or others complaining they've gained an unfair amount of weight."

"Now *that's* funny," said Descard.

People near the airlock began calling for Pars and Descard. They turned and headed that way.

I took a few minutes to just lean against a wall and watch the live camera views from the surface. It had begun to look like a standard construction site on Earth. I counted seven people in space suits rapidly changing the world around them.

The thought of Bishop gave me a pang of guilt. After a last look around I started up the ladderway.

B deck was a slow-moving mass of heavy people. Some were rearranging their packs because they were central dome people soon to be relocated, others were up and walking trying to embrace the new gravity, and some were still in their seats sleeping or staring at the ceiling wondering how they had gotten themselves into this.

Bishop was walking within them looking down at each, checking to be sure they were sufficiently enduring Mars reality. I headed her way. She looked up as I approached.

"How are you holding up, Amanda?" I asked.

"Better than some, Captain. How about you?"

"I seem to have slept without my consent, so I'm on the up curve."

"Yes, I'm due myself. I keep looking over my shoulder worried that Dumars will try to IV me. Have you seen her?"

"Not in the past half hour. Is everything okay?"

"I think Andrea went off to find some place to sleep where no one would bother her. I hope so anyway."

"Any serious problems here?"

"No, the fact the first dome group is almost ready to leave has bolstered spirits. We'll be okay. I should probably mention, Bob Banabalas is on the first group out. He's central dome because of his IT status. I hope we don't get any wild stories about life of the surface."

"You know I've been meaning to have a chat with him. Where is he?"

She pointed and I spotted Banabalas repacking.

I said, "Well, now's as good a time as any."

"Captain, if you find Andrea and she's sacked out please make sure no one disturbs her, okay?"

"I promise."

I headed for Bob. Banabalas looked up as I neared. He raised one hand. "Captain, could I possibly speak with you for a minute."

"Actually I wanted to talk to you, Bob. Let's step over by those packing cases where we can have some privacy. I see they set up a coffee cart. You want anything?"

"Fruit punch please, Captain."

I heated my coffee, collected Bob's fruit punch and met him at the containers. We sat.

"What I need to talk to you about Captain...."

"Let me go first, Bob. Maybe we'll cover some of what you have."

I sipped my coffee straw.

I said, "Bob, you are a teller of tall tales."

"There's been some misunderstanding there, Captain."

"You mentioned to some people you solved the airlock door problem."

"I meant to say that I was present when the theory was brought up."

"You also said something about holding the record for deep sea diving in a diving bell."

"It was a misunderstanding, Captain. I said I was present on the ship when the record was set."

"Where you?"

"Yes. I was ship's IT. The Amada. Jacques Cousteau's affiliate."

"Jacques Cousteau's expedition?"

"Well, no. But it could have been."

"You see, Bob? You need to keep it real, especially around here."

"I know. I know, Captain. It's the damn cheerleader, jock thing."

"Cheerleader, jock?"

"In high school, if you wanted to date a cheerleader, you had to be a jock. But if you had no chance of being a jock, you needed some other way to boost your status."

"This all started over a cheerleader?"

"I was a nerd. I even had tape on the bridge of my glasses for a while. I could get close to the hot women but they were just using me. I kept thinking I was about to be in a relationship but when the homework was done, or the laptop set up, they vanished. It was like trying to start an old car. You work and work and finally get the engine started but it quits and won't start at all. That's what it was like."

"So tall tales to boost your status?"

"It got to be a habit. It kind of works sometimes."

I sipped my coffee and nodded. "Bob, you've been missing the big picture all along."

"Yeah, what?"

"The beautiful people syndrome. It's not what you think."

"What do you mean?"

"The beautiful popular people, they go through years of everyone wanting to be their friend. People giving them things just to get close to them. One worshiper after another. They become used to that. It's the same for men and women. Eventually they decide they should marry someone rich or famous or both because that's the status they deserve. They spend a few years in the marriage and when the physical attraction becomes old news and boring, they realize they have nothing in common. Then one or both start becoming unpleasant because subconsciously they want out. That ends in an ugly divorce. The money is divided up and they're back out there, still feeling like they're the upper class. They go into the future with that same mindset and a shallow failed marriage and ugly divorce added. It's the same for nerds who become rich and end up marrying models. Is that the lifestyle you're trying so hard to achieve?"

"Well what about you? You're a jock."

"I loved aircraft and spacecraft so much I never had time for that crap. I had to keep my head in the books to make test pilot school. I was a test pilot before joining the astronaut corps. They send you all over the place in those positions. I never was in one place long enough to develop a serious relationship. I was lucky. But you didn't answer my question. Do you really want a life like the rich and famous? Go online and check the marriage, divorce and alcohol-drug patterns in that world if you don't believe me."

He sat silent for a very long few moments. He looked at me with a wrinkled brow. "I may have been looking at this all wrong."

"You think?"

"Captain, if only I had known you in high school."

"There's another thing, Bob. I don't think you realize it, but you are now a jock as you put it. You're an IT specialist on Mars. How many computer nerds will ever achieve that? You're already famous. You will go down in the history books as the first computer tech to set up the Mars internet which will probably remain in use forever. There are eighty-one people here using computers and computer systems. You are now one of the most important people on the planet."

"Oh my God! I *am* a jock!"

"Well, I hope our little discussion has been of some help, Bob."

I held out my hand and we shook, though he seemed to be in a daze. "I'll see you down there in Dome Central." I stood to leave.

He looked up and quickly regained his focus. "Captain, wait. There's something I need to give you."

Something in his tone made me take pause. I sat back down. Banabalas stood and raced over to his duffle bag. He pulled out a fanny pack and returned.

"It's Harold Bateman, Captain."

"Oh, yes, another of your ill-advised tall tales."

"No, it's not that. I mean, I really did play chess with him. We played on our laptops over the intranet. It's a bad way to play because it's so easy to cheat but I took a chance. I had to because Harold hardly ever came out of his module."

"And Security knows that, right?"

"Well, no. I shouldn't have said we played in public. After they checked the video files and saw we weren't there they wouldn't listen to a thing I had to say."

"So what about Harold Bateman?"

"You must know Harold was a computer nerd too, not hardware just software. That was another reason he never came out of his habitat. Anyway, he started messing around in his laptop's system32 DLL's and locked it up really good. He brought it to me to see if I could resurrect it. I had to pull the drive just to get into it but it was not a problem. I had it up and running the next day."

"Okay, so what?"

"Oh! Nothing. It's just that he left a flash drive plugged into his laptop when he brought it to me. I tossed it into my pack of drives and forgot to give it back to him. By the time I remembered he'd disappeared. So I thought I should give it to you in case there's stuff on it his family might want back someday."

Banabalas unzipped his fanny pack. There had to be at least fifty flash drives in there. He began rifling through them.

"How will you ever find the right one?" I asked.

"Oh, it's easy. It has the face of an alien on it. A Gray."

He held up a flash drive with the face of a large-eye ET on it and handed it over. "It's not really important, Captain. I glanced inside it. It's just a bunch of letters to his mother, a ton of them. But maybe his family would want them."

"Bateman's mother is not alive."

"Really? Then the letters must be like prayers or something. You know, talking to loved ones though they are no longer with you?"

"Thank you, Bob. It's very good of you to bring this to me. And I would like to keep the Harold Bateman incident out of everyone's mind so would you please keep this just between us?"

"I will, Captain. I promise."

"Okay, buddy. See you downstairs in the dome."

"Thanks, Captain. Thanks a lot."

I zipped the flash drive in a breast pocket and went to the ladderway. On C deck it was mostly Med people caring for the newly heavy. I passed by and kept going. Made it all the way to F deck and rounded up packets of scrambled eggs and bacon. I sat for real with hot coffee and wolfed the stuff down. Even in gravity it was still very, very good.

The Bridge was still deserted. With the stealth of a ninja I peeked into my office. Andrea was still sound asleep in the sleeping bag, faintly snoring. I smiled gratefully and eased the door shut.

At my command seat I checked the time. I had an hour before my scheduled surface work. I keyed the computer and plugged in Harold's flash drive.

The contents of the drive were exactly what Bob said they were: letters to Mom. At least they had all been automatically titled "Dear Mom." I had no reservations about opening one. At the least it might show Bateman's state of mind, or with luck who he might have had dealings with. I clicked open the first letter and read;

Dear Mom,

I think home is now keeping Patricia and Cathy alive living inside somewhere. Only now, they're over my estimates for outside understanding, never doubting, holding inside my inner neurosis, my yearning for consummation under both inner contradictions, lies, endless heretics. Earlier situations aren't instead denoting just ulterior semantics to address several enigmatic causes under rigid instability. You can have every calendar keepsake.

Harold

I sat back and winced, then reread it. My first impression was that he had gone crazy or was using hallucinogens. I reread it several more times looking for secret inner meaning.

My subconscious suddenly kicked in. This letter reminded me of something from a very long time ago, something in elementary school. It was a simple way of sending code, an easy way to conceal a message inside a message.

It took me a minute to work it out. You hide the real message by inserting the real letters within the fake message words. It could be that every third or fourth letter in each word was part of the real message. I took a chance and started with the first letter of each word, assembled them and immediately hit pay dirt.

Ithinkpacalisontomefoundhiminmycubicle hesaidjustasecuritycheck

I think Pacal is on to me. I found him in my cubicle. He said just a security check.

There was a brief moment of pride from deciphering the code. Then confusion. I reread the line several times trying to find a different perspective. There was none. My Chief of Security had been lying to me. There was no way around that. Maybe more letter codes would explain.

Half an hour later I had translated a dozen letters. The messages were all vague but indicated Bateman was on some kind of secret mission. He never gave a clue as to what that was. There were other mentions of Pacal and how Pacal was becoming more and more suspicious and following him. Alarm bells went off in my head. Was Pacal the murderer?

I rubbed my eyes and pinched the bridge of my nose in thought. There had to be some other explanation. We had made it through entry and landing safely so there could not have been a plan to destroy the Mars Base Alpha mission. I looked at my watch. I needed to be down in Engineering for pre-breathing and suit-up in ten minutes.

I unplugged the flash drive. The only real way to hide and protect something like it was to keep it on my person. Little things disappear too easily. I zipped it into the breast pocket of my flight suit. I'd switch it to the pocket tab on my suit undergarment.

All the way down the ladderway my head was spinning with possibilities. Pacal had mentioned a flash drive and that he hadn't been able to find it. That had been a slip on his part. Why was he lying to me? What was Bateman's secret mission? The reality of these things bewildered me.

The techs suited me up with two others, a mechanic and an electrician. The electrician's name was Dimtri Berenzin. He had a notable Russian accent. He poked me in the arm with one finger as the techs fidgeted with his backpack. "Hey Easton, we power up dome three, eh? Are you ready to blow up that giant balloon?"

I laughed as the techs lowered my helmet into place.

When his was twist-locked in place he tested the comm. "Easton, I think the people upstairs want their dome."

"The Hyatt Regency?" I responded.

"Hyatt, what is that?"

I smiled at him through the visor. "Luxury hotel."

He laughed a guttural laugh. "Let's go."

We lined up and entered the airlock. I could see the depress process had now become automatic for everyone involved. I made a mental note about warning them not to become complacent. As the airlock outer doors opened someone referred to them as Sam's doors. We took turns stepping out to the swinging man-basket. Being last I clipped on and slid the basket door shut.

An aerial vision of Mars once again flooded my eyes and mind. It was spellbinding. I stood scanning the horizon hungrily. Mars Base Alpha was a small dot on an endless red plain that terminated in distant hills and mountains. Far in the distance a dust devil swirled across the plain. Dimitri hit the down button and we jerked to a start-down.

I looked down. The ground around New Dawn was now disrupted from frequent visits of vehicles and people. The dirt road leading to Base Alpha was already well used. I could sense the cold on the outer skin of my suit. We descended along the smooth white body of our ship and arrived at ground level where an open rover waited. The driver waved and offered us seats.

As I stepped off the cage my comm squelched on. "Pars to Easton."

"Go ahead, Jan."

"Just an update. The mechanics have gotten into Cargo 5. The panel they cut out fell to the ground but no harm done. They are inside looking for the suits."

"Glad to hear that, Jan. Thanks for the update. Keep me posted."

"Will do. Pars out."

Dimitri and I made our way to Base Alpha central and spent three hours hooking power up to Dome 3 with the structural guys breathing down our necks. They were dying to blow air into the thing. I was called away once to figure out why the Dome 2 heater was drawing more power than expected. That turned out to be mechanics borrowing power from that system to work on Dome 1. When finally our shift was done, we caught a ride back to New Dawn. On the way another comm message came through.

"Descard to Easton."

"Yeah, Paul?"

"Mark, they are pulling those Mars suits out of Five. When they're done we need to get those cargo doors working. We can't leave the ship open to the Mars atmosphere. The thing will fill with dust and crap. I want to send Collins and Ansuri up there to get those hatch doors open. Then we'll have the mechanics weld or bolt that panel back in place. What do you think?"

"Sounds like a good plan to me, Paul. Keep me advised."

"Will do. Descard out."

Chapter 18

Dome 2 was a little slow warming up. Our second night on Mars was approaching. When the Dome's temperature was finally livable, the arguing began. Engineering did not want to move people in the dark. They could have convinced the Dome 2 residents to wait until morning except for one thing; the lights were on in Dome 2. Light was beaming out the windows. People knew their assigned rooms were down there waiting. Spacious air mattress beds and priceless privacy. Not all toilets were up and running, but there were enough. The energetic discussion went on and on.

"Descard and Pars to Easton."

"I know what you guys want so I'm not answering."

Pars' laugh cut in on the comm. "Come on, Mark, you're not sticking us with this."

"Well, what do you guys think?"

"The exterior of New Dawn is well lighted. They'd be using the rover lights to move people. We can set up outside lights for the Dome 2 airlock. That's the positive side of it," said Descard.

"Okay, I'm ready for the negative."

Pars answered, "These people would be taking their first step on Mars in the dark, or at least under the lights. For many of them it will be the first time they've used a spacesuit other than training. Someone could go into panic mode."

I thought about it. "What's your opinion?"

Pars said, "I think we should let these people go home."

Descard did not answer.

"Paul, what's it going to be?"

"I guess. We'll put our rescue guys out there as escorts. Even if somebody hyperventilates and passes out they can adjust the mix and still get them into the Dome."

"So that's it, then. Rather than have them all twisting and turning and pacing all night, we'll move them."

Pars added, "Security will have to get set up in there along with a Waste Management person. There's a general water dispenser available. The closed-circuit room sinks are just being unpacked."

"Two at a time in the basket with an escort?" I asked.

Descard answered, "We'd better do that. I wouldn't put three newbies in that basket alone."

Pars added, "That will be fourteen trips including the support people."

Descard said, "If we do this with minimal suit depressurization time they'll all be balloon boys in their spacesuits and it will be a five minute ride down, three minute ride to the dome, and ten minutes in the airlock. So eighteen minutes per trip will make this a four-hour deal. We'll finish up around 2:00 A.M."

I asked, "Can we do it?"

"I volunteer to hang in here and keep an eye on things," said Pars.

"I'll join you, Jan."

"Mark, you put in a regular work shift. You'd better rest," she replied.

"I'll make you a deal. I'll sleep if I can."

Pars replied, "I see your point."

"Well, Jan, you want to call Bishop and give her the good news?"

Descard said, "We may want to have a resuscitator there when you do."

The Exodus began.

If you want to set up a habitat fast put the people who will live there in it. Dome 2 came to life at the speed of light. Residents were in their rooms inflating furniture, unpacking their duffel bags, putting up pictures on the walls, checking their internet connections and staring out their windows at the black Martian night. In the morning, they would watch their first Martian sunrise from home. Then the closed-circuit sinks would become the next living-urgent furnishing. Everyone would be waiting for one to be issued. Sinks that require the user to fill the primary source bottle from the community water allotment dispenser, then later return the secondary recaptured water bottle to the water reclamation station to get a freshwater refill. Someday in the not-too-distant future, after the first deep well had been drilled, those sinks would be patched into the dome water systems and refilling would no longer be required.

The long night of lowering people down was more celebratory than laborious. Each new pair in the Dome cheered their own arrival. Although still tired and heavy, they quickly became busy residents.

I made it to my Bridge office around 4:00A.M. Dumars had straightened up the sleeping bag and left a giant smiley face on my computer screen. I kneeled on the sleeping bag on the floor and started to unzip my flight suit but never finished.

Once again no one gave me a wakeup call. Groggy, I unwound myself from the sleeping bag wrap and shoved myself out of my wrinkled flight suit and into a fresh one.

The Bridge was deserted again but bright Martian light was beaming through the windows. I thought to call down to Engineering but had trouble organizing my thoughts. Where had we left off last night? I climbed down to F deck and joined other half-asleep individuals at the coffee station. Some had found paper coffee cups and were pouring their heated coffee packets into them. A kind soul handed me one complete with hot coffee.

I sipped and decided to call Engineering just to see who answered. "Easton to Engineering."

"Andrea here, Mark. Good morning."

"Andrea? You're running Engineering now?"

"Descard and James are both still sacked out per my orders. I only got them to sign off an hour ago. They were up all night."

"I'm on my way down. What's our status?"

"We are getting ready to populate Dome number one. Maintenance has finished the daily crane checkout and the suit techs are setting up to send people down."

"Okay. On my way."

I drank quickly and left the cup on a table for someone else. The down ladder was easier today. I made all five decks.

Engineering again had become the busiest place on the ship. It was crowded. Numerous loud conversations were filling the room. The confusion bothered me. We still had power systems and life support running here, never mind waste and water. I needed to get a handle on this place before somebody who didn't belong accidentally leaned on a critical system console.

Dumars spotted me and came over. "They filled me in before heading off to get some sleep. I told them I could handle it but now I'm not so sure."

"You should have called me."

"Yes, but an overtired Captain can make serious mistakes too."

I went to the ladderway and stepped up onto the bottom rung. I had to yell to get over the noise. "Excuse me. Can I have everyone's attention please?!" I held up one hand for emphasis.

It took a good thirty seconds for the talking to subside.

"That's right. Over here. Let me have your attention please. I want everyone who is not part of the engineering staff to please vacate Engineering right now. I also want any engineering staff members who are not on this shift and not filling a position to also go upstairs. We will call you when you are needed. For those relocating we will call you as soon as we're ready for you. Please exit Engineering immediately. We are not going to continue relocation operations until this area is cleared."

263

I stepped down from the ladderway and got out of the way. It took them a minute to mentally adjust. To my relief a line began to form at the ladderway as the first few started up. The rest of us stood by and watched as the procession thinned the room greatly. It took fifteen minutes. When it was over people standing at their workstations took on expressions of relief. Someone clapped.

"Nicely done, Captain," said Dumars.

"Who is keeping the EVA log?"

Dumars looked dumbfounded.

I looked over the room. Most of them were still staring back at me. I held up one hand again. "Okay, everybody, listen up. Who is senior officer here right now?"

Reluctantly one of the suit specialists looked around and raised his hand. "Bremen, Captain. I think it must be me."

I waved him over.

"Bremen, you said?"

"Yes, sir. Scott Bremen. General Services Engineering."

"Okay, Scott. Do you have the EVA logbook?"

"No sir."

"Who has been operating the airlock?"

"I have been sir, with Chief Descard."

Dumars cut in. "I came down to check on things. I suspected Descard had CFS. He wasn't answering my questions adequately. I ordered him up to get rest. I told him I'd fill in."

I nodded. "I think I get the picture. Scott, find Descard's tablet he was using to track the EVAs. Hurry up."

I held up the hand again. "Okay everyone. Stop prepping people for EVA until we check the EVA log. Just stand by for now."

There were numerous silent stares.

Bremen returned. "It was next to the coffee dispenser, sir."

"Figures. Okay Scott. We are going to poll all the people outside right now, one at a time and bring that log up to current activities. Get ready to write."

I turned to Dumars. "Andrea, when did *you* last sleep?"

"I'm fine, Mark. But they do need me upstairs."

"Okay. I've got this. You go do what you need to do."

"Thanks. Did you get my smiley face?"

I grinned. She wiggled her fingers at me and headed for the ladderway.

Bremen and I moved over to the communications station. A tech was seated there staring up at us. His comm unit said McAllister.

"Mr. McAllister, can you patch me in to every spacesuit we have all at once?"

McAllister raised his eyebrows. "I've never done it but yes, I can."

"Please proceed, Mr. McAllister."

McAllister switched a few controls, tapped his own communicator to test the setup and turned to me and nodded.

"Attention all EVA personnel, this is Captain Easton. Would you please check in, one at a time so we can update our EVA tracking log. Standing by."

It was an unusual request. It took a minute for them to process it. Finally the first of them called in. Bremen began logging names, their time out and suit time remaining. Some of them did not know what their time-out was which was extremely annoying to me. In less than thirty minutes we were tracking all the EVAs in progress.

"So it's now your job to record everyone coming and going and why, Scott. If you have to leave you must appoint someone to cover for you. Understand?"

"Perfectly, sir."

"And go down that list and check on anyone out of suit and working in a Dome and update their listing. Okay?"

"Got it, Captain."

"I'm going to set up in Chief Descard's office. If you have any problems I'll be there. For now on all new EVA people have to go through me first. I'll tell you if they're approved to go out then you add it to the log."

"Yes, sir."

In Descard's office I found his large wall display screen was showing the schedule for Base Alpha's evolution. He had an actual coffee mug on his desk half filled with cold coffee. I made a quick trip and topped it off with my mix, very hot. I sat at his desk and relearned the schedule. Having become a lowly electrician over the past few days I had been away from it for too long.

The name next to the Dome 1 operations was Hilliard. I turned in my seat to call him but he walked in the door before I could.

"Ah, Captain, it's you now."

"Just in the nick of time too, Mr. Hilliard."

"It's Andre, if you don't mind, Captain. I've checked the Dome 1 telemetry this morning. It's stable at 73 degrees. We can start letting people in there."

"Very good, Andre. Have you slept?"

"Yes, sir. I finished in Dome 1 last night and set the heat to op mode and got a full night's sleep."

"Thank God somebody's got the sense to. I'm busy getting up to speed here, Andre. Can you set up the escorts yourself? Scott Bremen has the log. Let me know when you're ready and I'll approve the transfers."

"Great, Captain. I'm on it." With a thumbs up he ducked out the door.

On my master chart the coordinator's name for Dome three was Julia Barona. I sat back and pinched my communicator. "Easton to Barona."

This time there was a very long wait. I gave her a full five minutes. No answer. I turned to Descard's laptop on the desk and found the icon to his logbook tablet. I opened it and read down the list of EVA's. Sure enough, Julia Barona had gone out the door at 05:10 this morning. I tried again. "Easton to Barona."

"Barona here, Captain. Sorry, I thought I misheard the comm."

"Where are you, Julia?"

"I'm coordinator for Dome 1. I am there right now. It's beautiful in here, Captain."

"What's your status?"

"We will have enough toilets working by late this afternoon to start letting people in."

"Everything else is online?"

"Water, air and heat, all nominal."

"Emergency suits?"

"Already distributed to every room."

"Very good, Julia. Please keep me posted."

"Will do, Captain."

The next steady flow of migrants began about an hour later and did not let up. By lunch the ship was starting to feel deserted. The minor problems were also endless. Shipping containers that were supposed to fit through the airlock but would not. Food containers that seemed to want to stay frozen, people departing the domes getting in the way of people entering them, rovers being out of service for recharge, one cargo vehicle crane that would lower the shipping containers but then erroneously take them back up before they could be offloaded, a power connection that wasn't actually locked and had disconnected itself, people scheduled for work who were passed out in their new room because they hadn't slept in days, and in one case someone trying to demonstrate a standing long jump on Mars traveled past her target area and into the admiring crowd where they all ended in a heap on the Dome floor. I was told there was hysterical laughter that went on forever and fortunately no injuries.

Jeff James showed up around 1:00P.M. and a groggy Paul Descard about an hour later. There was so much going on we couldn't really keep track. We had to depend on the sensibilities of our coordinators and team leaders. My next shift came up at 3:00PM. I was to cover the preliminary cable layout for the future parking garage that would house the first pressurized rover and its two unibody spacesuits. I was all too ready to go and planned to steal some time for a tour of Dome 2 where my quarters and office were located. Though I was scheduled for 1500 hours there was a one hour wait to actually get through the line and the airlock. When I finally got my turn at least there was a rover ride to Dome 2.

The Dome airlocks are slightly larger than those aboard ship. They are more automated. You don't have to remain in them for the full re-pressurization period, you can exit and walk around the Dome's huge greeting area in your suit. In Dome 2 there is a large medical facility on the right along with my office and Security. Opposite those were the future Mars Base Alpha Administrative Council offices. Someone had already unpacked artificial plants and placed them around the open community area. The furniture was still not unpacked and assembled. It was a large enough open area that basketball could have been played there. Opposite the airlock a long wide corridor led past habitats. Large picture windows everywhere made the place striking to behold inside and out. Maintenance was working on the community bathroom shower section.

As I stood appreciating the wonder of it a sound suddenly came over my suit comm that sent chills up and down my spine. It was a shrill cry that sounded like a garbled "Help!" It could have been passed off as comm squeal but not by me. The hair on the back of my neck stood up and a bolt of fear hit me. I had heard that tone too many times before.

"This is Captain Easton. Is someone asking for help?"

The comm squelched on to someone gasping for air. A desperate sounding voice mumbled, "Oh my God!"

"This is Easton. Identify yourself."

I waited and just as I was about to insist again the voice answered, "Captain this is Samantha Ansuri. Laurel Collins has just fallen from the manlift."

"How far did she fall, Samantha?"

"About fifty feet."

"Stand by, Samantha. Everyone keep this channel clear. Easton to Dumars."

"It's about time Mark…."

"Andrea we have a medical emergency. You need to suit up and get out here as fast as possible with a med kit."

"What is the emergency?"

"Just get out here."

"I need to know what type of kit to bring."

"Someone EVA has fallen about fifty feet."

"Who is my contact?"

"Samantha Ansuri."

"Samantha, can you hear me?"

"Yes, doctor."

"I'm on my way to suit up. I'll be right there. Is the patient moving?"

"No, ma'am. She's on her back. She's not moving."

"Where are you?"

"I'm almost to ground level in the manlift."

"Do not move the patient, Samantha. Get me her suit number."

"Understood."

"Dumars to Easton."

"I'm still here, Andrea."

"We'll probably need half a dozen people and a makeshift body board. Do you understand? Oh, good, the suit techs are already here for me."

"I understand. I'll see you at the accident site."

Ansuri's voice cut in, "Doctor, she's suit number BB2875XKW. It's an EVA suit. It's not a Mars suit."

"BB2875XKW. Thank you, Samantha. As soon as my suit is powered up I'll patch in and take control of that suit."

I was still in my suit. I had to stop and think about depressurizing my suit immediately following re-pressurization. I stepped back into the Dome airlock and decided it would be safe to de-press.

Outside of the airlock I realized I didn't know where I was going. "Easton to Ansuri."

"Go ahead."

"Exactly where are you?"

"We are at Cargo 5. We were going up to fix the doors."

Dumars cut in. "How is she, Samantha? Is she moving?"

"I'm looking through her visor. She is unconscious, Doctor. She is not moving but I think she's breathing."

"Do not move her, Samantha. I'm in the airlock putting on my helmet. I'll be right there."

"Easton to all EVA teams. We need at least five people to group over at Cargo 5 immediately and we need one rover at New Dawn to pick up the doctor and the other to meet me on the way to Cargo 5."

There were several clicks on my comm indicating people had heard.

Outside the airlock I began a space-suited Mars run-waddle in the direction of Cargo 5.

"Samantha, does her suit still have pressure?"

Demars cut in, "I have her suit on my readout, Mark. She has steady pressurization, 6.6 pounds. Her respiration is shallow, her BP is high. We'll definitely need that body board."

"This is Prolen, Doctor. We have a habitat panel that will work as a body board. We're on our way with rover 2."

"Head directly to Cargo 5, Mr. Prolen. I'll get the Doctor."

Just as I started to get winded the second rover came up behind me. We threw sand into the air taking off.

"We've got to go pick up the Doctor. The other rover has the board."

"On it, Captain."

Two minutes later we met the Doctor bounding along with an escort. They loaded in.

"Where will we take her, Andrea?" I asked.

"We can't put her in that man basket and then hoist her up through the ship's ladderway. She's bound to have spinal injury. We've got to take her to the central dome."

"How will we get her out of the suit, Andrea?"

"We won't get her out of the suit, at least the torso. Thank God it's not a one-piece Mars suit, we'd have to cut the whole thing off. At least we'll be able to get her helmet, arms and legs off. We'll decide what needs to be cut then."

"Can you do body scans through a spacesuit?"

"Yes, with loss of definition, just what you don't want."

Ahead we saw the manlift lowered down beside Cargo 5. The other rover had already arrived. Several people circled the patient.

Dumars leapt out and almost fell from the lack of pliability in her suit. She hurried over, place both hands on the patient's visor to hold the head steady and stared down in.

She twisted around and looked at the rest of us. "Okay, we need to dig and slide that panel under her without moving her. Then a six-man lift if we can all fit in. We put her on the rover and then head for Dome 2 at a snail's pace. Everybody got that?"

It took us ten minutes to do it without budging the patient. The six-man lift worked then one person sitting in a back seat steadied the board next to the driver. We walked along in an odd off-world procession of spacesuits around the rover, all keeping one hand out to secure the board.

"Easton to James or Descard."

James responded, "We've been listening in, Mark. What do you need?"

"Organize a team to start transferring equipment from the medical lab to Dome 2. Doctor Dumars does not want the patient lifted into the ship. We'll need to make the transfer of the medical lab to Dome 2 a priority. She'll tell you what she needs."

Dumars cut in, "Make the scanning and X-ray equipment first on the list, Jeff. We also

273

may need to cut her suit torso off, so could you set something up to do that if we need to?"

"In progress, Doctor. Standing by for additional instructions."

At the airlock we somehow orchestrated the move inside without speaking. One man at either end of the board carefully moved her inside then came out. Dumars then entered and stood with her patient while they sealed and pressurized the airlock. The rest of us waited outside in silence as helpers inside removed her and transferred her to the mostly empty Medical Center.

I was the first into the airlock as soon as it was available along with three others. Inside the Dome I rushed my suit re-pressurization just a bit and hurried out of it as soon as possible. Still in my suit undergarment I hurried to the Med Lab.

There was at least an examination table. They had Collins on it with her helmet off. Dumars had stripped down to her suit liner and was lifting Collin's eyelids and peering in with a light. I had to bite my tongue not to ask.

Dumars finally spoke, "Yes, there is some concussion here. Jeff, are members of my staff on the way?"

"Two are out the door, Doctor," replied James.

Dumars said, "Okay, let's get her gloves off and see if we can unlock the suit and get the legs off without moving the spinal column."

The gloves were easy but the three of us had to maneuver to work on the suit torso and legs. We finally managed to hold the torso steady and uncouple the lower portion without turning the patient. A very slow, meticulous process lowered the suit bottom off her legs.

Dumars looked at me. "We're going to have to cut the rest off."

I tried not to wince. Another spacesuit lost.

"Dumars to James."

"Go ahead, Doctor."

"I need this suit torso cut off the patient. It will need to be cut through on both sides."

"We're on our way with a Dremel type of cutter, Doctor, but it will be a long, slow process."

"And how are you coming with my scanning equipment?"

"It's outside already, Doctor."

Dumars looked at me. "I'm going to start an IV. We'll use the left hand. Someone's got to hold the bag until a stand gets here."

I picked the nearest gawking Dome resident in plain clothes and motioned them to come.

"I have things I need to be doing," I said as an honest excuse.

Dumars replied, "I understand." She raised her voice, "Everyone else, it's time to clear this room."

I realized the crowd of Dome 2 residents had become large. I nodded to Dumars and help usher them out. Fortunately the exam room had a door that could be shut.

Samantha Ansuri was standing not far away, wet-eyed, still in her spacesuit, helmet on the floor by her feet. I went to her and looked around to be sure no one was nearby listening. Small groups of residents had formed here and there. They were all waiting for news.

"How is she? It's my fault I think," said Ansuri as I approached.

"I doubt that. Were you hurt at all?"

"No. I'm okay."

"What happened?"

"We were going up to work on the Cargo 5 doors. I'm certified to use the man lift, Laurel is not. I gave her the required safety lecture. We climbed in and clipped on. I started up. I didn't notice she had clipped onto the gate rail. Halfway up she must have been thinking about getting ready to get off and realized she was clipped to the sliding gate. She must have unclipped to switch over to a handrail. I noticed her unclipping. The rule is you cannot be moving in the manlift unless your safety line is attached, so I hit the stop on the controls. For some reason the manlift jerked violently like a seesaw. It threw both of us out of the carriage. I was still clipped on so I ended up hanging by my safety line but I watched Samantha fall backwards to the ground. It was the worst moment of my life. I was able to climb back in the carriage but it took everything I had. You know the rest."

"I don't see where you did not follow procedures, Samantha. I can't imagine any of us having done anything differently."

"But why were we thrown out?"

"My guess is the manlift was in just the right configuration, at just the right height and in the low Mars gravity the stopping motion was greatly exaggerated. Everything we do on Mars is a first-time experience. This problem will be now documented now so it doesn't happen to anyone else."

"You're sure this wasn't my fault?"

"It wasn't your fault but you're going to need to report to Dr. Bishop and let her help you with this. When you're up to it, write up the entire event just as you've told it to me. I'll need that."

"How is Laurel?"

"She is stable. They are moving equipment in to treat her. There's no reason right now to think she won't recover. Is your room here in Dome 2?"

"No. I'm in Dome 3."

"Are you sure you weren't hurt being thrown out of the carriage?"

"Just bumps and bruises."

"I'd like the Doctor to have a look at you when she's done with Laurel."

I searched the area and spotted a security officer helping out at the airlock. I caught his eye and waved him over.

"Officer, I want Doctor Dumars to check Samantha over when she's free. Could you find an empty room for Samantha to wait in and please stay with her?"

"Yes, sir. The Security office has furniture."

He picked up Ansuri's helmet and gestured her toward Security.

I turned in time to see the airlock opening and scanning equipment being moved in. It was time for me to set up communications here in my new office. I dearly wished the circumstances had been different. The first person to set foot on Mars was now in surgery.

Chapter 19

I sat in my office and stared out my plastic window at the main power stations and the Mars landscape beyond them. The work on Base Alpha had been delayed considerably by the accident. That didn't matter since we had been progressing at an astounding rate. We were actually still far ahead of schedule.

Collins was found to have a moderate concussion and three fractured vertebrae in her upper back but no detectable spinal cord damage. When the pressure on the brain had eased, Dumars awakened her. Her memory, speech and cognizance were all intact. She was apologetic. Using a traction device fabricated by one of the 3D printers she would be immobilized for several weeks. Her spacesuit had partially deflated on impact but then re-inflated itself almost instantly. It had somehow survived the fall but not the Med Lab.

In just three days all three Domes looked like they'd been lived in for years. There were posters on the walls, makeshift curtains here and there, paper plants that looked real and printed copies of The New Dawn Times Weekly in the community areas. It felt like one giant exhale of relief.

As usual my own room remained barren although I did inflate the bed and chair and put up the countertop. I did not have my closed-circuit sink yet nor my mini microwave. I'd probably be one of the last to get my mini fridge too. Bob Banabalas and the other IT guys had almost finished setting up our mainframe so the WiFi would come from Dome 2 instead of New Dawn. A few large screens had already gone up in the community areas. There were still occasionally wait times at the restroom facilities. Not all the units were up and running.

People were getting comfortable here. There had already been requests for EVA science missions. There was just one thing bothering me: Mick Pacal. Somehow through the entire Collins emergency I had not interacted with him. I had the feeling he was avoiding me.

Someone stuck their head in the open door. "Hey, you busy?" said Jeff James.

"Not at all, come on in. How'd you get by my secretary?"

"Now that's funny." He entered and sat.

"You guys have been extraordinary, have I mentioned that?"

James laughed and sat back. "I'll pass that on."

"What are we doing right now?"

"Mostly finishing jobs on the Domes and we're still moving equipment from the Cargo ships. We need to get our Dome freezer units set up so we can transfer some of the solid food out of Cargo 6 and into the mouths of the people."

"My God, that will be a day to remember."

"Expect excessive partying."

"Maybe we can make that the official moved-in celebration day."

"Great idea, Mark. There are a couple big operations coming up too that you know about, of course."

"The giant pancakes."

"Those're the ones now that Ansuri and Prolen have fixed the cargo doors."

I asked, "How did you talk Ansuri back into that manlift after what happened?"

"There was a clutch out of adjustment on that thing. They think it had something to do with the long-term exposure to the cold. Once she understood the problem was all mechanical she was okay with it."

"The woman has true grit as they say."

"We need to cut out a cross member between the Cargo 5 cargo doors just to get those pancake domes out of the ship."

"I haven't been thinking about those. Did the earthmovers actually finish laying out pads for them?"

"Yes, but we've walked and driven over them so many times we've got to redo them. No big deal."

I sat back and tried to imagine what was coming. "The recreational dome and the green house. That will be something. How long for those huge bases to unfold?"

"Six hours for each of them if it goes as planned."

"And we have the air already?"

"Yep, production has been ahead of estimates. And that reminds me, have the Bisleys bothered you recently?"

"Oh no."

"Get ready for it. They've hounded me twice about pulling compost out of cargo."

"Oh, God. Hide me."

"The deep well people are just as bad. They've barely moved in and they're all hyped up to get out there. They need the pressurized rover to do it, though, so you may be hearing moaning and groaning about the rover garage."

"Yeah, I was supposed to start in on that when the Collin's thing happened."

"Expect motivational support any time now."

I sat back and exhaled. "God, I need a drink."

A devious expression came over James. He leaned forward and looked around like someone with a secret. "That's another thing I need to tell you about. When the guys were searching Cargo 5 for the spacesuits they came across several crates that weren't on any manifest. They opened one to see what had gotten missed and you know what it was? Wine and hard liquor. Somebody got that by Inspection somehow. Five shipping cases of it. What do you want to do about it?"

"You're a great straight man, Jeff. I have a dozen different answers for that question. Do you think management actually did that on purpose or was it someone on this cruise who had inside contacts?"

"There's no way anybody got that stuff by Inspection unless they were very high up."

"So it was intentional. They just didn't want it to be advertised."

"That's my guess."

"We need to secure that stuff."

"You think?"

I laughed. "You'd better restrict access to Cargo 5 for now on."

"Already have."

"When we have our moved-in party we'll mysteriously release some of that stuff."

"There will be dancing."

I opened my mouth to say something about extra security when Paul Descard stuck his head through the door.

"Hey, are you in?"

"Yeah, Paul. Jeff and I were just planning a party."

"Is that because he told you about the contraband in Cargo 5?" Descard came in and sat.

I smiled. "That stuff is a blessing and a curse. You guys know that, right?" I replied.

Descard laughed. "More blessing than curse, I think. When's your party?"

I answered, "Undetermined at this point. We were also talking about the giant pancakes."

"Oh, yeah, those things scare even me. We know they're too big to handle but we're doing it anyway," replied Descard.

"The greenhouse has got to be huge," suggested James. "If all goes as planned we'll have another batch of people showing up in about two years. We'll need that thing."

"By the way, before I forget I stopped in to let you know the rover garage is up and can be used as soon as they finish assembling the pressurized rover, Mark."

"Are the spacesuits attached?" I asked.

"Yep, climb in, climb out. One piece, open the backpack to enter. What a trip," said Descard.

"Well that means I'll be having the deep well guys to deal with again. I guess I'll have to let them go scouting."

Descard looked over at James then back at me. His tone changed. "There's something else I stopped in to show you, Mark. Remember we had that conversation about conspiracy buffs and artificial objects on the Moon? Could you plug in this flash drive and put it up on the wall screen?"

I took the drive from him and plugged it in. It opened to a video file. I clicked *play*.

Two EVA people were walking the perimeter of the dirt pads for the next two domes. The person wearing the helmet cam we were watching looked over to see his counterpart pointing at the sky. There was a blurry swing around that stabilized to an image of the Martian mountains in the distance. It looked like there was a dark spec of dirt on the helmet cam lens but as we watched, the spec slowly moved from north to south. There was no detail to see on the spec and its shape was completely irregular but it moved in a straight line across our field of vision, then seemed to shrink and fade out of view. The three of us watched in silence.

"Want to run it again?" asked James.

We watched the strange effect a second time.

"What do you guys think?" asked Descard.

"You trying to say that was an artificial object?" asked James.

"I'm just asking what you guys think," replied Descard.

"It looked like a spec on the lens," added James.

"But it moved across that mountain range, Jeff," countered Descard.

"I can't argue that," replied James.

"Mark? What are your thoughts?" persisted Descard.

"I'll send it to Epstone and have it analyzed."

"Yeah, but what do *you* think?" asked Descard.

"I think there's not enough information to form a conclusion. Maybe it was something orbital."

"Did that look low orbit to you, Jeff?" asked Descard.

"I'm drawing a blank, Paul. I have no idea what I just saw."

"As I said, I'll pass this file onto Earth and we'll see what they come up with."

Descard rose. "Well, that's all I had. Anything you need, Mark?"

"I'm sure there will be, Paul."

The three of us laughed. Descard headed out the door.

"So I'll let you know when we can't put the giant pancakes off any longer." James stood.

"Are we really putting them off?" I asked.

"Only psychologically," replied James. He gave a half salute and left.

I turned in my chair and looked out the window at the Martian sky. The huge recreation dome and greenhouse dome were designed to go just beyond the three central power stations out there. Those domes would block my view of the horizon and sky. Base Alpha was designed around those power stations. It was meant to expand outward around them. The oxygen, hydrogen and water that would come from the deep wells would make that expansion possible.

I tried to envision those two big domes. There would be no airlocks in the recreation dome but two interconnect tunnels would attach it to both Dome 1 and the Greenhouse. The Greenhouse would have airlocks for the purpose of bringing in Martian soil and minerals. It would also have an interconnect tunnel to Dome 3, completing the first Base Alpha pressurized circle. People would jog that circle or just walk it for recreation.

"Anyone home?"

I swiveled to find Mick Pacal looking in the open door. A spike of tension shot up inside me but I contained it. "Have a seat, Mick. How's it going?"

"Thought I should stop in since we haven't resumed department meetings yet and it's been too crazy around here to try to catch you not involved in something."

"Isn't that the truth."

"I haven't had an update on Collins. How's she doing?"

"She actually fine, considering. She says the traction is punishment for her not being more careful. She's not blaming anyone or anything but herself."

"I was always bothered by some of those certs. Months on a starship where they couldn't put in refresher time on the machines, then out the door in a strange environment immediately using them for work. It always seemed like an accident waiting to happen to me."

"And as it so often is, there were several things that contributed to what happened. She clipped onto the wrong rail, the lift arms were at a critical angle and the cold had apparently affected a clutch system. Reminds me of the findings on many an aircraft incident."

Pacal looked out the window for a second. "That's right, you were a test pilot before becoming a rock jock, weren't you?"

"Hours of sheer boredom with moments of stark terror."

We both laughed.

"I read up on your background, of course. It was required for Security. You had to eject once, too, didn't you?"

"It's amazing how much damage a single bird can do to a turbine blade."

"How high were you?"

"I was just coming off the runway. That's where you usually meet up with birds. I made ninety feet I think I recall. There was shrapnel damage to the hydraulics. At least I didn't have to wonder about bailing. There was no choice."

"You bailed at ninety feet?"

"Didn't matter. I was in a zero-zero ejection seat, certified to safely eject from zero feet altitude and zero airspeed. I could have been parked on the runway."

"Any injuries?"

"Scratches from the bushes I landed in."

"A day in the life."

"Yep."

Pacal stood and went to the window. He stood looking out at Mars. "Have you heard anything else from Earth on Bateman?"

"Not a word. Have you?"

"No, nothing. And we haven't had any related incidents that I know of. It's like the whole thing never happened."

"No. It's not like that."

"You know what I mean."

"Someone else was involved. There's no getting around that."

Pacal sat back down and eyed me with a discerning stare. "If only we could have found his laptop or flash drive. There might have been something there."

"You keep assuming there was a flash drive."

"Everybody's got a flash drive or two."

"What would we find if he had, I wonder?" I asked.

"Probably just pictures and letters home that would mean nothing anyway."

I said, "Maybe he'll slip up and we'll still get him."

"Or maybe he's already slipped up and is still trying to cover his tracks."

"Maybe."

"Well anyway, I should let you know we've set up a new Security schedule. We have officers in all three domes in the security stations. We still have one person stationed in New Dawn. The comm emergency channel is operational. Let me know when you finally decide to power down New Dawn. They must be near to finishing in there."

"Yes, just about done moving stuff out. I'll let you know."

Pacal stood. "Nice talking to you, Mark. Sorry I didn't stop by sooner."

"It's fine, Mick. Keep me posted."

He waved and headed out the door.

It had been an unsettling conversation. In fact, it bothered the hell out of me. I already knew he was lying. Part of our exchange suggested he was fishing to see how much I knew. Then the reference to Bateman's flash drive. He wasn't guessing about the flash drive. He knew there was one. Next there was the suggestion it contained letters and pictures that would mean nothing. The letters on Bateman's drives were gibberish that meant nothing unless you spotted the code. Was Pacal telling me he already knew what was on that flash drive? His last exchange was just as telling. He'd suggested the suspect had already made mistakes and was still trying to cover them up. That sounded like first-hand knowledge to me.

It almost felt like Pacal knew I had the flash drive. How could he know? Banabalas gave me his word he would keep quiet about it. As precarious as that seemed, I trusted Banabalas. The only way Pacal could know I possessed the flash drive was if he'd been spying on me. I'd kept the thing close but I'd used it on a computer. If I was right about this it meant he and I were in that age old game of knowing each other knew with neither of us willing to admit it.

Maybe I'd be in a better position if I confronted him. Knight to Queen three, check. That would force his hand. The problem was, I didn't know what the game was. Why did Bateman think Pacal was on to him? What was Bateman up to? Why was Pacal stalking him? Why was Pacal keeping it all a secret?

I had to have answers before I forced the issue. I had to know what the consequences would be. No one else had been attacked since Bateman. There had been no sabotage that I knew of. The age-old Cape Kennedy motto came to mind; *if it works, don't fix it*.

Chapter 20

Big Domes Day arrived. The mechanics and engineers who make up transfer crews have always been the coolest people I know. I've watched their kind move huge solid fuel rocket motors on kneel down transporters like it was an everyday job, which for them it almost was. Lay it down, air pallet the thing onto a KDT, drive down the road at a snail's pace, then air pallet the thing back off and stand it up with an erector. All with live solid fuel just waiting for an igniter spark. I've never seen these guys so much as blink.

But even these hero-types were taking a cautious approach to off-loading the greenhouse dome. We'd had a very sober pre-op meeting. People listened intently. The engineering slide show kept everyone's attention. There weren't the slapstick foul mouthed jokes I was used to afterward. But I could tell they were sure they could do it.

They had cut out a cross member support to get the thing out of the ship. We had twenty of our twenty-two space suits in use. The crowd bothered me but there was a good chance we would need that many hands. Two men in spacesuits inside the ship helped guide the package to the expanded cargo door. It was up to the crane to drag it out. We were repeatedly assured that when the full weight of it fell onto the crane cables, the crane would hold.

We all stood well back. As the fat gray wheel emerged one hundred and twenty feet up, the two hundred-foot guide ropes slid out and unwound to the ground. A few minutes later the big wheel rolled on its flat side out of the opening and stretched the crane cabling to its fullest as it dropped and dangled in the thin air. It began to lower in jerks. Two mechanics on the ground approached with the greatest of care, grabbed the guide ropes and backed away to get tension. They held the big load away from the ship and helped guide it to the surface. Two feet from the ground the big wheel had to be positioned just right so it would lay down away from the ship. Ever so slowly the remote crane operator set it down on Martian soil. There was cheering over the comm and gestures of victory from the suits.

Cables were attached to special tow rings on the folded dome. Two earthmovers were positioned to receive the cables. Along the carefully prepared path the earthmovers dragged the big pile of disks at a snail's pace. It took two hours to reach the pad and another hour of manipulation to get the stack centered and orientated. The Bisleys had to be continually asked to get out of the way. Time was taken out for more cheering. The Greenhouse was ready to unfold and inflate.

I hadn't planned on it but by being there I got sucked into running the power conduit. After a long day of hook ups and checks we set the greenhouse pad to unfold and stood way back to watch. It was very much like watching paint dry except occasionally a large wall would

290

stand up and flop over. A unanimous vote was made to leave the recreation dome for tomorrow.

It took a full two weeks to place the recreation dome, fully inflate both, and set and couple the interconnect tunnels. On the day we were scheduled to unlock the Dome 1 emergency pressure door that opened to the Recreation Dome access tunnel, seventy-five of us were crowded into Dome 1 waiting for it. Six others were already on the other side of the door performing the certifications. The crowd noise was deafening. The mood was wonderful. The Bisleys had done their best to be first in line but their smaller stature left them submerged in the crowd.

When the door rolled open it was like spiritual decompression. The human flood rushed into the tunnel and out into the huge interior of the recreation center. There were cables scattered on the floor everywhere, no furniture installed, no equipment unpacked, but the expanse of it was enough to generate appropriate exclamations of, "Wow!" To the Bisleys' dismay, much of the hoard continued into the greenhouse connector and walked among the empty planting barriers that had erected automatically within the dome. A small stream of uplifted people continued ahead through the final corridor and back into Dome 3.

That evening we set up refreshment tables in each dome, with impressively large bowls of punch and solid foods defrosted from Cargo 6. Andrea got her ice cream. It was quickly discovered that the punch was spiked causing its popularity to suddenly skyrocket, so much so it would have taken Christ to keep the bowls filled. As Descard had predicted there was music and dancing. A few unexpected couples were discovered in other people's rooms. I woke up later in Andrea's room.

It took a full day to clean up but the population seemed quite sedate about it. Some people were late for their shifts. Nobody cared.

Martian life had become normal.

I sat in my office and through my open door watched a smaller sun rise in the sky. My laptop screen had too many request icons on it. We had two open rovers, one pressurized rover and a second pressurized rover being assembled. I was realizing the allotment had not been enough. We'd anticipated that during planning but starship space requirements had forced it to be so. We'd been lucky to fit the four in.

Amanda Bishop strolled in the door. "Hello, hero." She sat and smiled.

"I'm no hero."

"You were last night."

"They put in my coffee machine. You want coffee?"

"Oh, God yes. Any comfort food or drink will be accepted."

I poured and appraised her. She looked energized and online. She took the coffee with a nod and tested it. "Yum."

"So are you just here for moral support?" I asked.

"No, I'm good, actually. I'm getting some inquiries about when will the Base Alpha Council be set up."

"The sooner the better as far as I'm concerned."

"You and me both."

I poured myself a cup and sat. "It wouldn't take much, would it?"

"Their chambers would need to be arranged. They'd need those small offices to have tiny desks. Then it would just be each department nominating a person to sit on the council and you and I and Dumars counting the nominations."

"After which the Base Alpha science missions and expansions would be managed by the council. Hallelujah!" I added.

Bishop stuck her head in the door. "Along with disagreements and violations."

"Let's do it then!" I added gleefully.

"You got people to set up the offices?"

"Consider me motivated to find some."

"You'll become like royalty. You'll be an emperor with no power." Bishop leaned against the door and laughed.

I nodded enthusiastically. "No power. That sounds good."

"What was the name I once heard you use; Captain Dunsel?"

"Very funny, but I'll still be useful."

"To who? Andrea?"

"Oh boy."

Dumars stifled a laugh.

"Sorry. Couldn't resist." Bishop stepped in and snatched my coffee cup. "I'll return your cup as soon as you tell me council office space is ready."

"I do not need any extra inspiration."

She laughed and headed out the door. Andrea followed her, talking.

I went back to the requests. Too many asking for the pressurized rover. People coming up with creative reasons to ask for one. The deep well people were out in it right now. I looked out my mostly dome-blocked window and wondered how far out they were and what they were seeing, thinking I'd love to take one on a joy ride myself.

A small tinge of fear arose within me. I caught sight of the Bisleys heading for my door.

They stopped just outside and Mr. Bisley looked in. "Captain, we just wanted to stop by and say thank you for the early delivery of our compost. We've already begun mapping our portion of the greenhouse. Mr. James said you ordered a quick delivery for us. We just wanted to say thank you. We promise you Mars-grown food at the earliest possible date."

"My pleasure, sir. Keep up the good work."

They waved and went on. I breathed a sigh of relief.

"Shaw to Easton."

"Go ahead, Brent."

"We just got an emergency call from the survey team. They've had an accident. They were on a ridge and the ground gave way. One member slid or fell into a ravine. She is trapped and hurt. The second team member has no way to get down to her."

"I'll be in on this one, Brent. Have you recalled the other rovers?"

"Yes and we have maintenance setting up rope and cable to go with you. I've notified Security. They're sending someone."

"I'll call Dumars. We'll meet at the Dome 2 forward airlock asap."

"I'll have you set up there. Shaw out."

"Easton to Dumar."

"Yes, Mark?"

"Medical emergency. Meet me at the airlock immediately."

"Is it another fall?"

"Yes. This one needs rescue."

"On my way."

We needed Mars suits this time and the Maintenance crew knew that. They had four suits on racks open and ready to go in the short time it took me to get there. I was climbing in as Andrea arrived with her bag.

As they closed my backpack and the suit began to pressurize, the lead mechanic looked at me through my visor and held up his test mike. "We've already set the rope and cable into the airlock, Captain. Did you hear that okay?"

"Comm is good," I replied.

As I checked my readouts the third member of our party arrived for suit up. It was Pacal. We exchanged a wary glance. He stripped down and climbed in his suit without speaking.

The airlock time was quick but still excruciating. We couldn't send people already outside to do the rescue. They had time on their suits and we might need all we could get.

The rover was waiting. We slung the rope, cable and a rescue pack in and kicked sand spinning out. Pacal was beside me, Andrea in the back fussing with her med kit.

"What is the condition of the patient?" she asked.

"Easton to Shaw."

"Go ahead, Captain."

"We are en route. Would you set up a private channel between us and survey team so the Doctor can speak with them?"

It took a moment for Shaw to answer. "Okay, you're set up."

"Go ahead, Andrea," I said.

"Doctor Dumars to the survey team. Please respond."

"Greg Mathews here, Doctor. She is at the bottom of the ravine but is not responding to my calls. She has been moving but I think she's only semiconscious. Her right leg is underneath a large rock and it doesn't look good."

Shaw cut in, "I have her suit SN number, Doctor, from the airlock log. HHW73976PU."

"Thank you, Mr. Shaw," replied Dumars.

"You using the Mars positioning system?" asked Pacal.

I nodded. "Yes, and Mathews switched on their transponder so we have both."

"What the hell were they doing up on a ridge? I thought they were supposed to be surveying the plain for drilling sites?"

"I have her suit," interrupted Dumars. "Shallow respiration, rapid pulse, low BP. We need to get there."

I kept the pedal down. I added, "They're using the pressurized rover, Andrea, so they're in the hard-shell suits. That suit should have been really good protection."

"I don't like the BP, Mark."

We pressed on. It took fifteen minutes for the ridgeline to come into view. The ride got bumpy. I had to avoid large rock outcroppings. We could see their rover in the distance. I was driving at a fairly dangerous speed. My two riders were paying close attention.

We skidded to a stop at their vehicle. A trail in the sand led up the side of a hill. Pacal and I hoisted rope and cable over our shoulders and caught up to Dumars skip-running with her bag. It was a strange feeling climbing the hill in low gravity. It was steep but less difficult than it should have been. At the crest we saw Mathews waving off to our left. We hurried on.

The ravine was a good seventy feet deep. She was down there on her back, one lower leg covered by stone. Her arms were moving periodically but there was no voice communication.

"Maybe her comm is damaged," said Pacal.

"Her suit telemetry is five by five, so I doubt that," replied Dumars. "I've got to get down there immediately."

"Maybe I should just go down and try to set her up to be lifted out," said Pacal. "What can you do for her in a spacesuit anyway?"

"No. I need to get down there. There's damage to that leg. It needs to be immobilized."

"I'll go down with the Doctor to free her and set her up. When Andrea has her secured I'll send her up. I'll guide her as long as I can while you guys pull her up. Let's tie off these ropes."

I set up Andrea's suit for the descent with loving care. The entire ridge face was loose dirt. There would be no climbing. I went over the edge first so I could watch Andrea come down. I had to keep checking to be sure we weren't kicking more dirt down onto the patient. There was a chance of causing a new landslide and covering her over completely.

The bottom of the ravine was loaded with too many large and small rocks. It made stepping in the suit difficult. Andrea slid down next. I helped her unhook and followed her to the patient. The suit name patch said, Jemison. For some reason I remembered her full name; Eileen Jemison.

"This is Eileen Jemison, Andrea."

Dumars was on her knees staring into Jemison's visor. She fished in her bag for a light and pointed it at Jemison's eyes.

"Damn it. No dilation. Okay, Mark. Let's get this rock off her. No, wait. Let's set her up to lift right out as soon as I immobilize the leg. Mr. Pacal, can you and Mathews pull us both out at once?"

"I don't think so, Doctor. We'd be risking a rough ride for your patient."

"Okay then. As soon as we're ready, we'll get her up and out as fast as we can. Then get me up there fast. I suspect she has a compound fracture and is bleeding in the suit. I need her and me in that pressurized rover as fast as possible, and as soon as we're in one of you puts the pedal to metal to get us back for a transfusion. Got it?"

"We understand, Doctor."

Andrea looked at me. "So we set up her rope and when she's ready to lift only then do we remove the rock, got it?"

"I understand."

"And Mark, we need to lift this rock straight up, no jockeying it from side to side. Straight up and off the leg. Okay?"

"We can do that."

We tied Jemison off and took the best positions we could on either side of the two-foot rectangular stone. Andrea counted down from three and we lifted it off. From where I lifted, the sight of Andrea reminded me of one of those stories where a ninety-pound woman lifts a car off a kid to save him. It felt like she took more of the stone's weight than I did.

We pitched it away. There was a groan from Jemison. Andrea dove for the leg and unfolded a splint from her bag. She pulled a fat roll of tape out and taped the splint.

"Okay, get going!" She waved at Pacal.

We guided Jemison for as long as we could. To our relief it was a quick extraction but Jemison was no longer moving. Pacal and Mathews were gone for five or six minutes, then returned

"We left her in the docking station waiting for you, to save time," said Pacal. "Here comes the rope."

I tied Andrea off and watched the ascent. The threesome disappeared from the ridge peak.

There was a choice of large stones to sit on. I chose one, sat, and waited. It took a moment for me to put away my concern for Jemison before I could look around to see where I had ended up. This was a big, oblong-shaped crater. The far end was too far to walk to had I even wanted to, although there were cave entrances in the walls I would like to have explored. There were naturally formed pathways through the crater floor that would have set Descard off suggesting artificiality. If this really was a crater it had a very strange feel to it, something I could not put my finger on.

I leaned backward and looked up at the seventy feet to the ridge top. Still no one there. Suddenly my male ego kicked in and I made up my mind I would not call for them. Concern for Jemison took over.

"How are you doing, Andrea?"

The comm squelched on but I all I heard was a grunt. Finally Andrea answered. "I'm climbing inside; Mathews is docked. We'll pressurize on the way. He will drive while I get her out of the suit."

"You're going to take her out of the suit by yourself?"

"There's no other choice. I have to stop the bleeding."

"Take Pacal with you. Send someone back for me."

"No way, Mark. There could be more slides at any time. We could have trouble getting to you. I can get her out. Mathews will stop if we need to. No way we're leaving you."

I sat on my rock and stewed. "Okay, geologist Dumars."

There were faint clouds in the sky passing by. The only thing missing from my being in Death Valley on Earth was scrub brush. I waited and tried to imagine the hell going on inside that pressurized rover.

"Dumars to the Med Lab."

"We are patched in, Andrea. This is Doctor Davies. We are fully aware of your situation."

Dumars' voice was shaky from the rough rover ride. "Set up for a blood transfusion. Have it ready to go immediately. It's going to be close. Do you know her type?"

"She's AB plus."

"Well, you better find an AB plus volunteer really fast."

"I'm AB plus Andrea. I'm already getting set up."

"We'll be setting the leg and we will need an implant from the 3D printer."

"Understand. And there is concussion?"

"I am guessing it is moderate."

"We are standing by and ready, Andrea."

It started to seem like a long time for Pacal to not have returned. Then it finally dawned on me; I was trapped in a ravine and my only hope for rescue was a man who I suspected of murder, someone who had been lying to me throughout the trip. I asked myself, "How did you manage to get into this situation?"

I leaned back and looked up. Still no Pacal. Once again, I refused to call. The male ego is sometimes supreme. I got up and walked around to stretch my legs. The ravine wall really was all loose sand and dirt as far as I could see. Climbing would be like swimming in a spacesuit. Maybe we were in one of those manly contests where he was waiting up there, trying to force me to ask for his help.

Not gonna do it.

I checked my levels. Plenty of suit time left. Outside air temp minus 76. Nippier down in these craters, I guess.

Something hit me on the head and fell on my shoulder.

Rope.

I looked up to see Pacal leaning over. "Sorry it took so long, Mark. I don't think I can pull you out alone. It took everything we had to get Jemison up. So I repositioned the rover and attached the rope to the cable reel. You hook on and I'll use the rover."

"Sounds good to me. Easy on the pedal."

"Yeah, you'll have to tell me faster or slower. I'll keep it in turtle mode to start."

I wrapped myself in rope, took a position I thought I could keep and motioned him ready. It took several minutes before the slack in the rope began to pull up. I braced like a Martian water skier and fell into the dirt as the drag up began.

"That's about right, Mick."

"Okay. Tell me when you're over the edge."

After skidding over a few large rock surfaces, and leaving deep body trenches in the sand, I reached the peak. "That's it. Hold it."

We rode back to Base Alpha mostly in silence. In the newly opened parking garage I climbed out and waited for the place to pressurize.

"Thanks for the lift, Mick."

"Okay. You owe me a drink I think."

"I'll see what I can do."

Chapter 21

Andrea showed up in her room just before 3:00 A.M. She was dragging. She was still wearing blue scrubs and there were blood stains here and there. I handed her a bourbon in a short glass with ice from the community food court. She raised an eyebrow but accepted it quickly. She plopped down on the sleeper couch, drank the whole thing and let her head fall back. I took the glass and refilled it.

She looked at me for sympathy. "You know, we arranged all the unassigned rooms to adjoin the Med Lab so they could be used as long-term care facilities. The way it's going we may need more damn rooms."

"My room's right nearby. Maybe I'll have to give it up."

Andrea cast me a narrow stare. She stood, came to me and draped her arms over my shoulders. "Oh, but where would you sleep then, Captain?"

I wrinkled my brow. "Yeah, the cat would be out of the bag then."

She sipped her drink. "The chicken would have flown the coop."

"Our gooses would be cooked?"

"The van rocking like crazy in the church parking lot."

I winced. "Whoa, I think we've about covered it."

"I have more."

We fell to the couch and bounced a bit. She spilled her drink but did not care. After a long, exaggerated kiss she smiled approval to me.

"Sorry, but I have to ask, what's Jemison's condition?"

"Stable, finally. It was like a jugglers' circus in there. It was like the Hoover dam springing leaks everywhere with us putting our fingers in them, and I mean literally."

"What's the prognosis?"

"She'll be fine, I think. She was talking before I left. Dilation returned to normal. No permanent damage but low BP and concussion do not get along well, if you know what I mean. It was too damn close."

"You are an angel."

"You know I'm not but there must have been one or two around today. Why were they up on that ridge?"

"I'll be asking that tomorrow."

"Are you here for the night?"

"With your permission, ma'am."

"Stupid question."

The next morning I sat in my office waiting for Mathews to report. I was trying to look stern but the previous night had left me with a frozen, stupid half-smile on my face. Plus I had narrowly escaped losing someone yesterday. Her suit was really messed up but the suit guys would disassemble it and probably replace the right leg joints and fabric. So, all in all I had squeaked by again.

Mathews stuck his head in the open door and entered. I motioned him to close the door and sit.

"Okay, I'm listening, Greg."

"I know the project map envelope was of the flat plains area but when we got to the border we saw something we weren't expecting. We saw what we believed to be recurring slope lineae. You probably know there's always been a big debate those things are caused by sand, not water, but to us it clearly looked like liquid water flow. You know, they theorize this can happen when the temps are above minus twenty-three degrees Celsius. So of course we're out there looking for water, right? We felt we needed to see if we could find the actual source and photograph it."

"So exactly whose idea was it to go climbing without gear or approval?"

He hemmed and hawed in his seat. "I would have to say that I persuaded Jemison to take a look."

"Okay then, who was the first one up the hill to fetch a pail of water? You'd better be honest because there's probably ways to verify what you say, Jack."

He squirmed in his chair again. "Well, Jemison may have beat me up to the ridgeline."

"So it was actually Jemison's idea to make the climb."

"Well, it was kind of mutual."

"Okay, so here's what we're going to do. You are not allowed to visit Jemison or call her until after she is well enough to file her report. I've been told she may be able to dictate that maybe later today. You go write your report right now and email it to me. If your report doesn't match hers, there's going to be trouble. So you'd better be perfectly accurate in your report."

"I'm truly sorry about this, Captain."

"To be honest, Mr. Mathews, if I ask myself would I have gone up that hill if it had been me I'm not sure what the answer would be. I'll be slating that area for further study."

He gave me a look of surprise. I motioned to the door. He scooted out.

Before I could reset my brain two more guests entered. The lead was an attractive blond woman. Her flight suit label said, "Cursrick". She entered and stood at my desk.

"Yes, Ms. Cursrick. Good morning, or is it lunch yet?"

"Captain, I feel it's my duty to report something even though my teammate thinks I shouldn't."

I glanced over her shoulder at a slightly long-haired gentleman by the name of Raiken. "Please do proceed, Ms. Cursrick. There's no harm in reporting something."

She remained standing and proceeded. "We were out on geology mapping. We went quite a ways out. We were collecting samples when I looked up at a hill in the distance and someone was standing on it looking back at us."

I took a moment to digest the implications. "Did you see this, Mr. Raiken?"

Raiken seemed to take on a don't-ask-me persona. "Yes and no, Captain. It was only visible for a second or two."

"This person, whoever it was, turned and disappeared over the hill," added Cursrick.

"And you say you saw that, Mr. Raiken?"

"I think it was a dark shadow from some rock or something and as the light changed it simply faded away," said Raiken.

"I saw it clearly, Captain. It was a person," insisted Cursrick.

"Can you describe this person?"

"No. I could not make out any details. It was like a cloaked person. It was just a silhouette."

"You mean, not in a spacesuit?"

"They may have had a suit underneath whatever they were wearing."

"Did you check to see if another EVA team was out there at the same time?"

Cursrick replied, "Yes. All the other rovers were involved in the ground penetrating radar work or closing down New Dawn."

"So who could it have been?" I asked.

"I don't know, Captain, but I saw someone. Maybe the Chinese or the Russians have some secret mission here we don't know about. Don't you think we should check on this?"

Raiken looked at me and rolled his eyes.

"Ms. Cursrick, I never doubt my people. Easton to Pacal."

"Pacal here, Mark."

"Could you come over for a minute?"

"On my way."

I fidgeted with my coffee cup as they stood waiting. Pacal walked in and looked at me questioningly.

"Mick, Ms. Cursrick here feels certain she saw someone standing on a hill overlooking their work area but we had no rovers out there during that period. She's concerned we may have intruders we're not aware of."

"Did you both see it?" asked Pacal.

"Yes and no," answered Raiken.

"You must know in this type of environment there are tricks of light playing constantly."

"It wasn't a trick of light," persisted Cursrick.

"And you checked and none of our people could have been out there?"

"Yes," replied Cursrick.

"Well, this shouldn't be difficult to resolve. If you give me those coordinates we can take a run out there and check. In this sand if there *was* someone they would have had to leave tracks."

"I would like to go," said Cursrick.

"Fine. I'll let you know when a rover becomes available," answered Pacal.

The threesome turned and left.

I breathed a sigh of relief, got up and refilled my coffee and sat back down to contemplate life on Mars.

Amanda Bishop charged through the open door with Bob Banabalas in tow.

"Captain, Mr. Banabalas is up to his wild stories again. He is telling people Cargo 6 is going to fall over and crash to the ground." Bishop sounded desperate as though all of her psychology had been in vain.

Banabalas nodded his head energetically. He held up one finger in exclamation. "That's not entirely true, Captain. Doctor Bishop is the only one I've told."

I sat back under Bishop's glare and Banabalas' enthusiasm. "Bob, do you really think Cargo 6 is going to fall over?"

"There's no thinking about it. I've done the calculations. According to the Cargo 6 specifications, as loaded if it achieves an eight-point-two degree off-vertical tilt it *will* fall over."

"What makes you think it will tilt?"

"It is tilting, Captain. It's already begun to lean to the east."

"How do you know?"

"I was up on the EVA comm tower to reset the antenna amplifier system and looking out over the Cargo ships and the horizon I noticed Cargo 6 leaning."

"You climbed the EVA comm tower?"

"Oh, yes, that was a blast. Way better than the climbing walls in school. You're attached to a safety line so there's no danger. They didn't want to replace the amplifier so I volunteered to go up and do the reset there."

"Bob, why didn't you come to me with this?"

"I was on my way to tell you about it when I ran into Doctor Bishop. I haven't told anyone else."

"I'm impressed, Bob. But are you sure Cargo 6 is leaning or are you just guessing?"

"The Earth update said Cargo 6 landed with true vertical. I drew out an inclinometer from supply. That first day I measured it Cargo 6 was three degrees off vertical. It has gained another degree every day for the past two days. It's now five degrees off and progressing."

Bishop interrupted, "Mark, you don't really believe this do you? It's a very detailed story. It fits the pattern perfectly."

"Amanda, if Bob says Cargo 6 is leaning, I believe I have to go out and check it out."

Banabalas looked at Bishop. "The Captain is a close friend, Doctor."

Bishop looked slighted. "I'm your close friend too, Bob."

"Yeah, but he believes me."

"You still have your inclinometer signed out, Bob?" I asked.

"Yes, sir."

"Well, grab it and let's suit up."

"I'm coming too," said Bishop.

We suited up and waited quietly in the airlock. We exited, took a good vantage point and stood staring at Cargo 6 in the distance. As best I could tell it did look like it was leaning. I took the inclinometer from Bob, figured it out, and sighted Cargo 6.

It was leaning just over six degrees.

"Easton to Descard."

There was a sixty-second wait.

"Go ahead, Captain."

"Paul, please suit up and meet us outside the Dome 2 airlock immediately."

"Really, Mark? I'm eating real food."

"Immediately."

"On my way."

Descard joined us several minutes later. He stood with the inclinometer staring at Cargo 6.

"I'll be damned! I never spotted it! This is not good, Mark."

"So it really is leaning?" asked Bishop.

"Fuck. This is really bad," said Descard to himself though it came over the comm. He looked at me with foreboding. "Nobody can go near that thing, Mark. It could lay over at any time. We may need to just let it crash down and then scramble around to recover the food as best we can."

"Easton to Pacal."

"Pacal here. Go ahead, Captain."

"We need an exclusion zone set up around Cargo 6 immediately. At least a thousand feet."

"What's the problem, Captain?"

"Cargo 6 may fall over."

"I'll take care of it. Pacal out."

"Any better ideas at all, Paul?" I asked.

"This is just bad," replied Descard.

"How about we get an earthmover to slide its shovel under that leg and lift the thing back to vertical?" I suggested.

"Won't do it, Mark. As heavy as it is the back of the earthmover would raise up before the starship would lift."

"There is a way," said Banabalas.

We all twisted in our suits to look at him.

"The earthmover can't do it alone but the earthmover and the crane combined could lift it," said Banabalas.

Descard seemed to forget who he was talking to. "There'd be no way to keep the load on the shovel and the tension on the crane cable constant."

Banabalas suddenly seemed at his best. "They're both remote control vehicles Mr. Descard. A subroutine could be used to monitor and manage load on both vehicles."

"I'm not a programmer. I don't know if that would work," said Descard.

"I *am* a programmer. I know it would work," answered Banabalas.

Descard looked at me. "If that thing reaches eight degrees it *will* fall."

"Eight-point-two degrees," added Banabalas.

We all turned again to look at Banabalas, wondering who we were really talking to.

I said, "Well, the worst that could happen is we damage an earthmover. How long to set this up?"

Descard looked at Banabalas. "How long to write the subroutine?"

"An hour to write it but we'd have to test it."

"The rest of the day to set everything up for the test. Then several hours tomorrow to position the equipment. And, there's one part you won't like," said Descard.

"I'm listening."

"One man will need to go in to hook the crane up to the earthmover shovel. That'll take say twenty minutes."

"I'll do it," I replied.

"It can't be you, Mark. It's got to be somebody with heavy equipment experience. I could probably do it, but the maintenance guys are better than me."

"Will any of them volunteer?"

"They probably all will."

By the end of the day they'd done it. They'd proved the lift could be done with the earthmover and crane synced. As Descard had predicted the maintenance people had argued about who would do the hook up. They all wanted to go. In the end we allowed two to plan for the challenge in case one of them got into trouble. One mechanic to drive the rover, the other to hook up. In the meantime security set up a continuous watch on Cargo 6 and they documented the increasing angle every hour.

Sunup brought a very disturbing realization. Cargo 6 was leaning a full ten degrees. Heated arguing broke out between the structural engineers. They insisted that deviation was impossible. The rocket body should have fallen. We all stood in spacesuits in front of Dome 2 and wondered at the spectacle. There was no choice but to go ahead with the operation.

With the second earthmover standing by with a bucket of rocks and dirt to fill in the sinkhole, joystick operations in spacesuits brought in earthmover 1 and the crane. There was a long period of very slow heavy equipment dance. It took two hours to line up them up. We held our breath as earthmover 1 dug down and placed its bucket under the sinking landing leg of Cargo 6. With the crane positioned, we winced as the guys went in for the hookup. They were very good and very quick.

With all our eggs in that basket the lift began. The only one who didn't appear concerned was Banabalas. He seemed to have taken on a John Wayne persona.

The nose of Cargo 6 began to inch back upward. Three hours later the ship was vertical. We continued to watch, disbelieving it had worked as earthmover 2 gingerly slid rocks into the depression.

When it was over we went our separate ways, ignoring the structural engineers who were still trying to get someone to believe them that Cargo 6's lean had been impossible.

Chapter 22

The New Dawn Times Weekly

IT Tech Bob Banabalas saves Cargo 6!

Admittedly, the article was fun to read. Banabalas had bravely scaled the EVA tower in a desperate attempt to repair the communications antenna. During that daring undertaking while perched high above Base Alpha he had spotted the telltale signs of a calamity beginning to unfold with Cargo 6. His alertness had saved the Base Alpha frozen food supply. The story went on to review Bob's history and his vision for Base Alpha.

A subsequent article farther down the page read:

Celebration Organizers Insist No alcohol In Punch Bowls

Captain Easton Has No Comment

We planned to gather in the new council chambers at the horseshoe-shaped table made from former New Dawn habitat panels. It was an informal update meeting. The meetings that followed would be by the newly nominated Base Alpha Council members.

I was early. Only Jeff James was present. He looked up as I approached. "Mark, we put in a closed-circuit water and coffee machine. You want something?"

"I'll get it." I poured my coffee and sat with him.

"It's another starship dawn out there. I love the way the starships turn a gold tint in that light."

"How you doin', Jeff?"

"I'm okay. You know, I'm glad I'm not in solid waste management. I mean the system is incredible and all. The flat packs of waste come on that cart, no one ever has to even touch them. They're inserted into the processor which dissolves the pack and mixes the whole thing with Martian sand and other stuff and it comes out the other end as beautiful compost. Doesn't look or smell anything at all like what it was. From an engineering standpoint it is a miraculous system. But still, I'm glad I'm not in solid waste management."

"You know you're going to be eating food grown in that."

"Yeah, but when someone hands me a plate of French fries I don't think I'll care."

We both laughed.

James said, "Have you sat and watched the stuff going on in the recreation dome?"

"Just passed through so far."

"It's a riot. You need to take some time and check that out. When the real pros are playing ping pong it's so fast it looks just like it does on earth, but when the amateurs step up the balls are all over the dome. And the quarter court basketball, anybody can make the jump to dunk it but the rebounds off the backboard go crazy high and long. Every sport activity going on over there is like psychedelic."

"I'll have to call it up from the cameras. Are they online yet?"

"The IT rep will be at this meeting but I think so. Hey, you made the New Dawn Times Weekly again Mr. No Comment."

"Apparently some attendees think the punch was spiked."

"Very funny."

People began to enter and take seats. We exchanged brief greetings and waited for the chairs to fill.

I raised a hand for attention. "So where do we start?"

Descard spoke up, "Maybe I should start since the Cargo 6 event is still fresh in everyone's mind. We have completed filling in the cavity and added quickcrete as a stabilizing agent. Cargo 6 is now resting on the ground once again. We don't expect any further scares. We are now in the process of performing ground penetrating radar scans of all the Cargo ships and New Dawn which we probably should have done to begin with. We will also be covering the Base Alpha structures when we're done. So far, I think I can say we see no further danger from sinkholes. Anyone have any questions on that?"

There was a smattering of applause.

Jeff James jumped in. "I've been on the final shutdowns on New Dawn. All of the exercise equipment has finally been removed and set up in the recreation dome. We've tagged out almost all of New Dawn's systems. Please don't anyone use the bathrooms there."

James was interrupted by laughter but continued, "We should have all systems shut down except for some life support which will remain on indefinitely using power station number one. As you all know, New Dawn is to be kept ready in case we receive the refueling equipment during our next opposition phase with Earth after which it can be used as a return vehicle as needed. So everyone be advised the New Dawn elevator will be left in the up position to protect the cables. Access to it will be through the Security office."

James waited for comments or questions but there were none.

Dumars took the floor, "I need to remind everyone we're coming up on monthly checkups. These will be particularly important since we have been off our regular exercise routines for quite some time. I expect to be urging some people to get back on the treadmills."

Someone standing by the door called out, "Doctor Dumars, how are Collins and Jemison doing?"

"I guess I can speak to that without compromising doctor-patient confidentiality. Jemison's concussion has been managed successfully, the multiple fractures in her leg required a brace from the 3D printer. She'll be up on crutches very soon. She's doing quite well. Collins is still confined to bed and traction and will be for several more weeks. We are finding even in low gravity bones tend to heal much more slowly. Collins is keeping busy with survey data and satellite imagery. Let this be a lesson to everyone, however; do your exercises and do not take any unnecessary risks which could cost you weeks of recovery. That's all I have."

I turned to Bishop. "Amanda, the council nominations have started. How's that going?"

"You in a hurry to dump your job on other people, Mark?"

Laughter interrupted. Bishop continued, "It's really a good system. If someone wants to nominate a person in their work group they come into my office and we have a large touch screen on the wall. They write the nomination under their group's heading and they immediately see the nomination count next to that person's name. It's going well. There is a lot more turnout than we expected."

James interrupted, "Yes, but who's winning, Amanda?"

"Well I can guarantee you Andrea Dumars will represent the medical group. Granger is a shoo-in for the waste management people, Collins is beating out you two guys for Engineering being the first person to set foot on Mars and all and the rest is undecided except for one big surprise. Bob Banabalas is going to win the IT group."

Someone tried to conceal laughter but did not.

"Well, the next staff meeting is going to be very interesting," commented James.

I looked for our IT rep. "Mr. Brandon, how *is* IT doing?"

"The stacks in New Dawn have been completely shut down except for the sleep mode inputs. Our own Supers are installed and keeping the network room warm. We were able to transfer everyone's account without anyone even knowing. So as of now we are on Base Alpha networking and WiFi. The long-range antennas are also online."

James asked, "So all the telemetry channels are now based down here?"

"That is correct. All Earth receiving satellite relays are now handled here as well."

"Nice job!" added James.

"Thank you. I'll pass that on."

"Anyone have anything else?" I asked.

Smith from Supply raised one hand. "Captain, it's not that serious a matter but we believe a case of food packs has probably been pilfered somehow. We're still back checking the records but it does not seem to have been misplaced. The only explanation is someone took it without authorization."

"What was it exactly?" I asked.

"A case of beef and vegetables soup food packs, though we haven't found anything else missing."

"Somebody must really like soup," commented James.

"Is Security involved?"

"Yes, sir. They are assisting."

"Well, keep us appraised Mr. Smith. Thank you."

"Mr. Jenkins, how is solid waste management going?" I asked.

Jenkins looked up as though he was surprised to be called upon. "I really have nothing to report, Captain. As you know the system is designed to accommodate twice as many people as we have so our production rate is quite easy to maintain. In fact the only difficulty we are having is with some of the greenhouse people who are impatient for product. We even had an issue with one particular couple, the Bisleys I believe it was, hoarding compost so other growers were not getting what they needed for set up. I believe we have resolved that, however."

Half under her breath Bishop said, "I've heard that name before."

"Thank you, Mr. Jenkins. Let us know if you need anything. Amanda, you have anything?"

"I emailed you the personnel figures for the quarterly resource projection report to Earth. I assume you've received that. It's due tomorrow."

I slapped my forehead. "Oh God, I completely forgot about that."

"Sounds like someone's going to be burning the midnight oil," joked Bishop.

"Okay, what's status on the number two pressurized rover? Is Maintenance here?" I asked.

A stocky man in coveralls raised his hand. "In a word, Captain; finished. It's parked in the garage and ready for use."

"Okay, you all heard that. Everyone remember you must log in with Security before going EVA and you must have approval for the excursion from management. Okay, last call; anything else?"

I pushed my chair back and stood. Conversations broke out as the others began to leave. I saved a few notes on my tablet.

Dumars came up beside me. She spoke in low tone, "Somebody gave me a bottle of champagne. Want to come drink it with me later?"

"You mean instead of spending hours documenting every bean, every walnut and every other expendable item in stores and then charting the projected use for each of them for the next year? You mean drink champagne with a beautiful woman instead of doing that?"

"Tsk, tsk. I will save it for you."

"I'll be needing it."

I went to my office and tried to adjust the chair for long term annoyance. I began going through the reports sent to me by the various departments, intended to be compiled into a single report with matching database. I watched the Martian sunset out my semi-blocked window, replaced by the glowing lights from the central power station, recreation dome and greenhouse. As the clock on the laptop screen approached 3:00A.M. I sat back and wondered if I could stay focused long enough to finish. For a break and entertainment I set my wall monitor to step through Base Alpha cameras. The IT guys had been as good as their word. They were all hooked up and online.

I leaned back, stretched my arms behind my head and, as the imagery stepped from camera to camera, thought I spotted something unusual. I sat up and took manual control and stepped the camera views backwards.

It was the garage that had caught my attention. Someone was in there wearing the familiar white suit liner, messing with a pressurized rover.

There were no outside activities scheduled for after dark.

I watched the suspect closely. He or she was loading a box into the rover. It was a man. I held my breath waiting for him to face the camera, and when he did a bolt of fear shot through me.

Pacal.

Pacal was in a suit liner loading up a rover. I watched him climb up and check the two spacesuits attached to the dismount section. He climbed around and into the pilot's seat. The garage warning lights turned red. The bay door opened. The rover drove out.

Adrenaline coursed through my veins. I jumped from my chair and headed for the garage. Trotted along the Dome 2 corridor to the connection tunnel to Dome 1. A dash to the right to the garage entrance. The garage had automatically closed and re-pressurized. Inside I had a choice of the second pressurized rover or an open rover. I grabbed a suit liner from a locker and climbed into the pressurized vehicle. I fought to get my suit off and slip into the suit liner. In the driver's seat I called for the open door routine. The red garage warning lights came on once more. I tapped at the control wheel waiting for the slow door to open.

For a moment better clarity came over me. I couldn't follow him with lights off. Too many jagged rock outcroppings everywhere. I'd have to wait for him to get far enough ahead that he could not see my lights. But, if I was lucky, he would not have shut off his transponder. I powered up the rover and searched for rover one's transponder code. Once selected, a map appeared showing Pacal headed northwest at a brisk clip. His lead gave enough distance between us. I switched on my rover lights and headed out the bay door.

Even with lights the drive was harrowing. To my knowledge none of us had made an excursion like this in the dark. This was another first. I realized Pacal might check to see if he was being followed. I leaned over, opened the fuse panel and switched off power to my transponder.

The ride became ominous. Mars at night. A million small rocks in my lights disappearing beneath my vehicle. Occasional faint glimpses of mountains against a dull horizon. Off to my left the west ridgeline came into view.

Forty minutes into the chase the time element began to bother me. We were traveling a very long distance from Base Alpha. This was becoming new territory and in the dark there was no way to anticipate what lie ahead. I was forced to slow a bit. Pacal did not.

An hour into the pursuit, Pacal changed course to west then southwest. Once again, the distance bothered me. I was going to have to decide just how far to follow him before it became too dangerous. He seemed to know where he was going. I did not. I could drive off the edge of a crater without realizing it.

At the point where Pacal had turned westerly, I saw the reason. We were running along the west ridge. It ended just up ahead. He had looped around the last hill to head south on the other side.

I stopped at the turn off. Did I want to confront Pacal out here or just find out what he was up to? I'd get his coordinates off his transponder signal. I could check out that area with satellite imagery in the daylight. If I kept pursuing him I could inadvertently meet him returning. There was also an advantage to him not knowing he'd been followed and tracked. I set the rover to idle, climbed into a suit and detached from the rover. Outside I pulled a pair of suit binoculars from the equipment bin and climbed down. The hill was not too steep but it was loose sand. I had to ascend with a kind of paddling motion. It took ten minutes to reach the crest. A dark expanse of Mars appeared all around me. I scanned the south with the binoculars set to infrared and picked up Pacal far in the distance to the south. He was twenty-two miles away and still moving. There's was nothing else out there I could make out.

Time to get back before Pacal turned around and caught me. Using the headlights I followed the rover tracks back to Base Alpha. So much for stealth. Pacal was bound to realize there were now three sets of tracks.

Back in my room I set my wall screen to the garage camera and rested on the bed. It was somewhat a gamble that Pacal would actually return. A pattern had formed in my mind triggered by something Cursrick had said when claiming she had seen someone on that ridge. She had made the preposterous suggestion that maybe there was a secret foreign government presence on Mars. Suddenly the suggestion did not seem quite so absurd.

Pacal had been stalking Bateman. Bateman was afraid of him. What if Bateman had found out there was some other government's mission to Mars we didn't know about? What if Bateman had evidence of that and was going to blow the whistle and Pacal had stopped him? That fit the murder scenario all too well. Pacal, an agent for a foreign government, planted on the New Dawn mission. Then there were the disappearing supplies. Who had better access to the secure areas than Pacal? He could get in there anytime he liked. And what had I just seen? Pacal loading a case

Starship Dawn

into the rover and taking it somewhere. Taking supplies to a secret base? That would also explain Cursrick thinking she'd seen someone on that ridge.

The implications alarmed me. We were already far beyond opposition with Earth. For the next year and a half we were on our own. If some other government had plans to take over Base Alpha *and* they had planted an agent as our head of Security, we would be in deep crap. They could move in and occupy Base Alpha without a shot being fired.

Rover one pulled into the garage just before daybreak. Pacal must have been late. He rushed around to put everything away and secure the rover. Someone would wonder why the rover hadn't charged overnight so he left the power cable on the floor by the outlet to make it look like it had been forgotten. He pulled on a flight suit and before leaving felt the engine on rover two to see if it was warm. He went to the tablet on the wall and searched the rover two checkout logs, then strolled casually out the door.

I could have gone out and deliberately bumped into him and asked how it was going just to see how off balance he'd be but I'm not so good at that clandestine crap. I'd probably give something away. So I let him go. Better that he not know what I knew.

I followed Pacal along on the cameras into Dome 1, through the connector to Dome 2 and down the hall to his room. He needed a rest after a long night of lies and betrayal. There were no cameras in the rooms.

I considered my options. Jumping to conclusions had gotten me into trouble too

325

many times before. I needed more intel. But I was too tired to visually search satellite imagery of the areas Pacal had traveled to.

I stretched out on the bed.

Two hours of restless sleep were interrupted by my comm unit.

"Easton here."

"Hey, sleepy head. Are you coming to the morning meeting or not?" asked Andrea.

"Is Pars or Bishop there?"

"Both. What's going on with you?"

"Oh, up all night with the quarterly report. Can you get one of them to take it?"

"Yes. Then I'll stop by and give you a checkup."

"Thanks. I'll see you here."

An hour later she woke me again, this time in person. She sat on the side of the bouncy bed and deliberately made waves.

"Wow! I didn't think you'd really have to stay up all night!"

"What is your prognosis, Doctor?" I rubbed my eyes.

"The well diggers have chosen a spot and are ready to set up to drill."

"What else did I miss?"

"Security says they've discovered some other supplies missing. Items were taken out of a bunch of different boxes to try to hide the thefts."

"Suspects?"

"They don't know. They are planning to set up a trap."

"And they announced that at the meeting? Are you kidding?"

"Pacal wasn't there. It was one of his guys."

"Andrea, we need to talk. I need your help with something."

She leaned forward and pressed against me. "The doctor is in, Mr. Easton."

"God, you are the most hot-blooded doctor I have ever met."

She sat up. "Just how many have you met?"

"Seriously, I need to talk to you."

"Okay." She went to the counter and poured us both coffee. She sat in the chair by the bed and sipped. "This is starting to sound serious."

"As serious as it gets."

"What!?"

I recounted the entire sordid tale of Bateman, Pacal and the midnight riders. She cocked her head forward as though in disbelief.

"You think the Chinese or some other government is going to try to take over Base Alpha?"

"I'm having trouble buying it myself but it's the only scenario that fits everything that has happened."

"And you can't even go to Security with it because at least one of them is involved?"

"You see my dilemma."

"We need to bring the people we trust in on this."

"Yeah, but up until a few weeks ago Pacal was one of the people I trusted. We need to be sure. I'll study the satellite images of the area he visited. We'll see what's there. If there *is* something maybe we'll take a little excursion of our own just for recon. You must not let Pacal you know about this."

"Don't worry. He won't read me. I guarantee you that."

"Okay, then. Life goes on as normal."

"Right. Sure."

Chapter 23

The rest of the day was dedicated to studying satellite imagery. I logged into the rover's black box and pulled the exact coordinates Pacal had traveled. I began at the ridge area and varied the magnification down as far as it would go. There seemed to be nothing unusual but as I went further south, the full zoom of the landscape seemed unusual. There were pathways that did not seem natural. He had traveled way south, farther than I would have expected. He'd used the rover to its maximum range.

Near the end of his southward venture, there again seemed to be nothing there but to the east of that location, the imagery became odd. Blurry patches interfered with the definition. It was like something was there but it couldn't be seen clearly. My suspicions were bothering me too much. I had to do something.

Andrea and I met for dinner.

"You found nothing?"

"Maybe."

"What will you do? You can't take a chance and just wait for something bad to happen."

"I know. Tomorrow I'll take a rover out there and see what's there."

"I'll go with you."

"No. I need you here. No one can know I've gone. I'll need you to cover for me."

"Ah, you mean you'll have one of your migraine headaches and I've medicated you so you need to stay in bed in your room."

"Exactly."

"How will you steal a rover?"

"I'll sign it out under one of Descard's teams. I'll take it out before dawn. No one's ever in the garage then."

"Isn't it dangerous to go out that far alone?"

"You'll know where I am."

"What if that location is only a place he met someone and there's still nothing there?"

"They would have had to come from someplace close by. It's pretty much flat plain. I should be able to spot it with a scope."

She shook her head. "I sure would like to go."

"You know how serious this is."

"Yes. I do."

Before bed I packed a duffel bag with water, food, a range finder and a general-purpose scanner. I tried to sleep but it wasn't happening. I'd doze off but wake ten minutes later. Often, not knowing exactly what the danger is is far worse than knowing.

At 5:00A.M. I dressed and slipped out. I made the garage without being seen. The nearest rover was fully charged. Both suits were ready to go. I silenced the hanger audible alarms, climbed in and commanded the door to open. I pulled out slowly and quietly and watched the door close behind me. Headlights on, Mars GPS screen lighted, I headed for the darkness.

Sunrise on Mars marks an eerie passage of time. There are far more bizarre shadows everywhere. In some areas you come across a wide field of piled up stones that look like something that was bombed hundreds of years ago now petrified in time. The shapes and sizes of the stone seem impossible. In dim light they are even ghostly.

It was light by the time I reached ridge end. I would get to see what kind of topography was on the other side. I followed along the base of it and came around to find more of the same. Sand and fractured rock everywhere. Nothing new. I headed southwest along Pacal's previous path. Two hours into the trip I stopped and began scanning with binoculars. I heated up coffee in the rover oven and sipped and thought about what I was doing. If the arcane idea of some other country secretly having a base near here was true it was crucial they did not become aware of me. From here on I would need to advance cautiously.

I scanned the horizon more with the glasses. There was nothing to see. I resumed the southwest heading.

I dared another thirty minutes and stopped to scan again. The end of Pacal's previous path was maybe forty-five minutes ahead. Still nothing through the binoculars.

Slowing the advance, I looked for specs on the horizon like a fighter pilot scanning for the dots of enemy aircraft. Twenty more minutes and it was time to stop again. A quick survey revealed nothing. I heated my coffee and sat for a moment. I *had* to be close enough to see Pacal's rendezvous point through binoculars.

Ten more minutes of slow advance. I took my best position possible at the windshield and scanned very slowly with the glasses. At first there was nothing, but on the second scan something caught my eye. At maximum magnification something protruding slightly above the horizon line.

Excited, I dropped back into the seat and went another ten minutes forward toward that spot.

There was something there. It was a blunted cigar shape rising up from the surface.

Dared another ten-minute advance and looked again. It was just a dark silhouette but it was there. Something standing on the surface like a rocket body, no detail available.

A bolt of fear shot through me. It had to be a spacecraft. The ridgeline that ran along on my left would have helped hide a landing. There could be no other explanation for that shape sitting on the surface of Mars. I pressed the binoculars against the windshield to steady them better and tried to make out anything located around the silhouette of the ship. I was still too far.

Carefully I advanced, daring to glimpse through the glasses as I drove. There were obstacles coming into view between me and the ship, rock formations and small rock uprisings here and there. I needed to see who and how many were around that thing. I looked for symbols on the silhouette but could not make out any.

About a mile from the thing I turned the rover around for a fast getaway. It was time to use a suit. I grabbed the suit-up bar, pulled up and dropped my legs into the left-hand suit, wiggled into the torso and sleeves and hurriedly tapped the seal icon on my left sleeve. The back of the suit closed with a swish. I detached, grabbed a suit scope from the equipment bin and stepped down from the rover.

There were large rock outcroppings to my left. I could use them to approach without being seen. I shuffled along trying to stay bent over and held to the rock edge. The light was shifting. Steadied by a rough rock wall, I set the binoculars.

Astonishment! It was not a spacecraft! It was a tower! I had to reposition myself to get a better look, but there was no doubt about it. It was a stone brick tower maybe ninety feet tall. It was constructed of large bricks that formed light and dark bands from the base to the top. The thing was built on what appeared to be a giant cement block foundation. There were three large holes in the tower from bottom to top, evenly spaced. My first impression was that it was some kind of wind power generator.

There was much more. Beyond and just below the tower were three huge basins, stair-stepped above each other and connected by huge gates of some kind. Each stone-walled basin was the size of a football field. The highest of the three ended at a massive wide wall that looked like a dam of some kind. I was situated on a spot near the top of the dam just to the east side of it looking down on all of this. On the west side of the dam there was a large stone building with a V-shaped roof which seemed quite earth-like in design.

It took several minutes to believe what I was seeing. The place looked like it had been abandoned for centuries. I searched the perimeter thoroughly. There was not a living soul anywhere.

I stowed the glasses and considered the terrain in front of me. There was a possible path down to the tower. Without really considering the risk I maneuvered over the stone barrier and experimented to see how far down I could safely go. Sensibility kicked in for a moment and I switched on my helmet cam and set it to continuous record.

The descent was an exercise in cautious agility. Rock climbing in a spacesuit is not the best way to go. I had to be sure I could get back up. I slid a bit in places but there were always large stones to brace against. Ten minutes later I was standing at the base of the tower looking up at its ninety feet of precision stone architecture.

There was a dark, arched open door to my left. I went to it and peered around the corner and inside. My helmet lamp kicked on. Piles of collapsed rusty equipment and machines. I was able to step in and look up. Railing and equipment leaning against the wall all the way to the top. Light shining in the three large holes. Everything everywhere was of a dark rusty color. I looked for a souvenir but there was nothing small enough.

Outside there was a staircase that led down to the highest basin. I took it.

The basin floor was covered by fine red sand. I shuffled across it toward the V-roofed building and stopped at the discovery of something else. It had been to my right and below me from my first observation point. It looked like a spacecraft mounted against the side of the dam. Cigar shaped, pointy nose, fins near the base. I had a strong burst of desire to get into it to see but there was no clear path there. No way to get up to the base, no way to lower down to the nose. The thing was as ancient and abandoned looking as everything else. I continued toward the building.

It was another ten-minute climb to steps that led upward. I reached the top and found the front of the building wide open where large double doors must once have been. Like everywhere else no one had been here for centuries. I went to the entrance and peered in. My helmet light came on again.

Large collapsed equipment again. This time there were three car-sized, chest-high machines in the center of the place. They looked like giant generators or pumps. Rusted red equipment had fallen over and scattered everywhere. I backed out and turned to survey the landscape.

There was no explanation for this place other than it had been an industrial site for an advanced race thousands of years ago or longer. I had taken an Armstrong Step from wondering if there had ever been amoeba on Mars, to this. The place was too complex to describe in words. I did my best to scan everywhere with the helmet cam.

There was no shortcut back. I had to retrace my steps. The gears in my brain were turning. This place must have been why Pacal came here. He must have been documenting it for someone. Had Bateman known about this place? Was that part of it? I would have to try to stitch this all together.

The climb back took more than an hour. I was near exhaustion when I reached the upper rocks. A sudden pang of fear cropped up when I wondered if the rover was still there.

It was.

Backed into my docking station, opened the suit, climbed into the rover cabin and went directly for the water and food. I sat in the back too brain-drained to think any more about what had just happened. When my energy level had come back up to normal I scanned with binoculars in every direction once more to verify there was no life here.

The long ride back was a time to argue with myself. My mind did not want to believe I had just explored a long dead Martian installation. I kept glancing at the rover's power levels to help take my mind off it. This was the farthest any of us had traveled from Base Alpha. If the rover power meters suddenly dropped below fifty percent I could be stuck somewhere calling for rescue. There would be too many questions.

And what about questions? Was I going back to announce a Martian facility located just a few hours away from Base Alpha? Forget looking for fossils of tiny water creatures, guys. There were advanced people here before us. People not of Earth origin. How would that kind of Earth-shattering news affect us? Everyone would want to go there to see it. Our equipment couldn't handle that. There would be a serious psychological effect on everyone. What would the news do to Earth?

I felt anger that I was faced with these questions. I drove the red sand back toward Base Alpha and argued with myself the entire way. I reached the outer limits of the Base around 3:30 in the afternoon. I stopped and parked at the first sight of the big domes.

There had to be a decision about this now. I could cover up my use of the rover easy enough but was that the right thing to do? Was there a good chance news of a Martian facility not far away would disrupt life on Base Alpha? Definitely. Would it affect the psychology of the population? Definitely. Was it critical we continue setting up the Base to survive the next two years? Absolutely.

Then you can't go in there taking chances with people's brains, Easton. At least wait until the basic functions of Base Alpha were all up and running. There was no other choice. And what about Andrea? She'd keep the secret okay but would it affect her badly? She was a religious person. Her view of reality would be radically changed for the rest of her life the moment you told her about this. She was the lead Base surgeon. Her mental stability and focus could mean life or death.

When you're really not sure what the right thing is, it is often very dangerous to do anything at all because if you do nothing things usually gone on as they have been. But if you take a chance and gamble, it can be like driving off a cliff. You can never take it back.

At the least I was going to have to wait and think this through more. Plus I had Pacal to deal with. I needed to know what he knew. I stomped on the pedal and headed for the garage.

Maintenance people reentered the garage after pressurization. "Captain. How was it out there? We thought it was two of Descard's guys. We didn't know you went along."

"Just a boundary survey. I was going to take a couple engineers but changed my mind. Long dull ride around."

"Any problems with the rover?"

"No. Ran like a charm. Would you recharge her for me? I used suit 1."

"You got it, Captain."

I escaped to my quarters.

At my laptop I hurriedly called up suit 1 and got into the video file storage. I dragged my helmet cam video out of suit memory and onto a flash drive. I patted my chest and felt Bateman's flash drive still in that pocket. I added my flash drive to it.

I tapped my comm unit. "Easton to Dumars."

"I'm on my way," was the only reply.

I thought to lie down after that long excursion but I needed to make sure I lied convincingly. I sat at the terminal and went through my emails.

She charged in and sat on the bed, wrinkled brow, eyes wide open waiting for the news. "So? What did you find? What did you see?"

"Just mostly Martian sand and stones."

"That's it? No secret Chinese or Russian base?"

"Definitely no Chinese or Russian base."

"So what was Pacal doing there?"

"Maybe our theory was wrong."

"Or how about this; maybe he was scouting out landing sites for his comrades to come down."

"That is still possible."

"It's a ridge line along there, right? It would be hard to see a landing and people on the surface."

"That's true."

"So they're waiting for us to finish setting up Base Alpha before moving in. They're letting us do all the work before taking over."

"You realize we may be letting our imaginations run wild, right?"

"Pacal is up to something."

"You haven't leaked this stuff to anyone, have you?"

"Not a soul."

"'Cause you know this could set off a panic and that's the last thing we need."

"I have a degree in psychology, Mark."

"Good. You can keep us from both going crazy."

"I've got to get back to the Med Lab. What are you going to do?"

"Take a nap."

"I mean about Pacal, silly."

"I'll keep a close eye on him and see what else we can learn."

"I'll let you know if I hear anything." She rose and headed out the door.

I collapsed back into my seat then made a forward fall onto the bed. I slept to escape the trauma of my new life.

Chapter 24

New World Day 1 began at 05:30. I pulled on a clean flight suit and transferred the two flash drives into the breast pocket. The food area was nearly deserted. Two sleepy guests sat alone at tables. I heated up a double pack of scrambled eggs and precooked bacon, mixed my coffee and sat awhile in thought. We weren't settling a planet that had never had intelligent life; we were just the new kids on the street. I tried to place us in the solar system but the variables were too great. An hour later other people had come and gone and I realized I'd been sitting too long. I headed for my office.

No sooner had I sat down when my comm unit called, "Descard to Easton."

"Go ahead, Paul."

"Hey, are you free?"

"That's a relative question."

"I have a sentimental job for you."

"What's that?"

"On my way."

A few minutes later he stuck his head in the door and came in. He smiled down at me.

"What?" I asked.

"We finished offloading everything from New Dawn and all the systems except life support and one power center have been shut down with seals placed on them. The last step in the procedure is for the Captain to do a deck by deck final inspection so we can seal the ship up as off limits with special authorization needed for access. Want to go do it?"

"No sense putting it off. Let's go."

We regrouped at the airlock and pulled on suit liners. We selected EVA suits for their slightly smaller profile. Descard had a rover waiting outside. It was a cold clear Martian morning. This was just what I needed to take my mind off of things.

We left a dust cloud leading to New Dawn. The elevator was waiting. The ride up brought back the long distance Martian landscape. I found myself looking off to the southwest toward the big secret area. I could barely make out the ridgeline on the horizon. The airlock door had been left open. We climbed in, sealed up and waited for pressurization. We exited into Engineering and removed helmets.

The place was so quiet. The air was cold.

"The procedure is to keep this place at 68 degrees," commented Descard. "It's a little spooky here with no one aboard."

We helped each other out of our suit torsos. The suit liners were just enough to get by in the cold.

"I'm guessing you'll want to check the upper decks alone," said Descard. "I've already done it."

I nodded and turned for a better look at Engineering. All the dark consoles. Tags hanging off them. So many indicator lamps dark. So many gauges unlit. I realized I had never seen Engineering this cold and dark. I went to the ladderway and began the six-floor climb up. One third gravity made the climb easy now. It was a passage through areas of shadow and light until I reached the top and stepped onto the Bridge.

They had left the command, Engineering, and life support-communications stations fully intact, ready for departure. The reality of it swept over me. Had we really spent all those months here? All of us on a long journey through space? I stood at my command chair and remembered who I was. Test pilot and astronaut. The price of flying this ship had been a promise to take on a long stint as an administrator on the planet Mars. It had been a reasonable offer. As soon as the new ion drives were in use the trip here would take ninety days and there would be acceleration gravity all the way. I expected to be riding one of those ships back to Earth next time around.

But nobody had said anything about the discovery of ancient structures on Mars. What a loaded weapon that was. But as long as I kept it to myself Base Alpha would continue to be what was intended.

I looked in my quarters. The laptop and displays were gone. My skinny desktop was still there but the chairs had been detached from the floor and taken. The thought of Andrea crept into my mind. She was a very pleasant thought with complications attached. How to deceive the one person you care most about without destroying their trust in you. At some point I guessed I'd have to tell her.

On Deck F the food court was as ghostly as Engineering had been. Lots of empty bays and storage units. The ovens had all been removed and taken. Tables and chairs detached and transferred to the domes.

The exercise area was similar. It was now nearly bare. Everything usable had been brought to Base Alpha. Floor panels exposing the elevator crane components had been left open in case servicing was needed. This deck had never ever been quiet but it was now.

On D deck the walls for the Security office and Sick Bay had been removed and taken. Not one piece of furniture remained. The place was nearly a bare shell.

B and C decks still had toilet and shower structures in the room's centers. Everything else was gone.

I climbed back down to Engineering. Descard was putting a sticker on the number three power unit. He looked up and smiled. "I believe the word is...melancholy."

I nodded. "Having trouble getting my head around it."

"You wish we were still flying."

"Yep."

"Here you go. Captain." He handed me a tablet. "Just scribble under the line that reads, *'I have inspected the spacecraft's interior and do certify it is ready to be sealed for hibernation status.'*"

I signed with my finger.

We suited up and headed out the airlock. Outside in the man basket Descard attached tape seals to the doors.

"They'll be monitoring the interior and the ship's systems down in the Engineering Department in Dome 2. And we'll open her up for quarterly inspections."

On the ground Descard sent the basket back up to the top for storage and protection of the crane cables. We climbed in the rover and headed home. I couldn't help but look back.

Inside Dome 2 we were barely out of our suits when Jeff James appeared and flagged us down. "Hey, how would you guys feel about going back out?"

"What's up, Jeff?" asked Descard.

"They want to set the drilling equipment in place and maybe even start drilling later. Nobody wants to drive the crane all the way out there and back. It's too long a distance for that thing. We can do the offload with eight people. And we need an electrical type for some hookups. What do you think?"

"I'm game," said Descard.

I nodded but wondered if it was really what I should be doing.

Thirty minutes later Descard and I were in Mars suits making time across the Martian desert with two companions in the back. It was a forty-five-minute drive to the drill site, not far from where Jemison had made her death defying slide into the ravine.

They had brought an earthmover out to the site and dragged a makeshift sled behind it carrying the well equipment. They used the earthmover to clear and flatten a large area around the drill site. We spent the rest of the morning lugging equipment around, then took turns breaking for lunch in the pressurized rover in anticipation of the big stuff.

The drilling gear would have been too much on Earth, but five of us had no problem with it in the Martian gravity. Ground anchors had to be sunk for the drill base since its weight wasn't enough for a secure platform. By early afternoon they were ready to run power. I spent two hours following the procedure on a tablet. When I was done there was a surprising halt to the work as the drill team members seemed afraid to set the drill in motion.

Descard tried to get them going. "So don't we have to lower the drill point to the ground?" he asked.

"Oh no," replied the team lead. "This drilling assembly has pressure monitoring for the point. The system won't allow more pressure on the tip than is specified. It's the same with the screw. There's torque monitoring. If it takes too much torque to spin the drill the system will stop and automatically back it out and start again. They don't want us breaking drill heads here. It's a very smart system."

"So what are you waiting for?" persisted Descard.

"Just enjoying the sight of a completed drilling platform on Mars," was the answer.

Finally he motioned to his colleague beside the power station. The circuit breakers were flipped. The engage lever activated. Ever so smoothly the drill head lowered and began spinning. It was out of sight in less than a minute.

"Well that's it," said the team lead. He gave Descard, me, and the others a spacesuit salute. "Two of us will be here at all times while it is running. Everybody else is free to go. Thanks."

"How long to reach water?" asked Descard.

"No way to tell," someone replied. "Depends on the back-outs and head changes and the drill rate at different depths. Maybe three days, maybe two weeks."

The team leader added, "We'll be using a pressurized rover for this, so you'll be less one for a while."

We exchanged congratulations and headed back across the Martian desert.

Back in the comfort of my office, I leaned back and again began thinking about Martian neighbors when ironically my comm sounded.

"Pacal to Easton."

It straightened me back up. "Go ahead, Mick."

"Hey, I hear we are finally drilling."

"That is correct."

"How long before they hit water?"

"The estimate is three days to two weeks. My impression is the three days is wildly optimistic."

"Well that's going to be something."

"As long as it's not brine."

"Yeah. Hey, I've been checking the outer limits, no pun intended. After Jemison's accident I thought we ought to take a look around for more potential dangerous landslide areas. I've started a map of them. We may need to declare some areas off limits due to the potential for rock falls or avalanche threat."

"That sounds like a great idea to me. We should have thought of this sooner."

"So there's one particular area I've found off to the northwest I think may be very dangerous. You want to take a ride out there with me when you get time and we'll post it as a dangerous area if that's what we find?"

346

"Sure. I'll let you know when I get a window. How far out is it?"

"About an hour or so. Maybe a little longer."

"Okay. Thanks for the great input. I'll let you know."

"Pacal out."

The gears immediately began turning. He wanted to take me out on a one-hour ride to the northwest, exactly the direction he had gone on his mystery tour. There was nothing dangerous out there but he was telling me there was. More lies. Maybe he was planning on me not coming back.

A female voice interrupted, "Jenkins to Captain Easton."

"Go ahead."

"Captain, Mr. James asked me to tell you there is a problem with the main garage door refusing to open. They are opening it manually and will park the three rovers outside until it's fixed."

"What's the problem?"

"They believe the depressurization safety system is preventing it from opening for some reason."

"Thanks for the heads up, Jenkins."

"Jenkins out."

Andrea cruised in and sat. She studied me for state of mind but looked perplexed. "So what have I missed?"

I told her of my recent Pacal invitation.

"You're not going alone, right?"

"Maybe he wants to go out there to confess something."

"Oh, I doubt that. What's the harm in taking someone with you?"

347

"I might not hear the confession."

"Or you might not get killed."

"That's a stretch, don't you think?"

"It wasn't for Harold Bateman."

"The thing is, on a ride that long we are bound to get into the Bateman thing and he's a lot more likely to open up if it's just the two of us. We need to get to the bottom of this. We need to know why he went on that joyride. It's a potential danger to the entire base."

"Don't go."

"There's danger here too. If he wanted to kill me he could already have tried that by slipping poison in a drink or gassing me at night or something. There's more to this than we know. I'm betting this ride is just an excuse to talk privately."

"Maybe."

"I can't cancel his request. All I could do is postpone it."

"Set up an open mike in the rover. I'll listen in the entire trip."

"Okay. I can do that."

"But I don't like this."

"I know."

We sat staring at each other.

The comm sounded. "Pacal to Easton."

"Go ahead, Mick."

"Hey, I'm not rushing you but how about tomorrow morning? They're having trouble with the garage door so they're parking the rovers outside for the time being. I have a feeling the rover log is going to get screwed up by the users not being able to get into the garage. I put us down for tomorrow morning for the pressurized rover. I'll cancel it if that doesn't work for you."

"No, that will be fine, Mick. I'll meet you out there at 07:00."

"Great. See you later."

"Well, that's that," said Andrea.

Chapter 25

It was a frosty Martian morning at 06:00. An hour early I got into the rover and double-sided-taped a mike under the dashboard. It was set to transmit through the rover comm panel on a preplanned private channel. I exited the vehicle and stood outside the closed garage door waiting for my tour guide. He showed up at 06:30.

His comm was scratchy for some reason. "Here already, Captain? Wow! You're early."

"I woke up needing coffee."

"Man what a waste having to wear suits out here to pick up the rover. Now we've got two suits in the docking stations and the two we're wearing. I hope nobody needs a suit and can't get one."

"We won't be gone that long, will we?"

"An hour to the site, maybe thirty minutes there and an hour back. So maybe three hours."

"Shouldn't be a problem."

"Care if I drive?"

I held out one gloved hand. "Please do."

He was a skillful driver, weaving through the big rocks, putting the smaller ones underneath us, riding the edges of craters too big to dare. The mood was off. There was a pressure in the air other than the rover's. We had stripped down and changed into flight suits for the ride leaving the back of the rover stacked with spacesuit sections and undergarments. For the first twenty minutes neither of us spoke, instead acting as though the landscape was keeping our attention.

Finally Pacal broke the silence. "Well, I have to say, Dumars has done a spectacular job in surgery."

"Yeah."

"First in zero-G and now in Mars grav. It's surprising the operations she's had to do. Compound fracture in a space suit, fifty-foot fall from a manlift. She's writing the book on Mars medicine."

"True. Unfortunately bones don't heal so quickly out here."

"Hard to believe this place was covered in lakes and forests at one time."

"Do we know that for sure?"

"Well, they keep showing places that are former lakebeds and water flows. If you have that much water you gotta have plants, right?"

"Oh. I thought maybe you knew something I didn't."

"Well, I'm guessing this planet is loaded with secrets, don't you think?"

"Maybe. But why do you say that?"

"It's the microbe thing, you know? As soon as you announce you've found a single living microbe on another planet or moon, it's the same as saying there must be all kinds of life everywhere, right?"

"You mean intelligent life?"

"Has to be, Mark. A universe billions of years old, us having only been around for only a few thousand years and here *we* are."

I thought to argue I'd never seen any evidence of intelligent life off the Earth but stopped myself.

We rode on at Pacal's brisk pace. The ridgeline came into view in the distance. He maneuvered around and stopped at the end of it. We were supposed to be looking at rockfalls or landslide areas but none of that existed here, just sandy hills.

"You taking a break, Mick? You want me to drive a while?"

"Nope. This is it."

I had visually checked him for weapons out of the corner of my eye when we were de-suiting. He had none.

"I'm not seeing any rock-fall hazards anywhere, Mick."

"Oh, there're hazards out there. I promise you."

"Why are we here, Mick?"

He leaned back in the driver's seat and draped one arm over the back of it. He stared off into the distance. "There's an old saying that's a favorite of mine, Mark; *'The clouds never expect it when it rains.'* Ever hear that one?"

I played along. "Sorry, I don't know that one."

"It's by an American poet from way back when. I think their name was Nicks."

"But what's the point?"

"The point is sometimes just when we think we have a good bead on things, life suddenly changes and we change with it."

"Yeah, I'm going to need more than that."

Pacal shifted in his seat. "I think I should probably start this by telling you I'm the one who killed Bateman."

"You now have my complete attention, Mick."

"You already suspected that because you found Bateman's flash drive before I could get to it."

I looked out the passenger window and tried to sound as casual as he did. "Banabalas forgot he had it."

"Damn. I wrote him off too quickly. That was my third mistake."

"So are you trying to tell me you're a serial killer or something?"

"Far from it. Bateman's death was an accident. I was trying to stop him from doing something that would have caused great harm to a great many."

"You've lost me, Mick."

"Bateman was part of a conspiracy group. They called themselves The Universal Truth. A well-meaning, misguided bunch. They wanted to expose UFO cover-ups, all that kind of stuff and they were very, very good at it, better than all the other conspiracy types we'd managed. They operated in cells and none of them knew the names of many members. It made it hard to track the group as a whole. They used a lot of encryption in their communications and they sent the stuff through unorthodox channels. We've always been very good at keeping a lid on extraterrestrial stuff but this group was a challenge. They use high quality eavesdropping and tracking equipment. They are good at mapping alarm systems and bypassing them. They amassed a pretty good library of above-top-secret material. They wanted to release it to the world but we have an end game that's hard to beat. We can control what kind of extraterrestrial information is released to the public and we can contain anything that does get by us. In a worst-case scenario we provide a means to show pictures and documents have been faked even if they haven't been. We are hard to beat, believe me."

"Can I jump in here and ask, who is we?"

Pacal stood and went to the rover's water dispenser and poured himself a cup. He drank and sat back down. "Better if you just let me tell this in my own way, Mark. There's too much."

I sat back and folded my arms. "Okay."

"There's an old abandoned Martian water collection facility about an hour south of here on this far side of the ridge. It's a pretty big facility. Hasn't been used in centuries, of course. Bateman's group managed to get some really good hi-res satellite images of it along with coordinates. Their plan was once en route to Mars they would announce to the New Dawn population that New Dawn would be landing pretty close to this Martian facility. They'd spread the pictures around every way possible with the coordinates. Simultaneously on Earth the same material would be released everywhere. It was intended to be something we couldn't contain. Imagine everyone on New Dawn suddenly finding out there had been an advanced race on Mars which even meant maybe there still was."

"So you killed him to stop it?"

"No, but ultimately, yes. Our job is prevent harm to human society. What we usually do in these cases is we visit the individual during sleep. We introduce a special sedative gas mix to their room and make entry. Inside we IV them with a hypnotic that makes them ninety-percent receptive to questions and suggestions. We can interrogate them and find out what material they have and where it's stored and they willingly give us the pass codes if we need to remove any harmful data. We can also suggest to them very bad things will happen if they disclose the information they've seen. When we're done we've removed anything dangerous to the general population and the individual is usually discouraged from pursuing his plans. He never sees us or is aware we were there, other than maybe his computer has suddenly locked up and he feels a little strange. Problem solved. Society safe from the shock of extraterrestrials. At the same time, we try to allow those who have the capacity to accept the truth to see it. We carefully leak our own classified documents and then provide ways to dispute them. So those who have the vision to understand this stuff are not shut out."

"That's an ugly little story, Mick."

"Yes. It's one of those lesser of two evils stories, I agree. But we know things you do not. Anyway, I went in to interrogate Bateman without knowing about the illegal drug he was using. I found his drug stash shortly after it was too late. The combination of my aerosol and his illegal drug caused a seizure and blood clot. I'm not a doctor but I could see he was not going to recover. One pupil the size of pinhead, the other the size of a penny. That was mistake number one. I needed to cover it up. If I left him floating in his cubical Dumars would have figured out the drug interaction pretty quickly. She would have known someone else was involved because the second drug was inhaled after the first. So then I had to hide the body. Suicide by spacesuit came to mind. Getting him into the airlock was easier than you might think. I have access to everything. It took some time. Had the airlock door telemetry bypassed, the video cameras masked and the door all ready to open. I stood brain dead Bateman next to the airlock talking to him like he was fine until the right moment then just popped him into the chamber. Plan was suit him up and shove him out into space. Suicide by spacesuit. But there was a problem. I don't care who you are, you're not going to get an airlock outer door open without somebody noticing. Just can't be done. I thought if I was lucky Bateman wouldn't be discovered until after landing. The midcourse correction checkups were my second mistake. I forgot they'd be checking everyone. So then Bateman was missing and I had to lead the charge to find him. I stalled it as long as I could. I told those guys not to check the spacesuits. Told them I'd have suit guys do it, then I'd conveniently forget to do that. But my guys were too good. They didn't listen. You pretty much know the rest."

Pacal sipped his water and glanced at me for reaction.

"I'm curious about one thing, Mick. Did you bring me out here to kill me? I know you're a professional but I don't see any weapons and to be frank I don't think you can take me."

He laughed and shook his head. He took another drink. "Mark, I know how bad this all sounds but there's a lot more. The truth is, I don't have a problem, but when we're finished here, you will."

"You assaulted Bateman and your actions caused his death. You covered up the crime and repeatedly lied during the investigation. You don't have a problem?"

"Before you pass sentence aren't you going to ask why we're here at this particular spot?"

"I'm guessing it's because with a scope we could see the water processing plant you just mentioned. But that's not going to be necessary. I walked all over that place the day after you drove down there."

"So it *was* you who followed me. And you went down there? You've seen it?"

"My prints are all over the place."

"Go in the tower?"

"It's a pile of rubble."

"God, I am slipping. I kept an eye on the rover logs but you didn't have one reserved."

"I did, under Descard's name."

"So you've visited an old Martian water collection site complete with processing pools and wind turbines and control turrets."

"You care to tell me how it got there?"

"Okay, a short Mars history lesson. Ever wonder how Mars got the title Planet of War? Let's call it a million years ago. That's inaccurate but for the sake of telling it that will do. Mars was Earth-like, trees, rivers, lakes, forests. Mars was pretty heavily populated. There were different regions and different peoples just like Earth. Over thousands of years the Martian population became very advanced. They also had religion and racial differences. They were very successful for a very long time. But eventually there came the conflict that was too much even for them. It began as a localized clash but neighboring areas began to be affected and were drawn in. As the conflict grew, more and more regions had to choose sides. Eventually it became an all-out war that drew almost everybody into it. Some areas tried to stay neutral but the war affected them just as much. And guess what? Like all wars one side began to lose ground. The losing side just did not have enough soldiers and resources to hold off the winning side. When it got so bad the losing side was about to be overrun, they issued a warning that unless the winning side ceased attacks, doomsday weapons would be used to destroy everything. The winning side had a dilemma. If they backed off it would only give the losing side time to regroup and start attacking again. They decided they had no choice but to put an end to their enemy while they could, but the losing side decided death was preferable to being taken over. They kept good on their promise and struck back with doomsday weapons. Large areas of Mars surface were destroyed. The atmosphere ignited and burned off. Cities and people everywhere were subjected to instantaneous vacuum and dust clouds like the victims on Pompeii. A few survived off world and underground. Some scientists believed Mars would begin healing itself after a few months but the planet's core and magnetic field were affected. The solar wind swept in and prevented any chance of recovery.

"So how do you know this and what *is* your role in all of this?"

"Well, I'm not really a Chief of Security."

"No kidding."

"My actual title is; Nonterrestrial Agent or Officer."

"I feel like you are screwing with me Mick and you're pushing your luck."

"You know, Mark, it's a little bit embarrassing to me to have to tell you about real life because anyone with common sense and the slightest bit of deductive reasoning should already have surmised most of this. Did you think we would explore other planets millions of years old and never find any evidence of other former civilizations?"

"You're reminding me of an old rock song called, *Lunatic Fringe*."

"God, help me to open his mind." Pacal sipped his water and continued. "I'm only authorized to tell you a small portion of the truth. The truth is not made public to protect the many people who would have trouble accepting it. Believe me, there's millions of people on Earth who could not accept what you found yesterday. They want to believe they're only-children. It's much safer that way. Don't you ever watch Star Trek reruns? The noninterference treaty? What would this kind of news do to the religious community?"

"So you're trying to keep the faith?"

Pacal shook his head, drank, and caught his breath. "Stars and planets continually forming everywhere and yet you take it down to the tiniest of objects like an orange, for instance. It grows on a tree pre-wrapped and pre-sliced for you. No way that's not intelligent design. How do you get millions of intellects out of a mindless universe? Of course there's a primordial intelligence, so of course there's other life in the universe."

"You'd have trouble selling ETs to the Bible Belt."

"Yes, even though the Bible never misled anyone. All through the Bible the angels of God are descending from the heavens to help man, the voices of angels and God's helpers are speaking to man to aid him. Even the Sons of God who descended on the Earth and took wives of the son of man tried hard to help mankind. If you read Enoch, they gave man mathematics, art, and science. Remember that first time when the two Falcon 9 boosters returned to the Cape and landed at the same time? Were those pillars of fire descending on the Earth or not? The Bible never misled man. Some religious leaders decided they wanted history to be their way, not the way it was written."

"So what do you expect me to do now, Mick? What should I do with you?"

"That brings us to *your* problem. Things are pretty stable on Earth right now. People are busy with their lives. What happens when you announce all this stuff to the world? The people who have less vision and are less adaptable go crazy. They jump out of windows or shoot themselves. They run around with signs saying the end has come. Preachers lead their congregations to panic or genocide. And guess what? Not one thing on Earth has changed. Nature is still evolving. You still own property. Taxes are due. The price of gas is up. There's still food at the grocery store. The internet is running. The banks are open. Not one thing on Earth has changed except people now know and yet a lot of them decide it's time to go crazy. That's bizarre."

"You didn't answer my question. What do I do with *you* now? What does all of this mean to Base Alpha?"

"I am a Nonterrestrial Officer. I have a map for you with exclusion zones that are not to be entered by Base Alpha personnel. It's up to you to enforce it."

"Who says?"

"It's part of a very high level secret international agreement."

"And I have only the word of a murderer?"

"Bateman was an accident. If you arrest me you will open a can of worms literally beyond your imagination. Bateman's death was caused by him trying to do something that could have hurt a lot of people, especially Base Alpha. If you file this with your superiors, will you publicize pictures of the Martian installation and tell them who I am? If you do, you may cause some of your superiors to be removed from their positions by a much higher authority. They will be replaced by people who already have knowledge of everything I've told you. But if you say and do nothing, things will go on as you see them now. Which end result would you prefer?"

"I'm still having trouble believing this."

"You just walked around a Martian water collection plant."

"You've been lying to me this entire trip."

"And I just brought you here today to tell you everything."

"So you think the two of us are going to just go on as if nothing has happened and I won't say a word to anyone about your involvement in Bateman's death, and the Martian installation next door.

"You remember when we started this conversation I said when it was done *you'd* have a problem, not me? Well, here it is; for years the various world governments have been struggling to cover up the images of all the artificial stuff on the Moon and Mars and elsewhere. Now that we're here that job is becoming impossible. There's already undeniable stuff online. So far they've just pretended they don't see it. That can't go on, especially now that we have boots on Mars. When an evolving race is finally made aware of other life in the galaxy, that's called Disclosure. We are now in the elementary stages of Disclosure for Earth and guess what, as soon as it is announced a single living microbe has been found off the Earth, as I've said, that instantly means because of the billions of planets over billions of years there must be advanced life out there as well. You are going to be faced with Mars Base Alpha people coming to you having seen things, or even bringing you artifacts. What are you going to do about that, Mark?"

I sat back and decided he wasn't going to attack me, at least not physically.

"Anyway, Easton, act number one will have to be to make this area off limits. There must be large uranium deposits of some kind near here making radiation levels higher than is safe for humans, or something like that."

"So your idea of Easton's next act is to for me to lie to them all?"

"How do you decide what the right thing to do is, Mark? Hey, I'll tell you what. From here on out, we'll do whatever you say. If you want to tell the world about artificial structures on Mars, then that's what we'll do. If you want to arrest me, I'll go along peacefully. So that's it. Whatever you say goes. What you want to do, Mark?"

"The first thing that comes to mind is to get falling down drunk."

"First thing we've agreed on and in my office I've got just the bottle to do it."

We rode back in the comfort of the enclosed rover. Not another word was said. We pulled alongside the garage and silently got into our suits. When the rover indicated zero atmosphere, we climbed out and stood for a moment.

Pacal said, "How about if I grab the bottle from my room and meet you in your office, or would you prefer your room?"

"My office will be fine. We still have a lot to discuss."

"Fine. I'll see you there, that is unless you think I'm going to try to escape."

He gave a sly glance, laughed heartily, and headed off to the airlock. Although I'd acted unimpressed I had taken in every word he'd said. I'd left Base Alpha as an innocent ignorant and returned a completely different person.

Chapter 26

"I need to tell Dumars."

Pacal sipped from his short, ice-filled glass of bourbon. "Are you sure?"

"She knows everything about our little trip anyway. I taped an open mike under the dash."

"You mean the one I disconnected when I took the driver's seat?"

"What?"

"Have you told her about the facility?"

"No, no I haven't yet."

"That was wise. A controlled forced landing is more desirable than an outright crash."

"She knows about you. I can't go on covering this up from her forever. It would be way too much of a violation of trust."

"I agree, actually."

We looked at each other knowing what the confession would mean.

Pacal said, "She'll insist on being taken there. It's one thing to believe something. It's another to know for certain."

"When can I take her?"

"Any time."

"So exactly how are you thinking this should all go? If I agree to keep it all under wraps how do we do that?"

"There's another big issue coming up in the next few days. We'll have to deal with it."

"What's that?"

"The well. When they hit water, the biologists will find life in it."

I took a bigger drink and sat back. "God, that was supposed to be a big celebration."

"It's the turn of a key. The opening of a treasure box of secrets for some, a Pandora's box for others."

"So as I just said, how do we handle *that*?"

"It will take a long time for that information to make its way through the satellite relay network to Earth and then even longer to hear back from them. The news will be controlled on Earth by the higher authorities. It will be interesting to hear back from them on how they want this discovery managed, but here on Base Alpha there will be no containing that news. We will just have to play it down as a long-expected discovery that really changes nothing for us. We'll watch for anyone who seems to be having difficulty handling it. Some people who think they would be okay with that kind of revelation sometimes turn out not to be. Bishop will be center point for handling any cases like that."

"Yeah, and who's going to take care of Bishop?"

"Everyone here has been handpicked. There may not be much of a problem."

"I don't know. *I'm* still coming to terms with it."

"I need to get to a Security meeting. You and I will be having our own NTO meetings from now on. Non-Terrestrial Officers. Disclosure is always a giant step. We take it one discovery at a time."

"While trying to keep people from seeing things they're not ready to see?"

"That will be part of our first official meeting as NTOs. Remember, there are destroyed Martian cities in some places. Google Mars makes our job all the more tricky.

"How is it we have not spotted all that stuff before?"

"Censors prevent quite a bit of photos and video from ever being released. Even more is carefully masked and covered up by distorting the images. It is all intercepted and cleaned up before it is released. But that's getting too hard to do now. There's too many cameras and too much to hide. All a part of the evolution of Disclosure."

"Maybe the discovery of a war on Mars will be a wake up call."

"Yes. The message is, once you have nuclear weapons you can no longer conduct worldwide war. You are too advanced. You will destroy yourselves."

"Are *we* smart enough now not to let that happen?"

Pacal rose and gave me an almost sympathetic look. I stared back blankly. I watched him leave and called the Base Life Support, Communication Station. Brent Shaw answered, "Yes, Mark?"

"Brent, who do we have outside right now? I'm feeling out of touch."

"Two geologists out to the east doing regolith mapping. The well drilling is still in progress. We have four people there. Two are charting the well head temperatures. We have one Electrical engineer checking the back-up power feed to Cargo 6, and maintenance has repaired the garage door and two of them are outside bringing the remaining vehicle back in."

"So we have one pressurized rover out and both open rovers?"

"Right. The one pressurized rover is being recharged but will be available shortly if you need something. I have a feeling it won't be available for long."

"No. Thanks, Brent. I don't need to go anywhere at the moment. See you later."

"By the way, Mark. The Base Alpha council nominees are having their first informal meeting together in the Council Chambers."

"Thanks, Brent."

It occurred to me the Base Alpha Council members may be in for a rougher ride than they were expecting. I decided to visit the gathering.

They were milling about the room's center table with plastic champagne glasses in hand. There was so much idle chatter going on they didn't pay me any attention. Andrea tapped me on the shoulder and held out a glass of golden bubbling champagne which I dared not refuse.

"Where did this come from?" I asked.

"We are sworn to secrecy," she replied.

I sipped and surveyed the room. Bishop was talking to Banabalas who stood out like a sore thumb. Collins was live on a large wall display screen still in bed in traction. Two people with their backs to me were speaking to her. Several others were grouped in a small circle in some intense discussion I could not hear.

"So, any news?" asked Andrea.

"We need to have a long talk later and I'm going to reserve a pressurized rover for a tour."

"Not a three-hour-tour like Gilligan?"

"Funny you should mention that."

"What?"

"How is Council business going?"

"This is supposed to be just an informal first get-together but there's already discussions about access to rovers for people who don't have outside assignments."

"And so it begins."

"Yes."

"So, dinner at your place or mine?"

"Got a preference?"

"How about yours?"

"Okay. What time?"

"6-ish?"

"I'll be waiting. I'm overdue for that long talk."

"It's not that kind of talk."

"Really? You've piqued my curiosity."

I showed up at her room a little early. She'd managed to find a folding table and had used both our allotments to serve chicken and rice. There were even candles. We sat and drank her bottle of champagne with the food.

"So what's this mysterious talk we're to have?" she asked between bites.

"Let's not spoil an incredible dinner."

"Spoil? Now you have me concerned. This isn't about us, is it?"

"No. Not about us."

Her mood became impatient. We barely made small talk. We moved to the couch and took the champagne with us. She stared at me waiting.

"I would never violate the trust between us," I said.

"Good...."

"I didn't lie to you about the Pacal trip but I didn't tell you everything either."

"You did find something out there."

I stumbled through the story of the Martian water collection site. Her eyes widened. I finished that part of the story and paused to see where it left us.

"I want to see it," was her first reply.

"That's what tomorrow's trip is about."

She sat back and sipped. "It's going to take me a long time to get my head around this." She looked out the window, holding her champagne glass halfway to her mouth. "This changes everything."

"That's just it. It doesn't change anything at all."

"How can you say that?"

"Something Pacal said. Everything is exactly the same right now as it was yesterday. The only difference is that we know."

"You're saying we will go on just as we were?"

"We can't tell anyone else, at least not for a while."

"It's going to take me a very long time to come to terms with this. You're saying we've landed on a previously populated planet."

"Yes. It's a milestone in human development, an Armstrong Step. It's that period in a developing culture when they reach the point where they are ready to learn about cultures other than their own."

"Can humanity survive it? It's like taking another bite out of the apple from the tree of knowledge."

"I think I can handle it. Can you?"

"I don't know. We've been deceived all along. We've been led to believe there was no one else."

"Not really. A lot of material has been intentionally released over the years. Many of us chose not to believe it or we just ignored it."

"Can you sleep here tonight?"

"Wild horses."

Passion is one of the few things which can temporarily dispel fear. We spent the night taking refuge there, in each other. Our worlds and our fears became one, far removed from the shadowy valley of death and unknowns. There were no outside eyes peering in, no hidden dangers lurking. There was only us clinging together for safety and sensation. We made a long night of it then fell into dreamless sleep, wrapped in each other's arms, the best possible lifeline to hold onto.

She was up before light. She used the smell of coffee and food to annoy me awake. We loaded up and headed for the ridgeline in search of monsters and mayhem. And as we approached the tall tower she noted the loss of her human virginity by declaring, "Oh my God!"

We explored the tower and walked the reservoirs. We inspected the pump house and dam as well as the odd spacecraft-like structure attached to it. Back in the rover her attitude had changed.

"Wow! That was exciting!"

"Sounds like you're going to survive."

"I'll have to reread the Bible with a more literal perspective."

"Apparently it is a much more honest book than some people have believed."

"Can I drive?"

We returned to Base and she went into Medical. I headed for my office.

Pacal was waiting. He shut the door. "How did it go?"

"She handled it better than I did."

Pacal held up one finger for emphasis. "I've only scratched the surface on this stuff, remember."

"Time for soul searching, I guess."

Pacal nodded and left me to my thoughts.

Andrea had been right. She and I had taken another bite from the tree of knowledge. For the time being we were the Adam and Eve of a new human consciousness and the only thing that was certain was humanity would never be the same.